Grigg – PERFECTL ...

Dedicated with abiding love to Martha Livdahl Grigg, GEICO's long-time director of employee communications, as well as editor of its much honored "Steering Wheel" magazine. Also, most importantly to me, my wife. She contributed plot ideas and business acumen and encouraged and inspired this book.

Also dedicated to my mentor and friend, the late Washington Star/Chicago Tribune science editor Bill Hines and to the employees of the CDC, FDA and NIH who keep us safe. -- WG

Thank you, Ellen, for your reading of early versions of this book! And your good ideas.

A
PERFECTLY
NATURAL
MURDER
© 2019

By William Grigg

Listen, people, though I try not to use any of this as an excuse, I'm an ex-Marine who lost my twin brother and my lower left leg in a suicide bombing in Afghanistan. (America's longest war.) And I have this PTSD thing, Post-Traumatic Stress Disorder.

So, maybe you can see why I wasn't the *ideal fucker* – 'scuse me, I'm not long out of the service -- the ideal *Sherlock,* to determine if "The Case of the Perfectly Natural Murder of Evelyn Robbins," as Dr. Watson would have put it, was any of those things:

Perfect.

Natural.

Or, for that matter, even a murder.

I hoped to hell it wasn't. Though the lady lawyer who was involved in this with me is sure it was. Whichever it was, if I'm going to save my most cherished tail, along with the prettier tush of the red-headed Adrianna, I might have to shape myself the hell up and play detective. Adrianna thinks of herself as the brains of our two-person team (and enlisted me as the muscle) but I figure I'll have to use what remains of my brain, as well as brawn, if we are ever going to discover Who, How and Why (or even If) someone poisoned Evelyn Robbins, the bitch of the Athena Insurance Claims Department, at my dinner table. That's right: My dinner table, in my apartment, where Adrianna cooked the damn bouillabaisse from seafood bought by my lady boss, Mary Ann Howell. Plus, one of Athena's three founders and major stockholders were at my dinner.

And she, Bella Smith, might say that not only were my bottom and Adrianna's at issue but so was the company's bottom line.

Even if you don't work here, you've probably heard of Athena Insurance. Its ever-so-repetitive TV ads feature that cutesy, talking lap-dog, Athy. And, as Athy will tell you, Athena specializes in low cost, mail-order auto and life insurance for women. That's one reason so many of my bosses and colleagues are women, even with the one (and thank God only) Evelyn dead and gone.

Was her death perfectly natural? Or perfectly criminal? What's perfect, anyway? Not this *fu* — not *me* —by a long shot. But I have to try. And speaking of speaking, I've also been warned by my boss Mary Ann Howell that I have to clean up my goddam language and become more acceptably gentlemanly to remain at this women-oriented insurance company.

But give me a little slack. It's not like you never heard these words before, and as *Sergeant* Buxton "Buck" Grand, I've had a lot to curse about. A lot to scream in the night over. A lot to distract myself from with weekends of drink (and an occasional woman.) The shrinks spell all this as PTSD. To me that stands for I Don't Concentrate So Damn Well. I Blow Up "inappropriately." I Cry Over dying polar bears.

Also, my *eight*-hour job at Athena Insurance takes me *ten hours a day*. I hate that the most. I'm here before anybody else and I'm still here after everybody else is out having a beer.

The dead (poisoned it looks like) Evelyn Robbins was administrative assistant to the top honchoes in Athena's Claims department. I do a handful of low-level tasks in Athena's Human Relations, department and Evelyn had tried to play me for a personnel pansy. So, like most other employees I called her a witch, often spelled with a 'b.'

Her getting poisoned, though, particularly at my dinner table – I didn't ask for that!

And you want irony for dessert? I'm in charge of food safety at Athena, from the caterers for our executive dining room to the folks who load up the coin-fed machines that dole out cardboard coffee and taste-free sandwiches to us peons.

I guess "fired after poisoning a fellow worker" won't look so damn good on my resume, though, will it?

But rather than chase a possible murderer, I'd sooner cruise the singles bars, find me a willing woman. Raising skirts and swilling alcohol, that's my escape from PTSD on weekends. TGIF. Don't call it drunken womanizing. Call it therapy.

But there I go. I've gotten off the subject: Evelyn's death. I'm drifting. I do drift; that's part of the PTSD. I've got to try to concentrate on—

ADRIANNA:

That's okay, Buck. I'll take your case. I'll tell your tale (and do so without so many expletives un-deleted.) I'll Watson your Sherlock.   PTSD or not, ladies and gentlemen, Buck is a war hero; he's got the medals to prove it. Not much college but he's smart too in his own way: quick. And he is really, really big and tall. Big men aren't generally so handsome, though my Dad was to die for (and do for.) But Buck, when he's at his clean-cut best I've seen people just stare at him. And when he spreads that big grin of his, oh my—

But when the PTSD strikes, bang, he's wrecked. The looks, the strength, the smile—all gone.

So, he's no classic detective, no Holmes. No Peter Wimsey. No Poirot.

He's really more of a square peg stuck in the round hole of Athena's Human Relations department. I met him there when I was trying to get parking for Athena's cleaning women and other lower level employees. (Besides food prep, Buck supervises parking, another thankless job.)

But he helped us big. He talked with another ex-Marine who works at neighboring Macy's and they figured a way to share parking. (Macy's customers can spill into our lot at night and on weekends, while we can use part of theirs during our workdays.) After he worked that out, I saw he was more than just a handsome stud. I saw potential. I saw he might even be trainable if I handled him right.

Thereafter, I confided in him that I'd stumbled on fraud potentially costing the company millions.   He repeated "millions" about six times and then exclaimed "goddam" about three.

"Yeah, Buck, millions.," I said. I wasn't sure he believed me at first. But he said that "talking fraud" could be dangerous and that he had better cover my back (he said "ass," actually, and lightly patted mine) if things got dicey.

And things have! They certainly have.

My full name is Adrianna Nance Canter, *Esquire*. I'm a woman-lawyer (not a *lady* lawyer, Buck) recently hired in Athena's Claims Department, where we pay up when the drivers we insure have accidents.

Usually, it's routine. But if an injured party or that person's family asks for more than seems justified, we may make a counter offer. We may compromise. Or not. They may take us to court. Company profits depend on our keeping the final awards low, you can easily understand. We're not trying to cheat widows and orphans, you understand, just to keep the payments reasonable.

Lately, however, we've lost some big cases. I'm pretty sure somebody is leaking confidential material to the opposition lawyers to help them win. That ia not good for the bottom line.

Nor, I'm thinking, for Evelyn Robbins, if she got suspicious of someone. And they got suspicious of her.

The dead EVELYN, perched in purgatory, in an aside neither Buck nor Adrianna can hear:
What d'ya mean, if I got suspicious? — and someone got suspicious of me?

What d'ya think ya know? What d'ya think *I* knew? Buckeroo, baby, Man Up! You too, Adrianna.

You're alive. I'm dead. Find out if I was offed! And by whom. It's your duty! After all Buck, bereavement support is another of your little jobs!

And you two folks might live longer, if you figure it out. Who says whoever or whatever killed me won't be getting you two, too?

Part One: Death by Bouillabaisse?

Chapter One: THE LI'L LAWYER AS COOK

ADRIANNA:

Not knowing that Evelyn Robbins and I, along with the gentlemanly Athena Claims executive Maury Woodrow would need our stomachs pumped before the night was out, I arrived at Buck's apartment in northwest Washington, D.C., in early afternoon. I was humming a spirited song from "Hamilton."

I didn't know all the lyrics but I did know a key line; "I'm not throwing away my shot." I sang it aloud.

My shot at Buck, I meant, and my shot at the crook at Athena I hoped to expose. As well as my shot at showing all who would be assembling for dinner what a really fine bouillabaisse I could make!

I had been to Buck's place a couple times before, of course, but I was not yet important enough at Athena to be a *guest* at this private dinner marking the announced retirement of my super Claims boss, the straight-backed, stuffy Athena Vice President Jeffrey Spencer. No, I was there as *cook*. I had promised Buck and his boss, Mary Ann Howell, to cook the main course because Mr. Spencer loves bouillabaisse and because my French aunt had taught me the secrets to making the most genuine and delicious version imaginable. Yum.

I doubt Buck himself would have ever rated high enough to be guest or host, except that he apparently had kind of inherited such a knack for writing clearly (his father works for the *Washington Post*) that he had been chosen to ghost- or co-write VP Spencer's book of management stories, with which the Great Man wanted to crown his own career and help his successor. Some saw it as a parting gift to the company; others, me included, thought it was an ego trip, possibly for both men.

Whichever, the two of them working together, the poker-backed executive and the woman-poking ex-Marine hit it off.   And that had provided cover, I discovered, for Buck's boss Mary Ann Howell to secretly organize and pay for this party for Jeff Spencer without others realizing she and he were lovers, in violation of Athena's relationship rules or, more accurately its anti-relations rules!

I knew Spencer and Mary Ann were more than friendly but I didn't know the rest until I went by Buck's apartment that Friday afternoon to check out the cooking set-up. That's when Buck told me how he got stuck having the party in the first place.

I laughed, kind of choking on the outrageousness of the whole thing. "Your boss Mary Ann Howell coerced you," I chuckled, "into having this dinner to avoid anyone suspecting—if she gave it herself—that she was involved in a torrid affair with said Vice President Spencer, a relationship barred by Athena's no relationships rule?!"

I chuckled again. "A rule," I said to Buck "which might not hold up in a court of law but which at Athena is probably applied with especial strictness to you people in Human Resources?"

"Well, yes," Buck admitted. "You've pinned the tail right on the donkey. Ouch.

"But as it turns out," he said, "I've found that Mary Ann is a pretty nice person and Spencer's okay.   You know I'm helping him write a book of his own personal management stories. Working title: Lessons Learned. Everyone is supposed to think I wanted to give this party because we got to be good friends working on the book. In the end, it's almost true. I'm kind of glad to do this, even if I feel a little, er, let's say, *used* by my boss Mary Ann."

I told Buck, "*felt* used? .You *are* being used. But I guess I am also. But that's okay. Mary Ann asked me to cook because that hot bimbo Sibyl who lives with you might not be acceptable and couldn't cook anyway. I like to cook."

"Sibyl is no bimbo," Buck responded "She's a bright woman who teaches English. And to tell the hard truth, *she* up and left *me*. She implied that she and I weren't headed anywhere, like to an altar, so she was moving ahead with her plans to find work in her beloved California."

After saying this, Buck looked away and then added, quietly, "You know from my PTSD meltdown a couple of weeks back that I'm not steady enough for the kind of relationship she wanted. One with commitment, I mean.

"So, how do I keep her from making a terrible mistake? I contacted a cousin out West to help her in her job search.

"Her 'Dear John' note also suggested she thought that we—you and me—were starting to have a thing going." Buck looked at me for my reaction.

"People do make mistakes," I said. "Maybe she made one," I added, "and maybe I will too." I wasn't quite sure what I meant by that. I doubt Buck had a clue either.

"So, for dinner," I said, "you'll be having my big Claims boss Jeffrey Spencer and your boss Mary Ann Howell–"

"Discretely at separate tables," Buck said. "Most important of course, beyond Spencer, there's Athena Co-founder Wilma Smith—the one we call Wynken, who'll be representing her twin sister, Bella, or Blynken, and their older brother, Rosco, that is, Nod. Wilma'll present Athena's contribution to the perinatal research foundation Spencer's setting up in his retirement."

As I was a relatively new lawyer in Claims, I had not yet met the founding sisters but I knew they got their unfortunate nicknames from an occasional involuntary tic or twitch which was jolting to others but that they themselves seemed unaware of. Brother Rosco, on his part, got his nickname from a narcoleptic propensity to drift off to sleep at meetings. Nod had owned a majority of the shares in a small insurance company. His sisters conceived of renaming it Athena Insurance to promote casualty and life insurance primarily to women. They argued that women have fewer auto accidents and live longer than men so they could be sold insurance at lower rates, with more profit.

It worked. Government girls, as they used to be called, were quick to flock to Athena, and the company flourished from the beginning. (We ensure men, too, but don't emphasize it.)

"Who else will attend?" I asked.

"My friend and fellow ex-Marine George Brown and his pregnant Ramona. George plans to take pictures. Lots of pictures, the printable and the unprintable, if I know him!"

"Some for the *Herald* and others of people picking their noses or otherwise looking totally stupid?" I said. "I've heard he's good at that. Of course, I know him because we're doing parallel studies. I'm reviewing employees' telephone use, where I've found those fraudulent disclosures that I've told you about, while he reviews computer use."

"Well," Buck said, "for his photography, the company lets him have reams of film. He likes film's sharpness over digital. If you need to blow it up it is still clear—that's what he says. Uh, I might as well tell you up front that I once dated his wife Ramona."

"Who haven't you dated? And why would I care?" I asked, not expecting an answer. I had busied myself with my telephone/fraud investigation and used Buck as a sounding board. What started as a bit of tipsy smooching had settled into a routine that was friendly but not romantic.

I was sympathetic re his PTSD problems but put off by them, too -- his mood swings and binges, like the one he referred to. There had been another, lesser explosion of anger, luckily brief. And there were his women. Like some fishermen, he was "catch and release." He made no promises beyond a fun time, I'd heard, and he delivered that, apparently.

"How can you handle them all—the guests, I mean?" I asked.

"The bar will be in my bedroom. That room exits onto my long balcony. Folks can slip out there, hang, drink, enjoy the air and view the park. No rain is forecast. The other end of the balcony leads into this large combination living-dining room, with its adjacent open kitchen."

"Good circulation," I said. "That should actually be kind of nice, eating in this great room with your open kitchen with its red brick back wall adding to the atmosphere —"

Buck said, "As cocktails end, we'll pass out mugs of vichyssoise. I can't spell that any better than I can spell the 'bouillabaisse' but it's a delicious and easy bachelor recipe: powdered Idahoan Red Ball potatoes stirred into Half-and-Half.

Then, when they reach their tables, they'll find salads.

"For the main course, one person at each table will be asked to go to the divider between the kitchen and the big room and pick up the fish stews for their table.

"In her eagerness to keep her romance with Jeffrey Spencer secret, once Mary Ann helps you clean and cut up the seafood, she'll leave you to it. She says that at that point, this stew you're making doesn't take long, maybe 35 or 40 minutes, and that you're the expert and can handle it alone."

"I am," I agreed, "and I can. And I will."

I found paper and pencil. "Besides the seafood that Mary Ann is bringing, I'll need a couple of pinches of saffron, that's essential, a half dozen large tomatoes, and three big stalks of celery."

Buck took the note and left for the store, saying, "I'm going to owe you big for all this cooking!"

"Just listen to some more of the evidence I've dug up on the claims frauds," I said.

Mary Ann Howell arrived five minutes later with an ocean of seafood, extra silver and china, and some tiny pigs-in-blankets that "people love with their drinks," she said.

We worked easily together, slicing the fish, de-veining the shrimp, cleaning the mussels, and immediately refrigerating everything. When Buck returned, he was pleasantly surprised at our progress.

His friend George dropped in briefly with a podium he said would make a good bar.

Buck thanked him and went back to cleaning his bathroom, from which he removed two gross pictures of couples doing what couples get naked and do. He took perverse mannish pleasure showing me how, as your angles to the pictures change, the men's pelvises rise and plunge and the women's heads roll back in ecstasy, a "racy predecessor to the internet's porn gifs," Buck said.

"I wouldn't know about that," I said, "but I'll bring a couple of plaques to replace them. One is Bo Peep and the other is a copy of the Blue Boy," I fibbed. "They won't offend anyone."

"They'll damn well offend *me*," Buck blustered, that grin of his spreading across his face. "I'm not gay, as perhaps you know." Perhaps remembering that he was in Human Relations he added, "That's not meant to disparage those that are." He was still smiling broadly.

"Actually," I said, "my plaques are of sailboats on the Seine. If you like them, they'll be my gift."

"They sound good," Buck admitted. "And I won't have to take them down every time my folks visit."

Along with the seafood, Mary Ann had brought flowers. She put a small bouquet on each table. In addition, for the serving counter between the kitchen area and the rest of the great room, she had a vase of flowers so impressive it threatened to get in the way, obscuring my view of the living room from the kitchen and vice versa. After arranging the flowers to her satisfaction, she left to get her hair done and to dress.

I also got ready to depart. "I'll be back to make a bouillabaisse we'll all remember," I promised, not knowing how horribly true that would be.

As Buck seemed unusually up-tight about this event he was hosting for Athena's wheels, I added, "Don't worry. Everything is set. Just get a shower and relax."

Chapter Two:

A ROUSING THANK YOU

BUCK tells what happened next:

I was down to my Jockeys and had just removed my prosthetic leg for that prescribed shower when in strode Sibyl. Having lived with me for more than a month, she knew my front door was almost never locked. She marched straight to my bedroom, where she was neither surprised nor disturbed to find me just shy of naked, but otherwise not at all shy.

"I got the California job, Buck!" She was over-the-top happy, her eyes gleaming.

She kicked off her shoes. "You were especially generous to help me get the job after I walked out on you, and I'm here to thank you!"

She began to tug playfully at my Jockeys. I became quickly enthusiastic. *Hell, Adrianna said to relax!*

"You're about as faithful as a rabbit but you're still my favorite one-legged stud," Sibyl said as she fell into the bed, happy as a clam and much more open.

With both of us multi-tasking our wet kissing and foreplay, I soon reached a volcanic climax while Sibyl convulsed with pleasure beneath me. "Sibyl!" I said, in a hushed voice,

She whispered back. "I'll miss you!"

I think both of us free range rabbits were on the brink of a commitment we might soon have regretted when suddenly, Evelyn Robbins, the witch/bitch—*Evelyn the Interruptus*, I renamed her—barged into the apartment and right through to the bedroom, two hours earlier than expected. She bore the kind of wine that comes in giant, bulbous bottles, plus two of the largest bags of Fritos I'd ever seen.

She gaped at Sibyl and me. She also took in my ugly stump and artificial leg, the latter propped against the wall.

But she did not apologize. She was in a hurry. "Where's the bathroom?" she wailed. "I've got to pee. And more."

Sibyl giggled as I jerked my thumb toward the door next to us, and Evelyn rushed through.   Sibyl was still amused as I said, "I could happily strangle that woman!"

"I won't rat on you if you do," Sibyl said. "But now, my Lover, as a bonus, I'm going to bartend your party. I'll do that for you and then disappear. I hate fish, as you know, so I'll go eat red meat with old man Hal afterward."

"My gym-master, Hormone Hal?"

"That's who I stayed with after I left you. I thought you knew. I threw myself on his muscular mercies and took advantage of his good nature."

The bastard! But who could blame him?

We heard the trrrump of Evelyn's bowels through the bathroom door. There would soon be the flush and the washing up, so Sibyl quickly dressed and sped off to set up the bar.

Evelyn returned from the bathroom "re-freshed and re-lieved," as she put it. I was alone on my bed, a pillow between my good leg and my stump.

EVELYN:

So, I couldn't see his Avon calling. As if I cared. (When you've seen one mushroom on a stick, you've seen 'em all.)

Buck glowered and said, "If you *ever* tell people about this, I'll strangle you with my bare hands."

Ha! I knew I had him, and I let him know.   I smiled so very insincerely and said, "Really, Buck, we're all adults. Why would I tell anyone? —your Adrianna, for instance."   Buck saw my threat.

"My Ad–", he started saying, and then he just went nuts, hoarsely calling me the vilest names, really, just like that morning in his office when I had simply asked him to change a few dishes for that night's 20th anniversary dinner for my boss Jeffrey Spencer.   Only now he didn't scare me. I knew I had him by the short hairs. And I knew he couldn't move very fast or go very far on one leg, so I laughed at him—cackled, to tell the truth, and backed quickly out of his room. He threw the pillow after me and I turned to see him hop naked to the bathroom.

I admit he had a pretty rear end. *Hey,* I thought, *it might be fun to take that boy's anger to bed sometime.*

Never got the chance.

BUCK again:

Damn bitch. With Evelyn gone, I showered and was tucking a clean white shirt into my trousers when Adrianna returned in her party clothes. I whistled. She was wearing something filmy and sheer and very low cut. As short as she is, I almost felt I could see down her decole-whatsit to her belly button!

She read my thoughts. "Is the dress too revealing?" she said.

As an answer, I pulled her to me and kissed her in a major way. She didn't resist—until we saw the other two women in the doorway.

We drew back quickly.

Evelyn's eyes popped.

Sibyl, rolling the bar to its place in my bedroom, forced herself to smile.

I introduced the three. I had to. They looked at each other with undisguised curiosity and pasted-on smiles. They made some sort of automaton-type conversation. As for me, I felt like a shit.

ADRIANNA:
You should have. But enough about that.

Your boss Mary Ann re-appeared at 6:45 wearing a dress that matched her silver hair. She didn't like seeing Evelyn on the scene. Announcing to Evelyn that Buck had asked her to make sure everything was in order, Mary Ann paced up and down, checking the table settings three times, adjusting a knife here, a fork there, and moving the big flower arrangement on the counter between the kitchen and the main room first to the left and then back to the right.

George arrived with Ramona, who, even pregnant, was radiant. George had bags of ice, lots, in two big chests, which Buck helped him carry in. George was happy to hear Sibyl would bartend. "I can take more pictures that way."

The honoree, Jeffrey Spencer, arrived right on time. As Buck had been helping him write that anecdotal leadership guide for whoever would succeed him, the very controlled Spencer and the often-uncontrollable Buck were on quite easy terms. "Quite a nifty place you have," Spencer said. "Does Athena pay you too much?"

"Actually, Uncle Sam sends me a hefty disability check," Buck responded, "which almost makes up for Athena's stinginess."

Evelyn appeared at Spencer's side. "The bar's in the bedroom and the bathroom is just through there, when you need it," she said to Spencer, as if giving instruction to a child. "I'll show you."

"First let me see the kitchen and how the preparations are coming along," Spencer said. "I see the admirable Miss Adrianna Canter has everything in hand," he added, waving to me. He then spotted Mary Ann and said hello rather formally, keeping up the pretense that they were just casual work-friends.

Spencer's two chief assistants (and top rivals for his job) Lou Howard and Maurice Woodrow arrived within a minute of each other with their attractive and outgoing wives. Lou Howard brought a bottle of wine and he put it in the kitchen, saying, "It's something we like – nothing too fancy but I think you'll enjoy it."

Maury also headed to the kitchen with a wine – "a bottle for you and Adrianna to have sometime later, when you can savor its qualities"—and some bottles of Perrier. "I'll put half at the bar and half in the kitchen fridge to keep cold."

Claims attorneys Clifford and Newell arrived with their wives, and Maureen James and Viola Maaco arrived with their husbands. Representing the three siblings who founded Athena, Wilma Smith let all the men kiss her on the cheek as she air-kissed back. The party was soon complete.

Later, as the oil and tomatoes, celery, parsley, clam juice, saffron and other spices began to simmer, Jeffrey Spencer returned to the kitchen to taste this "bouillabaisse base." He pronounced it "excellent" and led me briefly out to the bedroom-bar where he got a drink for me.   He was hardly the only guest to stick their nose in. Almost everyone did.

I complained to Buck, "I'm half French and have lived in Marseille, the home of this dish, yet everyone's coming into the kitchen interrupting and interfering!"

"Sorry," Buck said. And here came Lou to add his two cents. 'The bar is out of Fritos."

Later, Stella came into the kitchen, said hello, opened the refrigerator and took a Perrier.

EVELYN:
I'll bet she was worried her drinking might spoil Maury's chances for Jeffrey's job.

ADRIANNA:

Rarely warning people, George took spontaneous shots of the kitchen scene, the bar scene, the balcony scene, the scene scene.

Maury Woodrow said sheepishly, "Hope we're not interfering. The bar is out of Perrier and, truth-telling time, I hoped to sneak a look or a taste. Nice of Buck to poll us last week to make sure none of us is allergic to shellfish."

"Two are, in fact. Buck has steak for them."

"I'm sure they'll appreciate that. My allergy, if you can call it that, is to highly spiced food. I'll be happy if the sauce isn't all red pepper."

"There's no red pepper in it at all," I said, trying not to sound annoyed, as Woodrow's position in Claims was considerably superior to mine. "Taste it," I said, giving him a spoonful. "But don't miss the vichyssoise – Buck's delicious cold potato soup," I said, gently ushering him out. "Evelyn is serving it on the balcony." Evelyn was also, it turned out, spilling it on claims man Clifford. He came into the kitchen for "some fizzy water, please, before that white soup sets on my tie and lapel."

I put a bottle of Perrier in Clifford's hand and told him to take it to the bathroom to use. To the others I said, "Out! Come back in 15 minutes and line up *on the other side of the counter!* and I will then scoop this masterpiece into bowls and pass it to you."

To soften my bossiness, Buck said, "With an appreciation of the grand job she's doing for us, let's all get out of here so our expert chef can finish her delicious dish."

My dish was delicious all right and brimming with color, while steam spread the smell of spices and the sea. Yum, yum, yum. No wonder it attracted so many visitors to the kitchen.

But Mary Ann in her nervousness had forgotten to bring the name cards she had laboriously prepared. She looked at Buck apologetically, and he laughed. He led Wilma Smith and Mr. Spencer to the head table and said to everyone else, "Sit anywhere – enjoy yourselves. And there's plenty of bouillabaisse. Plan on seconds."

Evelyn, of course, grabbed the chair to the right of her Jeffrey Spencer. Wilma Smith was already on his left. The Howards took the last two of the head table's seats. Maury and Stella Woodrow had to be content with seats at the next table.

When all were seated, Sibyl poured the wine. She poured a glass for me last and, dipping her head low, surprised me by whispering, "Adrianna, I'm off to another dinner—Take good care of our man. He needs someone, you know."

I was so taken back that I walked Sibyl arm in arm to the door, where she waved good-bye to Buck. He was trapped behind the counter, searing the two steaks, and couldn't get to the door. We two women hugged spontaneously, and Sibyl was off.

EVELYN:

I couldn't believe my eyes! Most women are a helluva lot more possessive than that!

BUCK:

I was damned surprised too. Before I could reach the door, Sibyl was gone.

Chapter Three:

BEST   BOSS EVER; 'HELP'

BUCK:

I realized that people were looking expectantly between me and the wine Sibyl had poured them. So that folks could dive into their salads, I managed a quick toast to Spencer that I hope was flattering enough but honest: "Some of you know I am helping Mr. Spencer write an informal book of tips for his successor and for anyone else who wants to succeed as a leader. I can tell you I am learning from this man that the skills of leadership include hard work, good ideas, humor, humility and compassion. Here's to you, Jeffrey."

Wilma Smith sang out, "Athena won't seem the same without you Jeffrey – and it won't *be* the same. You've contributed as much as anyone could to Athena's success!" We toasted again.

Maury and then Lou rose and their words showed none of the bitterness and anxiety the two rivals initially felt when Spencer had refused to endorse either over the other — and board members had insisted on opening the competition to outsiders as well. Both men spoke generously but briefly. *Everyone is being gracious, and mercifully short*, I thought.

Breaking the spell, Evelyn stood up and made a toast that rambled on and on about what "we" had done, year by year. But she did manage to end with a simple, "To the best boss I've ever had – the best boss that ever was!" People applauded these exaggerations—all but Adrianna, who suspected Spencer might have a hand in the frauds she was looking into, and now, having maybe amassed a million or more in kickbacks, was leaving before he was caught. Addrianna was standing half hidden behind the kitchen counter so that, I was pretty sure, no one could see she was not clapping.

The toasts over, I brought the beautiful, rare steaks to Dick Newell and Wilma Smith while Adrianna spooned out great bowls of stew for representatives from each table who carried them, two bowls at a time, on to their table-mates. The noise level rose as everyone drank and ate and shared stories. George was regaling the Cliffords with highlights from his trip to photograph Athena's oldest living policyholder in West Virginia, who, "grinning through broken teeth" had invited him back – "'for some good moonshine. We'll have a dern good time!'"

Sipping another bottle of Perrier, Stella told Dick Newell and Ramona Brown a story from her early marriage to Maury: "All I had to do was feed them once each day but I gave them extra and most all them died of over-eating. Maury soon replaced me with an automatic feeder!"

Maury laughed. "Just replaced you as regards the goldfish, my darling — for the sake of the Fantail and the Black Moor," he said, beaming at her. He blew her a kiss.

Evelyn ate quite enthusiastically, as I recall. Seated next to her boss, she sang, "'I'm loving it,'" the McDonald's slogan.

After finishing her first bowl of stew, she made a trip to the bathroom and on the way back to her table confided to Adrianna and me that she was enthusiastic about the seafood.   She said *"we"* loved it.

Spencer overheard the words "enthusiastic" and "seafood," and was on his feet. "I'll get you seconds, and some for me and anyone else." I think Lou and Maury joined him in heading to get seconds for their table from the kitchen. "There's a bountiful supply," Maury chimed in, I believe, as he jokingly, almost indelicately (for him) licked a big spoon before rinsing it in the sink. Adrianna had momentarily left the kitchen to eat at one of the tables, so some or all of the men — I can't be sure — may have gone into the kitchen rather than waiting to be served at the counter that opened into the Great Room. At any rate, they all returned to their tables with re-filled bowls. The eating resumed.

Later, after the dessert had been quickly consumed – "Everyone likes something sweet after seafood, or after a fine rare steak," Wilma Smith said – Adrianna headed out with decaf coffee to refill cups.

It was now time for founder Smith to surprise Spencer with Athena's hefty check for his childbirth research foundation, but she was waiting for Evelyn.

"She went to the bathroom again," someone said.

Doug Clifford whispered to me, "Great party – but Noel's not quite up to par. I think we better run along."

Adrianna set down the coffee pot. "My hands feel funny," she said, according to what Mary Ann told me later. "Tingly." She turned quite pale. "My tongue, too."

I could see how distressed she was. I went over. "You OK?"

"I feel awful. Is there no other bathroom except the one Evelyn's monopolizing?" she asked me.

"If it's urgent, there's a utility closet at the end of the outside hall. There are pails and a sink."

She covered her mouth with her hand and nodded. It was urgent all right. As soon as I got Adrianna to the utility sink, she threw up forcefully. I held her head and spotted a towel and wet it for her forehead. Meanwhile, Doug and Noel made their apologies to Spencer and Wilma Smith and were just at the front door, ready to leave. They were halted by cries from the bedroom. I heard the cries too. They were chilling.

EVELYN:

Those were from me! "HELP ME!" I screamed as I bolted from the bathroom. "OH GOD, HELP ME SOMEONE!" Still appealing for help, I staggered, splay-footed, through Buck's bedroom into the midst of the party.

"I think I'm going to die!" I wailed.

I wasn't kidding, either. I feared for my life!! I gasped for breath. My hands and mouth felt all funny; they were both tingling and numb. And my legs were weak and wobbly.

I lurched toward Mr. Spencer.

Chapter Four: 911

EVELYN:

"Help me! Oh, help me, please!" I croaked. I repeated, "I'm so sick!"

Spencer turned his chair around from the table to face the hubbub I was creating and grabbed me by my arms and shoulders as my legs gave out and I collapsed onto him.

And to my everlasting shame, though who could blame me, my failing body's bladder dribbled a bit on Mr. Spencer's shoes and pants cuffs. Wasn't much, as I had peed in the bathroom, but I'd have nearly died of embarrassment if I hadn't been pretty sure I was already dying from that wretched stew. "Oh, Help Me!" I cried out, "I think I'm Dying!"

BUCK:

Arriving on the scene, I punched the emergency number into my phone just as Athena's senior founder Wilma Smith yelled, "Somebody call 911!"

Cool executive Maury Woodrow must have already called. He got through first.

"Please, Miss-or-Madam," he explained, "THIS is an emergency, please. A guest at a dinner party has gotten VERY SICK and PASSED OUT – not from drink, I assure you — but after asking for help because – after eating the bouillabaisse – FISH STEW – she felt so weak she said she thought she was going to die! She's actually lying on the floor now, GASPING; breathing with GREATEST difficulty.

"I think we need more than one ambulance please.

"As I myself," Maury said apologetically, "I'm feeling – "

He handed his phone to me. "Sorry, Buck, I'm getting sick too. Will you give them your ADDRESS, please?!"

Despite his urgency, I nearly smiled at those "pleases." Even on his deathbed the gentlemanly Maurice Woodrow would probably say, "please," I figured. I gave the 911 operator my address and the nearest cross-street, while Maury, suddenly quite pale, made a panicky zig-zag to the kitchen sink, where he threw up. I told the 911 operator we now had at least three people throwing up and/or feeling weak and/or passed out. I remembered Noel Clifford and said, "Maybe four."

Maury looked both stricken and highly embarrassed. His wife Stella wet a dish towel and tenderly wiped his face with it. A tear ran down her cheek.

Meanwhile, Evelyn managed to rouse herself to look around and repeat, "So -- weak —can't -- breathe!"

I was plenty relieved when the 911 responders arrived and got Evelyn into the first of their ambulances in 13 minutes by my watch. I helped Adrianna into the second and Maury into the third and jumped into that one too. The aide said they would go to nearby Sibley hospital, the boxy, red brick cluster of medical buildings overlooking a city reservoir and the Potomac river.

I wailed to the aide in our ambulance, "I think it was my own fucking seafood dinner that made them all sick."

The aide, a sturdy, broken-nosed guy with a significant beer belly, half-smiled. "Probably not your dinner. Probably stomach flu. Something is always going around. They'll be ok. They'll recover quickly. You'll see. It ain't the end of the effing world."

I was not so sure. *It might not be the end of* your *effing world,* I thought, *but it might well be the end of mine!* The aide guy walked me to the Emergency Room desk and kept a reassuring hand on my shoulder as I sat there and told the clerk what had happened. I also helped a little with the necessary paper work but I felt as useless as when the suicide bomb exploded, and our jeep lurched and turned over on us. Indeed, my Post-Traumatic Stress Disorder was taking over.

I tried to speak calmly but I must have seemed more than a little agitated. Not enough for the psycho ward, I imagined one nurse saying, as she nudged a fellow nurse, "but pretty close."

"A nice-enough looking young man, too," I heard an older nurse say in a tut-tut tone of voice. I guess she meant me.

While my "victims," as I thought of them, had their stomachs pumped—and the contents saved for testing—I left the immediate ER area and haunted the institutional-green corridors of the hospital. I mumbled, prayed and cursed.

And I tried to get a grip. *Shoulders back! Stand straight!* I tried to shape up but felt helplessly disoriented—*Is this the hospital they took me to after the bombing? or the hospital in Germany where I was taken next? Where they amputated my leg? Or is this Walter Reed?*

Recognizing I was fast losing my last iota of control, I hurried into the nearest Men's Room, where I stared at the strangely frightened face in the mirror—mine! and then nearly wrenched one of the sinks from the wall.

I sank to my knees on the tile floor and pressed my forehead against the side of the cool sink for 25 minutes or so before recovering enough to pull myself up. Over and over I splashed water in my face. At length I dried myself and shirt and jacket with paper towels and more or less steadied myself. (I can't swear all this is accurate but it's the way I remember it.)

I knew this to be an "episode" of my PTSD. From a spot up at the ceiling, I looked down on the bathroom scene and saw myself in tears and blood. Beside me in that john lay my twin, *my better self, dead.*

Slowly the scene receded, and I was able to stand up and take charge of myself and return to a nearby waiting room where a policewoman and a health inspector located me and interviewed me, while a federal Centers for Disease Control officer listened. The CDC man had been at a meeting with the city health inspector and just came along with him. He gave me his card. Aitchison. Atchison spelled with an added 'i.' He had a nerdy plastic pen-holder in his shirt pocket and I found that reassuring.

Indeed, the interview itself was calming. I told them I thought my apartment might still be open but, just in case it wasn't, I gave them a key so they could examine and take samples of the food. (I said they could leave the key, after they finished using it, with Hal, owner of the gym just below my apartment.)

After that, what little rest I managed that first night was on an imitation-leather Lazy Boy-type recliner I wheeled into Adrianna Canter's room. I told one nurse who questioned me that I was Adrianna's brother. But because of Adrianna's fraud investigation, and now the poisoning, I felt more like her guard.

Like Maury and Evelyn, Adrianna had first had her stomach pumped and was then being "observed" and "supported with oxygen" until she could recover. I dozed and only woke up when her respiration changed or she shifted her position in the hospital bed. She snorted now and then and spoke unintelligibly in her sleep, but she didn't wake up and didn't know I was there.

Sometime in the night I had a nightmare full of blood, pain and death, but there was nothing new about that. Afghanistan always returned.

Evelyn's room was nearby, as was Maury Woodrow's. I'd have to look in on him. He had been surprisingly take-charge heroic, I thought. Quicker than me.

After that first night's restless sleep, without shave or shower I resumed my vigil, pacing about in the hushed waiting rooms, talking to myself or to strangers, God included, and I consumed quantities of stale pastries and heavily sweetened coffee that tasted like cardboard. The caffeine and sugar helped keep me going.

For an hour or more I knelt in the Methodist-plain chapel and sat or paced about in it. People stared in at me, but I guess they didn't think me dangerous.

Finally, I got a pretty good dinner in the hospital cafeteria. I then checked on "my" patients with the nurses. They said all was going well enough that Evelyn, like Maury and Adrianna, no longer needed a respirator! Whoopee! And Ramona and Noel Clifford had already been released.

Considerably relieved, I returned to the recliner beside the sleeping Adrianna, where I soon slept for real on this calm Saturday night.

But very early Sunday morning, *Damn!* I was wakened by shrill wailings from first one and then a second of those devices that monitor vital signs. I panicked but quickly realized these weren't Adrianna's alarms. I spotted Maury running to the nurse's station, probably, I thought, to complain about the alarms, false or not. A nurse hurried down the hall toward Evelyn's room. A second nurse followed briskly.

Malfunctions, I figured, *as weren't they usually?*

But then more nurses and doctors crowded into Evelyn's room. They rushed back and forth amidst the additional pulsing noise of a Code Blue, as I think it's called.

In a quick prayer, I promised God I would give up all sorts of minor sins (like masturbation, say, chocolate donuts, and pigging out on pizza) if "Evelyn Robbins" (I spoke her name aloud) would just be all right. (That seems frivolous in retrospect, though I wasn't joking.)

But, after a good deal of concerning commotion in and around Evelyn's room, there was, even more ominously, a good deal less: No action at all. No noise. That Sunday morning in the darkness just before a hospital really awakes, I heard one scurrying nurse whisper to another coming in the opposite direction: "Gone."

Evelyn was pronounced dead, I envisioned, amidst a circle of doctors and nurses who had assembled too late.

When the crowd of medical personnel dispersed, I crept down the hall and entered the now-quiet room and stood by her bed. There was one remaining doctor. "My sister," I mumbled to him.

"Sorry. Very sorry," he said and made no effort to get me to leave.

Evelyn was still warm when I touched her forehead, cheek and arm, but it didn't take a medical degree to know she was dead.

I was surprised that she looked pretty, oddly untroubled. Her face was relaxed and no longer mean or menacing.

Poor damn woman died without quite knowing what was happening to her, or why, I thought. *And the doctor seems as surprised and puzzled as I am.*

The doctor's hair and scrubs were rumpled; I supposed the doctors catch some ZZZ's somewhere in their scrubs while on night duty. He seemed to be talking to himself: "We thought we had her stabilized. We thought that she had come through. But she hasn't.

"Of course, we haven't had much experience with PSP—paralytic shellfish poisoning, a natural phenomenon. A lot of seafood-eating polar bears die of it, I understand, but not many people. There is no antidote for PSP and no treatment, really, except to support the breathing with oxygen and mechanically until the poison clears the body and the paralysis ends, usually within 18 hours, according to what's been published on it. Ms. uh, Bobbins had regained consciousness and had been breathing on her own without continuing support until this relapse."   I now saw the doctor was dictating into a small recorder. This was the all-important contemporary record, I guessed.

"We've had very little experience with PSP as it is very rare hereabouts," he continued.

Not rare enough for Evelyn, I thought. *She had put away a lot of the bouillabaisse—two big helpings, which could account for her being sicker than the others, but—*

I couldn't help momentarily thinking that, on the bright side, *Evelyn will complain, conspire and harass no more.*

"And the woman, this Evelyn, uh, Robbins (not Bobbins as I first said, sorry)" he said, with a glance towards me, "apparently was a heavy smoker for many years. The resulting lung damage could have exacerbated the effects of the lung paralysis apparently caused by the PSP, a diagnosis that is still to be confirmed by the D.C. Health department and the federal Centers for Disease Control."

And with that talk about smoking you are trying to cover your ass, I thought. Suddenly—my PTSD rising—I wanted to grab the doctor by his scrubs and bash him in his slender, over-long, self-important nose. Perhaps sensing this, he buzzed for assistance and slipped away. (No nurse ever came.)

I remained. It seemed only right to keep her company—until, after an hour, two technicians came to take her body to the hospital morgue.

As I left the room, I spotted Maury in his doorway across the hall. He was clutching his hospital gown modestly around him. He waved me over.

Chapter Five: MAURY WEEPS

BUCK continues:

I told Maury what had happened. The claims executive said, "I feared as much. I heard the alarms." He modestly didn't mention he had called the nurses' attention to them. Maybe he intended to talk about the alarms but suddenly he turned pale and stumbled backward toward his bed and almost fell into it. Catching his balance, he stood beside his bed, covered his face with his hands, and wept, wiping his eyes absent-mindedly with his gown. By this action he briefly exposed himself.

For once, Maury had shown no concern about how he might appear to others.

When he did realize this he pulled his gown down to his knees and said, "You know, in the Hellenic era the well-to-do had little weights sewn onto the bottoms of their tunics to keep them from blowing around and exposing their privates." It was typical that Maury knew that.

Then Maury turned back to Evelyn's death: "We had our differences, but, my God, Evelyn and I worked together for years. Please forgive me, Buck, but this is going to take some getting over!" Tears rolled down the executive's cheeks. He seemed wretchedly sad.

I gripped Maury by the shoulder. "I've shed some tears myself," I said, not mentioning they were probably caused more by my brother's death and resultant PTSD than by the loss of Evelyn.

We sat together on the side of the bed while Maury rambled on with story after story relating to Evelyn, none suggesting the woman was a saint or even a nice person. Instead, Maury presented a picture of a ruthlessly loyal employee "whom one had better never cross." He said it with a kind of admiration. But then he added, "She had the stupidity just recently to accept an invitation for me to attend a trial lawyers association lunch!"

"Lunch with the Enemy?"

"Precisely." Maury Woodrow screwed up his face. "I ask you: How would that look – the head of Athena Claims' technical team lunching with many of the same lawyers who sue us?"

"Hey," I said, "with your reputation for doing things by the letter, that certainly wouldn't be that disastrous."

"Well, perhaps," Maury Woodrow replied, rather pleased, "but look at that rear-ending case we just lost. Lost Big."

I perked up. This sounded like one of Adrianna's cases of potential fraud.

Maury continued: "Suppose it involved a trial lawyer whom I might have just been sitting next to at lunch! Wouldn't people have thought I might have accidentally given him some damaging angle to the case?"

Then he went Latin on me: "As Caesar said: *Meos tam suspicione quam crimine indico career oportere* – roughly, 'My people should be as free from the suspicion of a crime as from a crime itself.'"

I nodded and tried to look as if I hadn't needed the translation.

Maury produced a small smile. "Don't mind me, Buck. I like things a certain way, the correct way, as I see it — and that wasn't always Evelyn's way."

I nodded.

He didn't quite say, "She was a bitch but, by God, she was our bitch, and I was used to her," but that was the thought he left with me.

At length, needing to move along, I squeezed Maury's shoulder and excused myself.

I found Adrianna still asleep and breathing easily, apparently unaware of Evelyn's death.   In a couple hours they would bring her breakfast. And maybe the news, which she would take hard. I touched her cheek fondly and then walked through the dim corridors to the vacant hospital lobby. Its automatic front doors opened and, with a wheeze, wished me goodnight as they closed behind me.

I managed to drive to my apartment and collapse onto my bed before tears again coursed down my cheeks for all of the dead—Evelyn, my brother, our Humvee driver—and for myself and George (who had ended up without a spleen.)

But I slept. I did not awake until just after noon Sunday, when a *Post* reporter telephoned. I answered her questions, as best I could. Then I called the health inspector on the case to be sure he had been told of Evelyn's death. (He had. CDC's Aitchison had been notified too, he said.)

A *Washington Times* reporter called soon afterward and, while answering her questions, I zapped and ate a frozen dinner of meatloaf, potatoes and green beans. I was pleased the reporter seemed to know something about paralytic shellfish poisoning. More than I did, in fact.

The obvious then occurred to me and I called my father, who was quite conveniently *The Post*'s medical reporter. We talked for nearly an hour, with Dad now and then pausing to look up a factoid to pass along to me.

"As the guy in charge of food services at Athena, I'm in deep yogurt, aren't I?" I asked, twice. Neither time did Dad answer—or disagree.

When I had exhausted his knowledge, I returned to the hospital. I again spent a night, this being Sunday night still, and a little of early Monday morning, on the chair by the sleeping Adrianna, watching the rise and fall of her chest. I was guarding her, I figured, from whatever evil might be out there.

Chapter Six: URANUS STINKS

BUCK:

The only thing I could be sure about was that Adrianna would think we must find a way to prove Spencer guilty. And guilty, that is, not only of the leaks, fraud and kickbacks but of murder. I knew she would point out that Spencer picked up two bowls of bouillabaisse and ate one without effect while the other killed Evelyn.

Evelyn's death and Adrianna's and Maury's poisonings. I hated to think she might be right.

EVELYN: That's the way it happened all right. But I can't think that my boss and mentor, my one-time lover, my "we," would ever do such a thing --

BUCK:

I slept at last until a little past 4 a.m.   When I awoke, I climbed out of the recliner and stood beside Adrianna's bed, orienting myself.   I then stumbled to the john and used it. I also sniffed the air and realized, "I stink."

As kids, my buddy George and I learned that the seventh planet from the Sun has a sulfurous atmosphere, and we thereafter gleefully announced, at every opportunity, "Uranus stinks." Now, after days of crappy food, no shower and no change of clothes, mine did indeed.

So, hoping Adrianna would be safe now that Evelyn's death had alerted the medical staff to monitor their poisoned patients closely, I headed to Hal's gym and home. After some quick exercise, I showered hot and then cold, shaved and downed my Cheerios.

I got to work just five minutes before the first shift started.

The alert Athena public relations folks had come in early to put on my desk (as well as on the desks of my boss and my boss' bosses, and the owners' and who knew how many others) the news reports of Evelyn's death. I had read the *Post* story at least twice at home and now read the *Washington Times*, the AP and the rest of the material that had been assembled.   Then I returned to the *Post*.

The top of its front page was largely consumed by a story and commentary on a nuclear saber-rattling exchange between President Trump and North Korea's Supreme Leader Kim Jong-un. But just below the fold on Page One(!) the Post reported:

AREA WOMAN'S DEATH AFTER DINNER
SEEN AS RARE SHELLFISH PARALYSIS

Others Stricken, Seafood Danger Cited
By Edith Dimond

After a "delicious" private dinner featuring a fish and shellfish stew, a woman got so sick here Friday that she told associates she was having a hard time breathing and feared she was dying. She then quickly collapsed.

Rushed to the nearest hospital, the woman died there Sunday after treatment for what doctors called a very rare, food-borne disease called paralytic shellfish poisoning, which is sometimes associated with "red tides" of tiny poisonous organisms that experts say are taken up by some fish and shellfish.

The organisms do not harm these carriers but can paralyze consumers of the shellfish such as birds and mammals, including bears and humans. Cooking is no protection, doctors say.

District, Maryland and Virginia health officials said this is the first case in the area in five years and the first fatal case here in 18 years, but that there is a possibility other tainted shellfish might be in area markets. They said consumers should obtain medical attention if they experience difficulty breathing and/or tingling of the hands after eating fresh shellfish.

Usually, doctors said, even seriously affected people's breathing can be supported until the poison and its effects leave the body.

The woman, Evelyn Robbins, 49, a resident of Silver Spring, was administrative assistant to retiring Athena Insurance executive Jeffrey Spencer, for whom the dinner was held.   She became ill after consuming a bouillabaisse in a Northwest Washington apartment on Friday night.

She and several other guests were rushed to Sibley Hospital from the party.   Assistant   Claims Director Maurice Woodrow, 54, and Adrianna Canter, 28, a lawyer at Athena, were admitted to the hospital but late Sunday both were reported in satisfactory condition.

Some other guests were mildly sickened but recovered at home after brief checks in   the   Sibley emergency room. Others contacted by The Post said they had no symptoms whatever. These included Wilma Smith, co-founder of Athena, who had a steak instead of the seafood.

Buxton Grand, an Athena employee who hosted the dinner, said the fish and shellfish for the soup were bought fresh that day and refrigerated until they were cooked.

The host is the son of Post medical reporter Peter Grand.

The elder Grand, who was not at the party, said, "Paralytic shellfish poisoning, if that's what this is, is rare but potentially fatal. The shellfish do not taste 'off' and cooking does not counter the poison, which can travel in the water as a 'red tide' of tiny organisms and infect mussels, clams, crabs, oysters and scallops when taken up as food. A federal-state program of testing potential seafood harvesting sites has largely, but not entirely, eliminated the threat of the poison reaching seafood retailers."

The Centers for Disease Control in Atlanta has obtained samples of the bouillabaisse and of the consumers' vomit for testing.

According to William Shapiro, a physician and toxicology expert at Sibley, the potent toxin can develop in shellfish in the presence of toxin-producing dinoflagellates, one cell creatures, in an algal bloom, which often turns the water brown or red. This is most likely to occur in warm water of low salinity – as in the Chesapeake Bay after a summer rain, he said.

Victims may suffer nausea, dizziness, trembling, and numbness and tingling of lips and tongue, spreading to the face, neck, fingertips and toes. In its severest form, Dr. Shapiro said, the poison can paralyze the lungs and result in death.

The twenty dinner guests were Athena employees and their spouses. Besides Robbins, Woodrow and Canter, Ramona Brown, wife of Athena computer service superintendent George Brown, was kept overnight at the hospital as a precaution as Mrs. Brown is pregnant.

(Her husband, George Brown, took the pictures accompanying this report of Miss Robbins toasting Mr. Spencer just before the group began eating the seafood and of her subsequently collapsing. He allowed The Post to develop his film.)

Several guests said Robbins was enthusiastic about the dish, called it delicious, and had two large helpings. Despite the poisonings, the guest of honor, Vice President Jeffrey Spencer described the main dish as 'an authentic French bouillabaisse with great flavor. Very tasty.'

Acting assistant vice president Mary Ann Howell bought the seafood for the party earlier that day and said she kept these items refrigerated until they were to be cooked.

At Athena she supervises the dinner's host, Buxton Grand, who is responsible for employee services at Athena insurance. Among their shared duties, the two are responsible for food service and food safety. Howell and Grand had no ill effects from the meal.

BUCK set the paper aside and said to himself:

No ill effects? Except Getting the Blame, as the butt of colleagues and the social media, likely Unemployment, and, according to Adrianna, I expect, the Threat of Murder to me and her!

Next to the main story, a short side-bar said the symptoms of PSP warrant immediate medical attention. The brief article said that a city and federal investigation will be carried out to determine if other tainted shellfish might have slipped through the state and federal network of testing "that has greatly reduced the occurrence of PSP-related illnesses, with deaths in the Greater Washington area at zero in many recent years."

"Doctors familiar with PSP said there appears to be a great deal of variability in the reactions of people to the poison," the side-bar concluded.

As the "responsible host," as one associate called me, I re-read that last sentence several times. It seemed the only explanation of why one person was dead, several were recovering and a good many who ate the stew appeared untouched.

About then, an intern from the Athena PR office ran in with a second memo. It said that WRC, the local NBC-TV outlet, had been following the story almost all weekend.   I guessed this was because one of their staff was a neighbor of mine. She probably had heard and seen the arrival of the ambulances and followed up.

The memo said the local channel, its affiliated cable station MS-NBC and the national Fox news had Evelyn's death first, on Sunday afternoon or evening, all of them using one of those "BREAKING NEWS" banners that sweep across the screen to assure viewers this isn't information from a prior year, I suppose. The banners were followed by live interviews with the young doctor I had seen in Evelyn's room.

I cringed at how much media attention Evelyn's death was getting.

With Dad being a reporter, I should have been used to these sudden explosions of news, which were often followed by silence in a day or two.   But as I shoved the papers aside, I wondered if this story might not have what reporters call "legs"—meaning longevity.

I feared that George's photograph of the vomiting Evelyn would appear on the Post's website and would, from there, go viral on social media – which I soon found it did. Why in hell had George given the Post his film?! I wondered, but I wasn't about to make point of criticizing my "damn friend." From the hallway, my boss Mary Ann Howell overheard my cussing, but for once let it pass without comment.

Pretty Danyel Lemon, our company news editor, soon intruded. She wanted advice on what to tell Athena's workers in her Bulletin Board News. These "news flashes," as she called them, were distributed on Athena bulletin boards as the name implies and also through internal emails. "Is it safe to eat in the cafeteria?" Danyel asked. "What have you done there?"

"Tell them not to eat anything that doesn't have an 'R' in it," I said before remembering Danyel had no sense of humor. "Just kidding," I assured her. As patiently as I could, I explained all I knew about PSP.

"The bottom line is that the food served at Athena," I said, "comes from an entirely different source, and anyway, by coincidence, no seafood is currently on any of the menus."

As soon as Danyel left I called the caterers to make sure that would be the case. Then, not totally sure that our preparers could tell a tuna sandwich from a hamburger, I walked down to the cafeteria to be doubly sure.

In the halls I could tell that many people were gossiping about the poisoning. Some employees stopped talking entirely as I approached. Others awkwardly sought a new subject.

In a couple of cases, they tried to be funny:

"Going to make these little seafood dinners of yours a monthly affair?"

Or "How do I get off your guest list, Buck?"

Not wanting to make light of the death or, on the other hand, to shame the jokers for doing so, I tried to maintain a non-committal expression. I nodded and passed along.

Back in my office again, I called my friend George. "How's Ramona getting along?"

"She says she's fine, that it was worry about the baby that made her nervous and scared. But the baby is not harmed, the doctors say, and neither is Ramona. She only had a tiny helping, just to be polite. During her pregnancy especially, she's not had much appetite for either spicy stews or seafood, so she had passed most of her bouillabaisse on to me. I ate a lot."

"I won't worry then!" I said. "I'd probably be the only person at your funeral, and that would only be because bereavement is part of my job.

"Seriously, mi amigo, this whole thing has been hell, and Adrianna is still in the hospital, and Maury, the Virginia gentleman, is too, I think, and he is as distraught about Evelyn as if he liked her. "

George said, "He just about died of embarrassment from throwing up in front of everybody! I got a picture, you know." I had to laugh. My first in days.

By Tuesday, although we were still awaiting reports of the tests at the Centers for Disease Control and George's picture of Evelyn collapsing on Spencer in a shower of vomit still seemed everywhere on the Internet, my boss Mary Ann Howell seemed to have stopped worrying full time about our reputations. Or maybe she was just spouting her own wishful thinking. At any rate, she called me in and told me, "Nobody in management is holding us responsible for what happened, and nobody has asked me what I was doing buying food for the party in the first place. I think everyone is just pleased that only the *Post* and the *Washington Times*, along with the local TV, covered the story at any length.

"The AP story that circulated to other papers was brief, according to our pr people's computer search. It hardly mentioned the company.

"Thank God for Donald Trump!" Mary Ann continued. "He's helped by tweeting a very personal attack on a female NBC commentator who he said was 'bleeding' after a facelift. He followed with a video manipulated to look like he's beating up a CNN reporter. All that is a great distraction!

"We should consider this whole unfortunate 'Evelyn thing' water over the dam or under the bridge," Mary Ann said. "Evelyn will be buried in a family plot in Ohio somewhere, near the little college town of Delaware—Ohio Wesleyan college is there—and Athena will have a rep there and a wreath of flowers. Period. The less we dwell on it the better."   She picked up a salary report and began to study it, dismissively.

I took the hint and got up to leave, hearing Mary Ann Howell add unnecessarily, whether to me or to herself, "I think it's high time we got back to work and stopped discussing this affair with anyone."

I nodded but thought, *Lots of luck*. Who did she think was sending those flowers she talked about? Bereavement services were a part of my Employee Services job, so my work related to Evelyn's death wasn't done. And Donald Trump's crazy tweets wouldn't keep the focus off us if there's more "breaking news" from CDC about the poison. That would just lead to a revival of George's gross pictures.

Returning to my desk, I found that my smart intern, Dill Dixon-Price, had also thought of the tasks ahead. "Shall I order flowers for Evelyn's funeral?" she asked.

I said, "I'll be meeting Evelyn's mother and father at Dulles Airport. I think we should have a small bouquet in a nice vase waiting for them at their hotel, and then order a larger-than-usual spread for the funeral. Have the card on the little one say, 'From Evelyn's many good friends at Athena.'"

At "many good friends," Dill glanced up to see if I was joking. I coughed and went on: "The big one for the funeral should be from the three founders, the Smiths."

"What about flowers from Jeffrey Spencer?" Dill asked.

"Good thinking. Ask the temp replacing Evelyn to see if Spencer wants us to send flowers to the parents or the funeral in his name."

When Dill left, I phoned Adrianna at the hospital: "How are you? When are they letting you out? I've been by to see but you were always asleep. Well, except yesterday when they stopped me because they said you were talking to a public health investigator."

"A nurse told me that my 'brother,' as she called him, slept in my lounge chair. She volunteered he was quite tall, and almost handsome.   Since my brother is just over average height, not what I'd call beautiful and lives in Vermont—I thought they must be talking about you."

"Yeah, it was me," I admitted. "'Handsome,' she said, did she?"

"Well, 'tall' anyway," Adrianna said. "You must have really needed sleep too, or you thought that Evelyn, Maury and I needed protection."

"I wasn't much protection," I said, "for Evelyn."

"But you guarded me! I'm alive! Thank you!"

"You're welcome. I'm very glad you are."

"As to my condition," Adrianna said, "having my stomach pumped was no fun, but I'm lots better. I hear Maury has been released. And I'm well over the tingling and breathing difficulty. They had me on oxygen for a little while, but no longer. And I had a big fat-free dinner last night and poached eggs and oatmeal this morning. Solid food. I've even, ahem, passed gas, which seems to be a prerequisite to getting out, which I'm allowed to do, leave that is, in about an hour."

"I'm on my way," I said. I grabbed my jacket.

An hour and a half later, I had Adrianna in my Miata, the jump-seat behind us filled with sweet-smelling flowers from me, and from her land-lady Mildred and big boss Jeffrey Spencer. We sped toward her place, her red hair streaming and shining in the sun.

.

Adrianna said, "I didn't talk about this to the investigators from the city or the guy from the Centers for Disease Control, but I've been wondering if Evelyn's death could be deliberate—and Maury's and my poisoning too! Or maybe somebody wanted to kill me before I manage to pin the fraudulent leaks I've found on a specific miscreant. Maybe Evelyn and Maury got in the line of fire, so to speak."

"You're kidding!" I said, "but no, you could be right. It's a credible idea. I guess we'll soon know. CDC is testing the contents from Evelyn's stomach, and yours and Maury Woodrow's, too. And in the stew and maybe specifically in the mussels or the other shellfish. And looking for reports of a red tide occurring anywhere. We'll soon know if it was a natural phenomenon."

Adrianna said, "My instincts tell me otherwise."

I replied, "*My* 'instincts' told me not to have that party in the first place, and not to have Evelyn at it, so instincts can be right on.   I'll ask CDC about testing for other poisons."

My mobile interrupted with a text message from Spencer. "Understand yu meetg M/M Robbins' plane 2 hrs. Pick me up office 45 mins before. Want to see what help I can be. But Buck: I'll send my own darn flowers!"

Adrianna said she would like to go to the airport too. I waited while she put something on that she considered appropriate. Then we picked up an Athena SUV and Spencer. He was surprised to see Adrianna and said he hoped she felt strong enough. However, he added, "Good idea, a woman's touch." Then he sat, arms folded, and said no more until we reached Dulles airport.

Chapter Seven: WHERE THERE'S A WILL

BUCK:

I had made a sign with "Mr. and Mrs. Robbins" printed large on it, but they weren't hard to spot. They were red-eyed and more than middle-aged, and very plainly and conservatively dressed. They came off the ramp from the plane holding hands.

"Thank you for meeting us. We just want to accompany my little girl home," Mrs. Robbins said.

Her husband patted her hand and said, "And tie up any loose ends."

Mrs. Robbins had clearly been crying but she wiped her eyes, sniffled and said, "If it's possible, we would like to stop by and see Evelyn's apartment before we go to the hotel. I called the super and he said he could let us in." Adrianna nodded almost too enthusiastically, I thought. Spencer seemed more reluctant but agreed.

As we entered the apartment, I wasn't surprised to hear renewed sobbing from Mrs. Robbins. It's tough losing a son or daughter, even when they are adults and have lived at a distance. Adrianna teared up as well, and the two women clung to each other and marched into the kitchen to get glasses of water.

Left to ourselves, we three men looked around. My eyes widened and if the occasion had been different, I'd have whistled or even exclaimed, "Jesus!" The apartment was outrageously large with separate living and dining rooms full of what looked like very expensive modern Scandinavian furniture, maybe design originals as Adrianna described them later, in teak, chrome and glass. Evelyn's collection of Swedish art glass looked pricey and the abstract paintings hanging on the walls in impressive frames didn't come cheap either, I figured.

The main bedroom looked very Hollywood, with a suite of bleached furniture, including a king-sized bed with a silver satin covering. There were two more of the abstracts plus a massive mirror in a heavy, rococo frame, white and gold.

All paid for by blackmailed executives or grateful lawyers for Athena's adversaries? I had to wonder. That would be Adrianna's view, too.

A smaller bedroom contained a desk and other rosewood furniture, plus a small bed-sofa. There was a 42-inch flat screen Sony mounted on one wall. Probably Evelyn used the room as a den and occasional guest room.

Luckily, Mr. Robbins joined his wife in the kitchen just before I spotted in this den-bedroom a coffee-table-sized collection of photographs by Robert Mapplethorpe, open to a page so graphic that I quickly shut the book and, for good measure, slipped it under the bed.

There was some other racy stuff lying around that I also quietly hid, but the desk in this room soon drew my attention, and Mr. Spencer's. The desk held a stack of folders filled with papers.

"I guess we should leave these papers for Evelyn's folks to go through," I said, reluctantly, as I felt an itch to dive in and learn more about the woman.

Spencer nodded but said, "I'm pretty sure she would have had a will, and it would be useful to find it. Better ask Evelyn's mother if we should look for one,' he said to me.

I thought he seemed eager to find it but he turned away and looked out the bedroom window at the scene below. Over his shoulder I could see a dog was pooping on the neatly cut lawn and a well-dressed woman was readying one of those plastic bags *The Post* comes in to pick the pile up. The scene was nothing to draw anyone's attention, so I assumed Spencer was trying hard not to get into the stack on that desk and into the drawers.

In those moments, I poked my finger around and spied an envelope on the desk that had "To My Darling" written large across it. Without thinking, or rather, thinking it might prove as embarrassing as the Mapplethorpe photos, I slipped it into my pocket.

I asked Spencer, "What do wills look like?"

"Usually they are in distinctive envelopes or blue or brown folders," Spencer said. "Copies may be kept at home and/or at an attorney's and/or in a lock box at a bank." Abruptly, perhaps thinking I had seen something that looked like a will, he left the window and moved to the desk. "Let me look."

He started through the stacks and then the desk drawers.

Belatedly I headed to the kitchen to ask Mrs. Robbins if this was all right.

She was again sobbing on Adrianna's shoulder.   I retreated. I returned to find Spencer sticking a plain white envelope in his jacket pocket, much as I had.

I didn't say anything, and I was pretty sure Mr. Spencer didn't think he'd been seen.

"Mrs. Robbins is crying," I said. "I don't think this is a good time to ask about a will."

But at that moment Mr. Robbins appeared, saw the open drawers and demanded, "What are you doing?"

"I'm a lawyer," Spencer said. "I thought it might help if we found Evelyn's will—and, say, I think this might be it." He pulled a brown folder from the pile. "This says, 'legal documents.'" He started to open it.

"Wait just a gosh-dang minute!" Mr. Robbins roared loud enough to bring his wife and Adrianna to the room.

"John, what's going on?" Mrs. Robbins wanted to know.

"This Spencer feller has got into our daughter's drawers—papers. First their party food kills our girl and then he rifles through her things!"

"I told you," Spencer said, "I'm a lawyer and I just want to see if this is a will. I don't mean to read it! And—and I didn't kill anybody!"

"At home in Ohio we've never eaten a damn mussel or a damn clam and neither had my daughter until she came east to work for your women's insurance company," Mr. Robbins said. In his resentment he pronounced the shellfish as if they were unnatural foods and "women's insurance company" as if it were a subversive entity.

"As for that envelope, *I* will open it," Mrs. Robbins said, pulling the document out of the folder: "'Last Will and Testament of Evelyn Patricia Robbins'—Patricia was her grandmother, my mother, so we used that for her middle name—'I, Evelyn Patricia Robbins do make, publish and declare—'"

"Legal gobble-de-gook," said her husband.

Jeffrey Spencer advised, "There's an attorney's name on the cover. Perhaps he should read the will, tell you if there's anything more recent, etc., etc. That may be a photocopy, you know, not the original, and it may not be the latest version."

But Mrs. Robbins was reading silently on. Suddenly, she screamed. "No! No!" She started to tear the will in two.

"Stop!" we all cried, Adrianna and Mr. Robbins included.

"Don't tell me what to do! This gives everything to *him*. You got Evelyn to leave everything to *you*!" she said, pointing to Spencer. "No wonder you were so eager to meet us and, and, and," she sobbed, "to go through my Evelyn's things and fly back with us and Evelyn's body!

"Did you kill her? Kill her for her money – or because you tired of her? Did you make love to her, take advantage of her? I can see by the look on your face: You did, didn't you? – take advantage? And now you're feeling guilty – as well you should!"

Spencer paled. "Stop. Please. You don't know–"

"Do you deny having a love affair with my daughter?" Mrs. Robbins asked.

"Whatever relationship your daughter and I may have had—"

"Then you *were* in her pants!" Mr. Robbins hissed.

"—ended amicably a long, long time ago," said Spencer, plowing ahead, "when she decided I was too old and stodgy for her, which I guess I was. I'm nobody's prize, though ironically she grew to appreciate my business skills in subsequent years just as I came to admire her work-time abilities."

"I'll bet," Mr. Robbins said.

"Mr. and Mrs. Robbins," Adrianna quietly but firmly interrupted, placing a hand on both their arms, "like many loving parents you think of your Evelyn as 'your little girl' but your daughter was well over 21—she was a grown woman—and she was bound to have had some attachments. That's only natural. I didn't know her well and I don't know anything about her and Mr. Spencer, but in the short time I've been at Athena, in the same Claims Department with them, I've seen nothing to suggest anything more than a professional relationship."

"Exactly!" Jeffrey Spencer said.

"And," Adrianna continued, "as Mr. Spencer says, this may well be an old will. Invalid, quite possibly. I'm a lawyer too. I'd also advise that this will may well have been supplanted by a more recent one that her lawyer—I assume that's the man whose name, address and phone number are on this folder—will be able to tell us about.

"It's not yet quite five," Adrianna said. "Let me," and she pulled out her phone, "call him right now and see if we can get an appointment early tomorrow before you return to Ohio."

"Well, um, yes," Mrs. Robbins said, "maybe that's a good idea, isn't it, John?"

John looked like he was used to acquiescing to his wife, and he did.

Adrianna made the call and the appointment, and I ushered them all to the company car. With a degree of relief, I delivered the Robbins to their suite and agreed on a time that evening to take them for dinner. I then dropped Spencer at Athena and took Adrianna to her home. Both were distracted and silent.

After Spencer got out, I asked Adrianna, "Any chance you feel up to going to dinner with me and the Robbins? You'd be helpful. And Athena's paying and I'm sure I can squeeze you onto the tab."

"I don't know when I've had such a flattering offer," she said, "but I'm exhausted. I'll eat a Stouffer's frozen dinner and go right to bed. Remind the Robbins I'm meeting them at the lawyer's office at 9 — he is close enough for them to walk from the hotel.

"You'll remember to tell them?"

"Sure, I'll remember, Adrianna, if I can just get over the image of you lying in bed in a lacy negligee, all alone."

"Put a fluffy flannel nightgown around that image, Buck, and you'll be right on the money."

Chapter Eight: LEFT-OVERS

BUCK continues:

At the restaurant with Evelyn's folks, I saw there was bouillabaisse on the menu, but none of us mentioned it or ordered it. Mrs. Robbins had lamb, and Mr. Robbins and I had steak. There wasn't much small talk, but I did remind them that Adrianna would meet them at the lawyer's office. I drew them a map. "Two and a half blocks, is all."

Then I explained that regardless of whether the will was valid (as next day it proved to be) Evelyn had made them the beneficiaries of considerable Athena insurance. That seemed to mollify them somewhat.

We ate quickly and skipped dessert, so I dropped them at their hotel and was home early. I strolled about my neighborhood streets, happy to have a little quiet time alone.

Next morning, I exercised and was having my standard bowl of Cheerios when my twice-a-month cleaning woman, Maria Gonzales, arrived.

"Senor Grand," she said, "Theeze place is a terrible mezz, jus' as I was expecting.   I see the news like anybody else! I'll do what I can in my half day, but don't you think you'll want me back for another half day—say Friday? My Friday morning lady has gone to her daughter's, she's minding the grandkids, and she won't be needing me."

"Friday would be great," I said. "Here's your money for today. And there's bread and some sandwich meat in the refrigerator for lunch before your leave."

"No seafoods left over from the party?"

"Ha ha," I said flatly, but I tried to be a good sport. "I'd find you a poison lobster, but I'm late," I said. "Gotta run."

My car was low on gas so I drove straight to a discount gas station on River Road north of Athena and a little out of way. I hate to pay full price.

As I pulled my wallet out of my jacket to pre-pay, I felt the "To My Darling" letter I had purloined. I set the pump on automatic and read.

"Dearest,

"If only you realized how hard it is to see you so often and not to have you. Just tell me—give me a sign— that our glorious times mean something to you still? What must I do—tell the world about our times together, just to get your attention? Well, this may be the last time I write you about this. Next, I'll act. That seems to be the only way. A thousand kisses XXX from Your Adoring Evelyn."

I concluded that this "Dearest" letter was likely meant for Vice President Spencer.

So, it won't hurt to admit to him I took the letter thinking I might spare the Robbins pain. I'll see how he reacts to that. I'm sure he'll think I did the right thing. But will he admit the letter was for him? Or that he pocketed another?

I put the "Darling" letter back in my jacket.

At work, I assembled an estimate requested by Athena's directors and finished a report Mary Ann Howell wanted, leaving it on her desk along with a copy of what I'd done for the directors. I headed for the cafeteria to eat lunch with Danyel Lemon, who wanted to talk about Evelyn's obituary, which she was preparing for the *Athena Herald,* the employee news magazine.

"All of the employees know it was food poisoning she died of, of course, and your food and your dinner," Danyel said, "so I thought I'd just state 'poisoning' right off in the obituary. No need to be obscure, to say 'died suddenly,' I don't think."

"Hmm," I said, "'died suddenly' usually implies a heart attack or an accident or a suicide. 'Poisoning' might sound like something deliberate, like murder. And don't you think 'food poisoning' implies dirty hands, poor food handling, or a sick food handler? — none of which is true. Why not just say 'died of suspected paralytic shellfish poisoning' and explain how it's naturally occurring and so on?"

"Yeah, with you being host and all, I guess it would be good to make that clear."

I said, "We'll hear from the CDC before your deadline and so may have a confirmation of the natural paralytic shellfish poisoning angle."

"That would be good—something new to report," Danyel said. "It is kind of funny, though."

"Funny?"

"Not the death and the illnesses. It's that you, the person in charge of food for Athena, are the one who gives the party where everyone's poisoned."

"Oh, ha, ha, ha. You got the joke! How about a nice story about how ironic that is! Actually, how about a story about how good the food service is. There has never been a case of food poisoning in the history of the Athena organization. And the facilities themselves get the highest marks from the inspectors!"

"Sounds a bit self-serving," Danyel said, "and not much human interest."

"Keeping my job — no human interest in that?"

"Keeping your job? Bad as that! Well, tell you what, Buck, I might even write what you want, but later, maybe a couple months from now. Now would be too obvious." (She wasn't as dumb as I'd hoped.) "I'll trade you that piece for some good ideas I can use right now for a series I want to do on hobbies people have. That photo of the oldest policyholder will do as a kind of small feature for this issue, but I'm not sure what else we'll have, you know, of real interest to people. You find me a great hobby, and I'll not only write a nice piece on food services, I'll buy you lunch, elsewhere." She laughed.

"You're on. I'll find you something," I said. "Definitely."

But by the end of the day I hadn't thought of anything. I turned out my lights and sat in my dark office, my thoughts jumping from Mr. and Mrs. Robbins to Adrianna to Evelyn's death to Adrianna to Danyel's search for a hobby, and back to Adrianna. The phone rang, and, speak of the devil, it was Adrianna, and she was whispering: "I'm glad I caught you. I'm sitting at Evelyn's desk and—"

"You're here at the office?"

"Yes. I met the Robbins at the lawyers, and the will we saw is the latest, so Spencer gets the money, but the Robbins seemed less concerned."

I jumped in: "Maybe because I explained to them at our dinner last night all the insurance that she'd made out to them."

Adrianna continued: "And Spencer has now gone with them to the airport to fly—all three of them, with Evelyn's coffin in baggage—to Ohio, so I thought I'd look around in her desk while he's gone."

"You can't do that. You can't go through people's desks. Especially those of dead people."

"Nonsense. You and Jeffrey Spencer did it in her apartment. And I work in Claims. This is my chance to do it here. So, come on up. Hardly anybody's here and they think I'm looking for a lost file."

I took the stairs as fast as my legs, real and artificial, could take me.

There were two claims examiners at their desks as I slowed and entered the department. Both were straightening up their desks to leave. "Good luck finding that file," one told Adrianna as he departed.

"You see," she whispered to me, "as an assistant manager looking for a file that I need, I can rummage through Evelyn's desk and no one thinks anything of it." So that the remaining examiner could overhear, she raised her voice and said, "Mr. Grand, I think that personnel folder you want may be on Mr. Spencer's desk. Come with me."

I followed but as the door closed, I spun Adrianna around and asked, "Just what in hell are you pulling?"

"Nothing. Just wanted privacy to show you this: A list of numbers I found in Evelyn's desk."

"So?"

"These claims numbers are for dead files – the very files, the big settlements, I was telling you about."

"Maybe Spencer asked for them, the files, a list of the big cases."

"All the big court cases that happen to involve the very law firms with the phone numbers I'm investigating?"

"Okay, I'm impressed. Anything else?"

"I think somebody might have beat me to some stuff in the desk," Adrianna said, "but I did find another list too." She held out another slip of paper. "These are claim numbers I hadn't seen before. I think they're pending cases, and they're all made out to Spencer, but I haven't been able to find the files anywhere in his office."

"You've looked through his desk and his files too?" I asked. I was incredulous.

"What's the problem with that? Everyone comes in and out of Spencer's office with messages, etc., whether he's here or not. The mystery is why aren't these files in his office? They were signed out to him."

"Don't ask me!" I said.

"Why don't you ask me?" Jeffrey Spencer boomed from the doorway.

Adrianna gasped. "W-we would have, but we thought you had gone to Ohio."

"What files are you talking about?"

"These." Adrianna handed over the list.

"I don't know the files by their numbers," Spencer said. "Leave the paper here and I'll look around."

"Okay," Adrianna said. She smiled. "I guess that's it." She started toward the door.

Spencer nodded toward me. "Did Buck here come up to help you read the numbers?"

"We were going out for a drink," I said.

Spencer slammed his fist on the desk and yelled in his most imperious manner: "You expect me to believe that you were taking this girl out for a damn drink when she's barely out of the hospital? Damn it, I know you both. I like you both. But, even in this Trumpian era, I also like a little truth. Those numbers are on Evelyn's notepaper. Where did you get those claim numbers—and if my guess is right, what were you doing in her desk?   And, as for that"—he turned to me — "I think you also have some explaining about the paper I saw you take out of the desk in Evelyn's apartment the other night."

"Hold on," I shouted. "If anyone needs to do some explaining about that, it's you, 'My Darling,' it's you." I thrust the "To My Darling" letter into Spencer's face. "You explain this—and at the same time let me read what you pocketed at Evelyn's." *Man*, I thought, *am I going out on a limb.*

But after Spencer silently read the short "Darling" note, he sat heavily onto his executive chair and said, "I can see you and I have things to discuss, Buck. To share, if you like. Why don't you go home, Adrianna? You shouldn't be at work, let alone in my office."

"You've got to be kidding!" Adrianna replied. "I'm not leaving. Buck has told me everything about this 'Darling' letter," she lied, "and I want to hear your side of it right alongside him."

Spencer glared but said, "Very well. The three of us will talk. Ironic isn't it? I dropped the Robbins at the airport but didn't go with them to Ohio, because I suddenly thought that maybe I should look through Miss Robbins' office desk tonight myself? So, I told her parents I'd fly to Ohio tomorrow, instead of today, and I will."

"What did you think you might find in Evelyn's desk?" Adrianna asked.

"I wanted to make sure she didn't have anything personal about me, like info on me and Mary Ann, or some other, made-up romance."

Some other? I remember thinking. But Spencer continued:

"I guess it is obvious from the way I fumbled and failed to deny Mrs. Robbins' accusations that I violated Athena's sacred no-relationship rule with Evelyn. She and I, long ago—long, long ago—had an affair. What you may find hard to believe is that Evelyn was then a warm and seductive creature—and I was a hot-blooded young alpha male with, well, raging hormones and no previous outlet. She wasn't my secretary, just a file clerk, nor did I then have a big job, of course. But I knew that what we were doing was, er, irregular by Athena's standards.

"I brought wine and candy and flowers to the one-room apartment she had then, for the dinner she invited me to—a dinner she cooked with her own hands on two electric hot plates and which she literally fed to me, sitting on my lap. And afterwards" — he paused before deciding to share more, but then let it all hang out: 'we undressed each other, piece by piece, and did what young people who attract one another do much too readily, without weighing the consequences.

"She let me have my way with her, with no reluctance; and she enjoyed herself. She was very passionate. I had never had sex even once before. I was so thrilled, honestly, at losing my virginity that when she said she could go on a vacation with me, perhaps to the Homestead or the Tides Inn, I eagerly agreed. She made the reservations, and we spent a week together at the Tides—a week of paradise I could not afford, but I had a credit card even back in those ancient times and I was in thrall of Evelyn and ran eagerly along the garden path with her. She already knew every stepping stone. Every twist and turn she showed me took my breath away, along with my good sense. But I never hesitated. And I never regretted until much later.

"It never occurred to me to wonder where she had learned some of those things!

"Nor did I suspect then that she was insatiable, could never let go. Am I making sense?"

"Definitely," I said, "You must have been getting it really good. We saw that bedroom, the black negligee on the bed, the book of Mapplethorpe photos—"

"The vibrator," Adrianna contributed.

Spencer said, "She didn't have all those things then, as far as I know, but she did like having sex—a lot. I soon learned she never got enough of anything—sex, gifts, flattery, my time.

"That's what killed it. Her drain on my time. I could never have completed law school with her hanging on. So, as much as I hated to miss the hot sex, I stopped seeing her. It wasn't, what I said before, that she tired of me and found me too old, though I was older. It was that I wanted to succeed.

"And also, luckily for me, about this time I also met Marilyn, who became my wonderful wife. She was as supportive and unselfish as Evelyn was demanding, and soon I was wondering what I had ever seen in Evelyn.

"Evelyn threatened to interfere with my new relationship, and they did meet and talk, but, whatever Evelyn told her about me, Marilyn shrugged it off. And Evelyn eventually settled for the chances I gave her to move up at Athena.

"Don't get it wrong: She was qualified.

"And I think— I'm sure after seeing that fancy apartment—that she quickly discovered other profitable love interests, though she still wanted my attention at the office. Luckily, as I say, she wasn't the worse secretary in the world, not by a long shot.

"When my wife died, Evelyn was sympathetic but must have been seeing someone—possibly Lou, when he was temporarily separated from his wife. Anyway, whatever the reason, Evelyn didn't try to get back with me.

"However, more recently, whether she suspected something about me and Mary Ann or not, some of the old, grasping Evelyn seemed to roar back to the surface. I'll admit that a part of my pleasure at taking an early retirement was that I'd get away from Evelyn for good. Plus, of course, soon I'll be able to say goodbye to Athena's old no-relationships rule re Mary Ann. I'll admit, my life will be easier."

"And the money?" I began.

"I was almost totally surprised by that. She told me once she was leaving 'something' to me in her will, but I thought that was just talk, another of her ploys, another way to hold on. And I'm really surprised to be left so much! I don't know how she accumulated all that. I will see that all of it will go to the foundation and be put to a very good cause. Still, I'd hoped a later will would be found that left me out of all this.

"I am surprised, believe me, at this 'To My Darling' letter you just showed me. And I was surprised, too, by the note that I myself found and pocketed. I thought it might be another of her tricks, so I borrowed it, you might say, and read it. I even toyed with showing it to her parents but thought better of it.

"Since we're all three in this together – going through Evelyn's things, that is, and taking things we shouldn't, maybe, I will, as you asked, share it with you. Here. Read."

This envelope was addressed, "To My Partner."

I read aloud, "Dear Partner, I love that word so much. Partner. I don't want to upset your plans, but I've discovered your secret! There is no reason, however, that I have to tell other interested parties about this, if you know what I mean. Don't let me down and I won't let you down. But if you disappoint me, I might have to do something neither of us will like.   Partner."

"'Partner!'" Adrianna repeated. "What does that mean? Is that you, Mr. Spencer?"

"Me? No, that wouldn't make sense; it must be someone else though I can't imagine who.   She had that annoying habit of saying, 'We' wanted such and such or 'We' thought this,' but she never called me 'Partner.' I don't know anyone else she called that either. I can't fathom what she is referring to except that it sounds a bit shady."

Spencer re-examined the "To My Darling" note. "In this one I recognize Evelyn's way of talking and writing – and I guess it could have been to me at one time. But, unless she knew I'm serious about Mary Ann and it really stirred her up, I can't imagine her writing anything like this to me currently, or even in recent years.

"I believed I had become the Noble Father Figure. I still believe it.

"And it does seem odd," Spencer continued, "that neither letter was sent. Had she meant to send them but died first? Or was she just planning how to manipulate people?"

"You have no idea who else she might lately have been fu-funning with?" I said.

Spencer cut me off. "No idea, Buck. None at all. In recent years I've deliberately kept myself away from her private, non-Athena life."

"Sounds to me," I said, "like 'dearest' was someone she saw a lot of, and she thought the person liked her, too. That's not a very wide field, is it? Haven't you been surprised at how few people appear to be mourning her? Maury, for example, seemed quite moved—but had nothing good to say about her except that she was loyal.   Another thing: The note hints at previous attempts to get back in intimacy with this person."

Spencer said, "I assure you I've not been hounded by Evelyn to revive our fling. As to sympathy and shock, I've felt remorse but" – and here he again slammed his hand on his desk — "honestly, thank God Evelyn is finally out of my life. Of course, I suppose I'll have to own up to some of this to Mary Ann."

"What's past is past," I said. "Maybe Mary Ann will shrug off the past as easily as your late wife did." Attempting to wrap things up, I added, "What shall we do with the notes?"

"Before we get to that," said Spencer, "I want to know something. I've lived up to my part of the bargain. Now, what about yours? What files were you looking for in my office and Evelyn's desk? And why?"

"I was looking for evidence of possible fraud," Adrianna declared, much too honestly.

"Fraud!" Spencer exploded. "Looking for fraud in my papers? What the hell are you talking about young lady?" Spencer's face had turned bright red. I was surprised that Adrianna was so forthcoming— and hadn't planned a cover story. (She was a lawyer, wasn't she?)

Adrianna back-tracked. "Fraud may be over-stating things," she told Spencer. "You know I'm doing the telephone half of the telephone/computer audit as you asked me to. And I have found some unexpected long-distance calls from our multi-user telephones in Claims. I would like to track them down. And, more to the point, I wondered—you know how Evelyn could latch onto things—I wondered if her curiosity might have led her to question some of these calls herself."

"Oh." Spencer said. "I don't doubt there's some occasional abusive use of our phones and computers. But what were you looking for in my office?"

Adrianna was now quick to shift her story. "Well, Buck showed me the letter he picked up at Evelyn's," she claimed, "and I was going through her desk here to see if there were others, much as you meant to do, and I came upon the list of numbers. File numbers. I thought I'd see what they were related to and where they were— somebody might need them. So, rather than bother you," she said with all the humility she could muster, "I took it upon myself to look on your desk and chair, where everybody leaves things. The way staff uses your office, it's almost public space, really.

"I apologize if I overstepped, but I'd still like to know where those files are."

Noting Spencer's continued frown of annoyance, she added, "It's not like Evelyn was just your exec. You took Mary Ann Howell's advice and made Evelyn super-secretary-administrative assistant-whatever for your assistant VPs as well as for yourself."

She added, "Mr. Spencer, please give me some slack. I'm a lawyer, like you, and I just want all the facts—to see all the cards Evelyn held."

Spencer was still frowning but his face had returned to its natural color and he appeared somewhat appeased. "If it's somehow important to your audit, I'll locate those files for you myself. But stay out of Evelyn's desk, my office—and Lou's and Maury's offices too, for that matter! You should know better!"

"I do know better now," she said. "I guess I've read too many John Grisham novels!"

"While you're reforming," Spencer said, "please remember to keep any relationship you have with this young man," he waved at me, "out of the Claims Department!"

"Don't worry. The tall woman tending bar at his dinner for you has given him everything he wants!"

Sibyl had already headed for California and maybe I should have let that remark pass, but I've got PTSD, remember? "What did that bitch Evelyn tell you?!" I blurted out. "I told her I would kill her if—"

All three of us gasped and suddenly we were all laughing at this all-too-common expression. Our tension eased.

Spencer looked at us anew, seeming to see us as colleagues, not mere serfs, I think.

"Say," he said, "if you two are so darned interested in Evelyn, maybe you can help me clean out her apartment. I promised Mrs. Robbins I'd have Evelyn's things listed and stored until she could decide what to dispose of, and how. Evelyn has brothers and sisters who might want pieces of her furniture, for example.   I'll talk with the family some more when I fly out to Ohio tomorrow."

"Mr. and Mrs. Robbins have accepted you?" I asked.

"Surprising, isn't it? After the appointment at the lawyer's that Adrianna here smartly arranged, they looked around the apartment some more, and I think they may have seen some explicitly sexual items that persuaded them that Evelyn wasn't the innocent who left their home twenty years ago. And with that realization came the further thought that maybe I wasn't the wicked seducer I first looked to be."

"And," I said, "they now know about all the insurance money that was outside the will and that they, not you, will get.

"But what shall we do about Evelyn's notes?" I asked again.

"Certainly, we mustn't destroy them," Spencer said, "in case they might be evidence of some crime. Let's hold on to them for now, at least until the CDC confirms Evelyn's death was from accidental shellfish poisoning, a red tide. If it is confirmed as a natural event, then eventually we could just list the notes as 'incidental correspondence' in hopes Mrs. Robbins will say to toss them."

He looked at Adrianna, who suddenly seemed beat. "Adrianna, I don't want you at work tomorrow. Stay home. Rest up. I mean it. And since you sometimes take orders to be mere 'suggestions,' I'll add this: If you disobey me and come in here, I'll fire you, do you understand?"

"I uh-understand," she said. "I'll be good. And no more snooping where I'm not wanted, I swear."

"And now, I myself will drop you at your home," Spencer said to her, "since that Sibyl may be waiting for Mr. Grand here. What kind of name is that, anyway? Sibyl? Sounds like a siren."

"Sibyls were women who divined the future," I said, and I wanted to add that her future had already started in California. But no one was listening.

I went back to my hastily abandoned office, finished what I had been doing, straightened my desk and departed. When I reached my apartment, my land line was ringing, and it was Adrianna insisting that I read the "Dearest" note to her immediately and in full.

"No more snooping, indeed!" I said. But I did read the note to her. I read it slowly enough so that she could copy it down.

"Well, well!" she said. "That Evelyn! Do you buy Spencer's story that the affair was over years ago?"

"Maybe not quite so many years ago as he suggested," I said. "He may have a creative memory, like many of us, or a creative memory blank, like an accused politician. Speaking of Evelyn, what did she tell you about Sibyl?"

"She asked me if I knew about you and this Sibyl, and I said, 'Sure,' and she said, 'Well I'll be damned.' That was all."

"I'm glad Evelyn mentioned her," I lied. "That gives me a chance to get one thing straight: Sibyl's a nice girl. But she's gone. After staying with me a short time she stayed with Hormone Hal, the owner of the gym downstairs from me, and she came back the night of my dinner-party, uninvited but just to help and to thank me for supporting her job hunt and to tell me she had got the job in California and was leaving almost immediately. Don't give her another thought."

"Why would I?" Adrianna said. She hung up.

I fell into bed – quite alone.

Chapter Nine: A LIBRARY, A LUNCH AND A LIFT

BUCK:

The next day, after Spencer flew out to Ohio for real, I got a call at work from the supposedly resting Adrianna Canter. "Meet me at *Café Sur Le Parc* in half an hour, can you?"

"You've been ordered to rest. What if Spencer spots us?"

"He's in Ohio, remember? And it's important."

ADRIANNA:

At the restaurant, I told Buck, "I've spent the morning at the public library in Wheaton. You know they have stacks and stacks of specialized medical books? I read up on shellfish poisoning and found its symptoms are remarkably like some other poisons, such as strychnine, which I learned is a plant-based poison.

"'Once used in a very diluted form to treat constipation and as a stimulant, strychnine at higher levels can paralyze the lungs,'" I recited for Buck's benefit, "just like PSP. So why couldn't strychnine or maybe some other easily obtained poison have been added to my pot of bouillabaisse? Or just to Evelyn's bowl, Maury's, and mine?"

"Why are you so eager to make Evelyn's death a murder?" Buck said. "But I did talk to the CDC, and its assays, as I think they're called, will pick up those other poisons, if present."

"Great. Can you do me one more thing?" I asked Buck. "Last night, I left that little piece of paper from Evelyn's desk behind—the slip of paper with the file numbers on it with Spencer. It's probably still on Spencer's desk. But I promised I wouldn't go near his stuff again.

"Can you go in while he's away and find and copy the numbers? He's got a copier right by his desk. Cut the copy so it looks like the original, leave the copy, and bring the original to me.   Might prove to be evidence one day!"

Buck made an ugly face but nodded.

"Thanks. Now, have I made it clear to you how these claims frauds might work?"

"You've got more?" Buck asked.

"Here's a really sad one," I replied. "Florida. A small child dashes into the street in the middle of the block just as our policy-holder, a young mother, is driving along. The child freezes. The mother, the driver, isn't texting, her cell phone is off, and she doesn't even have the radio on, but she can't stop in time. The child is killed. Later, when the driver talks to our representative, she mentions that her own child was in the back squirming to get out of his booster safety seat but that she said she was used to that.

"None of this is in the police record," I told Buck, "but somehow the lawyer representing the dead child's family takes us to court and homes-in on an allegedly squirming child in the back seat. Showing our insured a picture of the child who died, the lawyer says, 'Didn't this beautiful child die because you were distracted by your own child's trying to get free from his safety seat?' and the mother, tears suddenly running down her cheeks, says, 'I don't know, I hope not.' How did the lawyer know to ask about the child in the back, much less that it might have been distracting the mother? You know the answer, don't you Buck, as sure as I do?"

"Yes, "Buck agreed. "That's as impressive a case as that rear-ender you told me about. I'd like to hear more. But right now, to keep my alleged job, I'd better get back to work."

"But you'll go by Spencer's office and get the numbers?" I asked.

"Absolutely," Buck said, "I'm beginning to feel that you and I've been dropped in the middle of a crime novel. Maybe the only way to get you and me out alive is to solve it. To play amateur detectives—defective detectives, you might say. But remember, if I do get you out alive, you'll owe me big."

"I'll owe you?" I laughed. "No, you'll owe me for making you the hero of Athena, which may get you out of 'parking, puking and pensions,'" I said, proud of my alliteration, "and into a real job.

"But don't let Mary Ann pile any more work on you, as you have another job to do, on top of that book you're ghosting for Spencer. Spencer called me on his way to the airport to say he left Mary Ann Howell the key to Evelyn's place to get to me. As a backup, the building's super has a key and knows I'll be going through Evelyn's things. Since I'm resting today, as he said to, I'll start on her apartment right after lunch tomorrow on company time. That's probably a lot sooner than Spencer figured I could get on it, but I don't see any percentage in delaying, if, as you say, we're in the middle of a mystery to be solved. You'll join me when you get off work?"

"Join you? He said I should do that?" Buck asked.

"He said if I found anything licentious, immoral, obscene or salacious, as I'm sure to, I should give it to you to dispose of. That'll be easiest if you are there, working, say, on the Spencer book on your laptop."

"Well, something there could also give us a clue," Buck said, "something we badly need."

"So, can you drive me over to Evelyn's tomorrow at lunch?"

"Where's your car?" Buck said.

"Haven't got one. I take a Metro bus to work."

"But your parking committee – what was that all about?"

"Just didn't like women employees without seniority and big degrees getting the shaft," I admitted. "I do thank you for helping us."

Half under his breath, Buck mumbled the F-word. "If you don't get yourself killed investigating this claims stuff, I may kill you myself!" he told me.

I just laughed. "Get along to your so-called work. Since I invited you to lunch, I'll pay the check."

"Do that." Buck jumped up and hurried off. I think he was more amused than angry at being conned into helping me clean up after Evelyn. (But he would indeed bring his laptop along and write on the Spencer book until I needed him for some specific chore.)

BUCK:

Back at my office, I immediately called CDC to confirm that its testing would specifically pick up strychnine or a variety of other poisons Adrianna had mentioned—if they were present—and that the results might be ready the next day. "Yes, yes," Dr. James Aitchison said, perhaps annoyed I'd think CDC would do a sloppy testing job.

I then assembled data on Spencer's personal pension and, to be on the safe side, wrote a memo asking him a series of questions for our book. If anybody asked what I was doing in Spencer's office, those should provide cover enough.

Chapter Ten: DEFINITELY

BUCK:

Next morning, I got what I thought was great news from CDC: I caught it on tape on a little recorder I attached to my phone:

"No, it wasn't arsenic, it wasn't strychnine. It wasn't any of the other possible poisons that you mentioned, or a host of others, Mr. Grand," Dr. Aitchison said.

It seemed like many weeks later, considering all the media reports that had piled up on my desk, plus the TV I had seen clips from, and what I had begun to call the "anti-social" media. But only a few days had really passed and here was Aitchison saying, "It was definitely paralytic shellfish poisoning. I'd stake my reputation on that. I couldn't be sure if it was carried by the mussels or just which other seafood; it's hard to be sure from partially digested stomach contents or a cooked stew.   Everything gets kind of blended."

My stomach turned. "Envisioning that, I might throw up," I said.

Aitchison guffawed. "But PSP should be a relief to you and your Miss Trotter—no, sorry, that's Canter, isn't it? —the lawyer-cook? — in that no amount of cooking or preventive handling would have changed the outcome.

The only odd thing about the poisonings of the deceased, and your executive, and the little lawyer-cook (I love saying that) is that they are the only cluster that has been reported. Ordinarily, you'd expect a bad batch of seafood to reach a good many dinner tables and there would be other sick people taken to other hospitals from other dinners. We've checked.

"Nothing.

"But the Division of Marine Fisheries did recently see some Maryland test results that while not reaching the actionable level, did approach it. You could speculate that perhaps somewhere near where our sample was taken there may have been a higher peak that affected a few shellfish, and that these could have gotten clustered at your market and your table.

"CDC has informed all the Eastern coastal states of your cases and will continue to look for any other possible illnesses, of course. It should also help that your poisonings have been reported so widely in the newspapers and on TV along with alerts as to the symptoms and the need for immediate medical care. We don't want any additional deaths marring our safety record!"

"No," I said. "Nor mine. You'll be glad to hear that everyone else who got sick has fully recovered."

"Maurice Woodrow and even the Canter woman? We did confirm PSP in samples from both their stomachs, as well as from the dead woman."

"Yes, Maurice Woodrow and Adrianna Canter are well again."

"Maybe," the expert said, "they ate less stew or had stronger immune systems."

I asked a few more questions and then called Danyel, confirming to her that the CDC saw the poisoning as a natural shellfish problem, with no other poison detected. "No strychnine, no mishandling involved." I played her the tape of my conversation with Aitchison. I also called Adrianna and played it for her.

Then, with my "cover" forecast of what Spencer could expect as a pension, as well as some pages from our book, I went to Spencer's office to follow through on my promise to Adrianna.

But as I walked past Evelyn's desk I saw and heard a line she had shared with Spencer and others blinking and ringing. There was a claims man at the other end of the big room, but he didn't attempt to answer the call, whether or not he had the call on his phone as well.

I'm compulsive about ringing phones, I guess. I picked it up after the ninth ring. "Mr. Spencer's office," I said.

"Oh, thank *heav*ens, I do have the ri-yut number!" The voice was female and Southern, turning single syllable words into doubles.

"Yes, but I'm sorry," I said, "Mr. Spencer's out of town. Can I take a message?"

"Whya, yey-us you may," the voice said. "Would you ask him to call Mrs. Phyllis Gyraud." She spelled her last name. "He has my numbah," she added.

The number Mrs. Gyraud was calling from showed up clearly on Caller ID, and began with 804, which I knew was the Richmond area code in Virginia, so I read the number aloud and asked, "Should Mr. Spencer call you back at this number? It's company policy to have a call-back number on all messages—in case, for example, Mr. Spencer might call in for his messages but not have your return number handy."

"I see," Mrs. Gyraud said. "He's not heyah in Richmond by any chance?"

"No ma'am," I said. "He's in the – ah – Midwest." No need to say he was in Ohio to attend a funeral. Satisfied, Mrs. Gyraud said, "I do think you," and hung up.

I was completing the "While You Were Out" slip when Lou Howard approached.

"Well, Buck," he said, "what brings you up here where we actually get work done?"

I said, "I have Mr. Spencer's pension figures, plus some questions for him regarding his book, and I want to put them all where he'll see them first thing when he returns from Ohio.

"Plus, arriving here to leave this stuff, I heard the phone ring and none of your so-called 'workers' were answering it, so I picked it up. The line just dripped with Southern honey – a Mrs. G-y-r-a-u-d for Spencer. Ever heard of her?"

"Not a claimant I'm familiar with, but there are Southern belles among them, I'm sure. Or she might be a friend or relative—or what about a ladylove?" Lou said, leering. "I know he enjoys the company of women, though Jeffrey's social circles and mine don't overlap much."

He stared at Evelyn's desk. "Can't believe she's dead. She could be a pain in the backside, but she was kind of a fixture. And to die at a party we all attended!" Lou looked at me and seemed to realize that for me, as the host, the whole thing was a lot worse. "Sorry. I guess you've heard more than you want to on that subject."

I told Lou, "I got the official word from the Centers for Disease Control down in Atlanta today that Evelyn and Maury and Miss Canter were definitely victims of a natural poison, specifically paralytic shellfish poison from something like a red tide, that no amount of cooking or refrigeration could have prevented."

Lou said, "I think Jeffrey would like to know that. Leave a note in his desk chair when you put the other stuff on his desk. Whoever takes his call will pass the information along. That's our routine. He's due back late tomorrow or the next day."

Why did I have to run into Lou, the social animal? He'll never leave so I can retrieve that slip with the numbers!

And now, Maury approached. "What's going on with you gentlemen?"

Lou said, "Buck has some stuff for our esteemed retiring leader, and he stopped to play secretary when the phone rang."

I pointed to the telephone message from Mrs. Gyraud. "Ever deal with a policy-holder named Gyraud?"

"No. It's a French name, I suppose," Maury said.

With that, we three men seemed to have run out of topics to discuss. We stood looking at each other.

Finally, Lou said, "Three-handed poker, anyone? What's on your mind, Maury?"

Maury sniffed. "Probably the same thing as you, looking for projects Evelyn was involved in. This has been a terrible week." Maury did look beat. "Not much fun having my stomach pumped, and I may never look at a mussel again without angst, anxiety and dyspepsia!"

I stepped toward Spencer's office. "I'll put this stuff and the telephone message where Spencer will see it."

With that said, I at last got into Spencer's office. I looked quickly about as I put my information on the desk and the phone message in Spencer's chair. *Phone messages, the last use of carbon paper in this computer age,* I thought, but I didn't think to take a copy.

As for the list of case numbers Adrianna wanted duplicated, I looked atop, beside and under the desk. Nothing.

I lifted a stack from the desk and looked quickly through the "in" box. Nada.

Outside, Lou was saying, "You do look tired, Maury. You better take a few days off. Take your boat out and just go! That's what I enjoy doing."

Maury replied, "Not the best time to be out of the office. Not trying to get rid of me prematurely, are you? Besides—"

"You have a yacht?" I butted in. *I don't think Danyel has done boating.*

"Had," Maury said. "Past tense, I'm sorry to say. I'm surprised you would remember it, Lou, but I had a nice little sailboat for cruising the bay, 32 feet, and I loved her, almost as much as I love Stella. There's nothing like sailing a sweet sailboat, but I sold it. Stella gets very, very seasick. Whether over the side or over the captain," he said, "there's not much that takes more of the fun out of sailing than *mal de mer*! Lou, you and your son are the sailors now."

"I'm just surprised, Maury, that you would ever sell anything that nifty," Lou said.

He turned to me. "Maury is the guy who they wrote that bumper sticker for: 'He Who Dies with The Most Toys Wins.' Maury has this really cool MG – one of the really old ones. He has a greenhouse, a gigantic swimming pool marked with lanes and all, and exotic trees and flowers, political pins, and more steins than I've ever seen before. It's a wonder *House Beautiful* hasn't featured his grounds. The interior of the house is special, too – though that's Stella's doing, pretty much, I guess. She bought that set of Audubon bird pictures, didn't she Maury? I wish to hell I'd married a rich wife!"

Maury looked miffed, but I was all smiles.

"Political pins?" I said. "Steins? I'm looking for an unusual hobby or collection for Danyel to write up in the *Athena Herald,*" I said, "in return for promoting the safety record of Athena's food services."

"Ah, well, yes, Buck, I do enjoy my political memorabilia and my steins, and I enjoy sharing them. So yes, I'd love to see them, or our fish(!) written up. Stella just bought me a beauty of a fish I call Jaws, so I'll admit, as Lou says, it's nice when a wife has a little money too.

"But Buck, as to your needing an article, you know Mary Ann Howell could just ask Frederica Pulsudski to order Danyel to write up food services. You don't have to bribe her!"

"Ah, I can guess what kind of half-hearted, begrudging effort that ordered article would be," I said.

"Well, maybe you know best," Maury responded. "*Quid pro quo.* As for a spread on my collections, I hope you might do the writing yourself while George does the pictures. Anyway, you must come to see my treasures and have a swim, whether Danyel wants a story or not. Bring a date too."

"Say, I have a collection of odd socks," Lou said. "Any story in that? Seriously, we too have a pool and you and Adrianna are welcome there too!"

Adrianna! I remembered. "Got to dash!"

"Hot date?" Lou asked.

"I have to prepare for a meeting I'm hoping to have tomorrow."

I had decided that after Adrianna and I worked at Evelyn's apartment, we should have dinner at my place as it would be too late to find a place to eat out at nine o'clock or so. I would buy everything tonight—a Sauvignon blanc, lettuce and a choice of Ken's bottled dressings, plus eggs, bacon, tomatoes and milk for an omelette we could make together. (Don't they say, The couple that cooks together, copulates together? No, they don't, but I like to think it.)

"I would also stop by the neighborhood deli and get its rich pomegranate and dark chocolate ice cream, a specialty.

"For afterward."

If the murder mystery no longer needed solving, I'd try to crack Adrianna.

Chapter Eleven: I MADE MY BED

BUCK:

With the poisoning cleared up, I strode into work Thursday morning feeling happier than I had since Sibyl departed and Evelyn died. It was a bright and beautiful day, and I knew my apartment was clean, comfortable, and ready for the night and Adrianna. So was I. I had made my bed with care. Just anticipating the evening perked me up, even if Adrianna would spend the first hours working on Evelyn's apartment and I would work on the Spencer book.

I drove Adrianna over to Evelyn's at noon, as planned. Along the way, with the top down, we each munched a pre-packaged sandwich from Athena's Taste-o-Matic. (Danyel and I had sponsored an employee contest to name the set of machines. "Taste-o-Matic" was the best of seventeen entries.) After the bland sandwich, I figured Adrianna would readily agree to dinner at my place when we finished at Evelyn's. I was right. She readily agreed.

Happy and whistling, I left her at Evelyn's place, and five and a half hours later, still happy and whistling, I was back. I hurried down the eleventh-floor hall and pushed the buzzer at Evelyn's. I couldn't hear any ring, so I knocked.

"Adrianna?"

"Buck?" came Adrianna's muffled voice from the other side of the door.

"Yes, it's me. Open up."

Her words rushed out: "I can't! Someone was in here when I arrived and hit me, knocked me out, at least briefly, and locked me in here using the deadbolt. When I woke I couldn't reach anybody to help me because whoever broke in stopped long enough to take my phone, and the landline doesn't work. Discontinued or cut." She sounded as if she had been crying.

"Sit tight," I said. "I'll get the super!"

I ran to the elevator and quickly reached the building superintendent. According to a plaque on the counter, his name was B. D. Jones. I explained in brief what had happened. "Do you have a pass key of some sort?"

"Course. That's how I let her in. She said a key was supposed to have been left with her but it wasn't. But I had heard from Mr. Spencer that a woman would be coming to straighten and sort Miss Robbins things, so I let her in. How did she hit her head and get herself locked in? You have to lock those double cylinders from the outside to do that."

"Let's not worry about that. She's pretty scared; we need to unlock that door pronto."

We hurried back to the eleventh floor, Jones all the while complaining about the building's obsolete security. "We should have cameras at the doors and in the halls, and exterior doors that automatically lock and signal if someone's propped them open. Maybe when some lady tenant gets raped or killed the management will wake up and get security conscious." We reached the door and freed Adrianna, who embraced me tearfully and thanked the super. She was shaking and disheveled and had a cut over her right eye.

"Thank God you've come," she said. "Somebody must have already been here when you let me into the apartment, Mr. Jones. The curtains were closed and the lights didn't go on, but by the time I knew that, you had already gone. Someone, probably the intruder, had pulled out the circuit breaker, it seems. Each apartment has its own, I discovered."

"Yep," said the super. "They're in the kitchens."

"I finally found it and got the lights to come on. But before I found the circuit breaker, I was feeling my way around in the dark. I heard a noise in the main bedroom, and went toward it –"

"You should have turned around and left!" I said.

"I had no idea, at first, Buck, that it was an intruder. I thought a member of the family, maybe, or someone else helping from the office. I called out. But something came hurtling through the air at me and I stumbled and fell and blacked out, dropping my phone. I wasn't out long, I guess, but then I found myself locked in somehow, and my phone gone. I had no way to reach anyone. And I couldn't get out. So, I panicked, at least at first.

"Then, as I said, I groped around, opened the curtains and finally found the circuit breaker, and so I got the lights on. And since I was stuck here until you arrived, Buck, I just went ahead and sorted and catalogued."

"What a trouper," I said.

"I got a lot done actually, but since the electricity had been off, the clocks didn't tell the right time and my mobile had been grabbed and taken as the person fled—did I already mention that? —so I didn't know what time it was getting to be and I began to think you had forgotten me." Adrianna began to sniffle.

The super said, "I had better go down to my office and call the police."

"Tell them I think the burglar was going through Miss Robbins' dressing table and/or bedside tables. The drawers were open. I probably surprised the thief before he got anything of value—except my phone, of course."

I jumped in. "Look, B.D.," I told the super, "take Miss Canter's card and mine, here, too, and tell the police they can reach her, wherever she is, on her iPhone. Meanwhile, I'll get her forehead patched up at an emergency room and get her a drink and some food." The super decided that was a good plan.

"I'll come back to the apartment later," B.D. said, "and let the police look around if they want, and make sure things are properly locked up afterward." He left.

Adrianna was rattling on nervously as we got ready to leave, but I was staring at a piece of paper sticking out of a page in Evelyn's personal telephone book. It read, "P. Gyraud."

Well, well, well. The name of the Richmond woman with the Sou-ther-ren accent!

Adrianna was at the door. She opened it and let out a cry at a cloaked figure standing there. The person, he or she, ran down the hall. I took off in pursuit.

The intruder ran through a door with a lighted "exit" sign—a door to utility steps of steel leading down to the other floors.

I barreled after the intruder through the door and paused at the top of the stairs.

Uh, oh.

I heard Adrianna yell something like, "Careful!" or "Watch out!" and felt the foot of my artificial leg catch on something.

Was I tripped?

Pushed? It happened too fast to know. But I felt fear like never since Afghanistan as I flew—hurtled toward sure death! I thought — plunging spread-eagle toward the steel and concrete landing a flight below.

I've had it! I'm a dead man!

I desperately thrust out my arms to grab the iron railing that ran down the right wall. *Thanking God for all the weight lifting I've done at Hal's gym,* I got both hands on the railing and almost held on. Afghanistan flooded back. I felt the sudden rise of the Humvee and its sickening rotation, as I crashed to earth.

My brief hold on the railing managed to slow my fall but I ricocheted into the wall, smashing my nose, which I had previously been rather proud of. I half-slid, mostly crashed to the floor. I felt a lightning strike of pain to my head that riveted the length of my body, with a special intensity in my chest and shoulder, as if something had burst there.

I couldn't breathe but I was hurting so much, I guessed I wasn't yet dead.

In that instant though, I lay on a primitive dirt road beside my dead twin brother Jens.

And something very bad had happened to my leg.

ADRIANNA, with tears in her eyes:

I heard him scream, just as the intruder came back into the upstairs hall and ran to another exit. I rushed pell-mell down the steps to help Buck, almost falling myself. Buck lay crumpled up on the landing. He had to be dead after such a fall.

But he was moaning.

Then he must still be alive. His face and head were a mixture of blood and snot, but there were no exposed brain cells as far as I could tell. I gingerly sought an undamaged spot on his face to kiss. And I wept.

I could see his hands were abraded and bleeding. His shoulder, which must have taken the brunt of the fall when he hit the landing, was wrenched and twisted, maybe broken. And he would be terribly bruised, probably from head to foot. Foot singular. I saw his artificial leg had been torn loose from the stump of his left leg and looked damaged. The stump itself was bleeding through his trouser leg.

I rifled through his clothes and found his phone to call 911, but the phone didn't work. And mine had been stolen! I just screamed and screamed. Miraculously hearing the commotion, the Super, B.D., showed up, sized up the situation with a "You again?" kind of look on his face, and called for an ambulance.

Buck remained unconscious except for two moments when he stirred and mumbled. He first pronounced his favorite F-word, adding, "Got to be more to this than a red tide." Later he roused himself to say, "'P. Gyraud.' Don't forget. Ask me about 'P. Gyraud.'"   I almost laughed. Buck started out trying to avoid becoming involved in solving Evelyn's poisoning, but now that he was half dead, at least I hoped just half, he seemed determined to unravel it!

I rode with him in the ambulance to Sibley Hospital's now familiar emergency room. He was given pain-killers and his hands were cleaned and treated. He would need a plastic surgeon to restore his patrician nose. His clavicle, or collar bone, was broken, and three ribs.

He would be admitted and watched for concussion. The broken bones would be immobilized until they knit back together. His jaw would be wired and, eventually three badly broken teeth would be replaced.

Reversing roles, he was now in a hospital bed, and I, with a mere four stitches in my forehead, lay in the Lazy Boy recliner beside the bed.

We had been handed a list of concussion symptoms and problems to watch for – confusion, blank stares, delayed answering of questions, slurred speech, clumsiness – can't walk in a straight line. "In addition," a nurse said, "watch for extreme emotions – crying or getting very angry – of repeating things, asking the same questions over and over, and failing to remember words or objects. Finally, watch for loss of consciousness beyond ordinary sleep."

"With a few drinks, I can get like that any weekend," Buck said, slurring the words but trying to smile.

"That's no recommendation, you know," I said, and the nurse nodded.

But when the nurse had gone and Buck said, "Aw, gimme a kish, A-dri-anna, I just nearly got killed," I did kiss him, several times over.

In the morning, after looking over his battered body, I kissed him again—with tears in my eyes and with what I figured was a sort of post-coital warmth. Indeed, after the violence and danger of the night before, I felt like something had been consummated, though nothing of the sort, at least of a sexual nature, had happened.

Maybe Buck had the same feeling of connection, for he kissed me back with gratitude. "You're a jinx and a pain in the, uh, rear, you know, but you are very good at picking up the pieces," he managed to say.

He must have been in great pain, but he exerted himself and managed to stand, intending to dress and go to work.

The fool!

He collapsed by the bed.

I screamed for the nurses, and they got him back in bed and had the staff doctor check him again. The doctor said Buck's spleen, lungs or other organs, or his blood vessels or bones had apparently been so bruised and banged up that he was bleeding inside, a common occurrence if you lived through such a fall. The doctor advised it was better to see if things healed over time on their own rather than to cut him open to find out what the source was, unless the bleeding didn't stop on its own or got so bad they had to go in. So, Buck most reluctantly spent a week in the hospital just lying there hurting (without much in the way of pain-killers, as they tend to slow clotting) while being observed for internal bleeding.

The doctors also concluded he indeed had suffered a concussion. At first, Buck could not   remember chasing anyone down the hall and into the stairway, nor his flight down that stairway, nor his plea that I ask him about someone, whose name he could no longer remember. Nor could I.

A couple of days passed before I thought that I "kind of" remembered what Buck had said. I told Buck, "You said to ask you about somebody sounding like Gerald. It wasn't really a man's first name but sounded like that."

He couldn't remember even that.

Besides the bleeding and concussion to worry about there were his collar bone to be kept immobilized in a sling and his ribs (wrapped uncomfortably to keep them from moving around) so these fractures could heal.

But neither Spencer nor Buck saw any reason for Buck to just lie there when there was the book to be completed so, as soon as possible, Spencer began coming by regularly at 7 a.m. Both all business, Spencer talked about the book (and Buck mumbled his replies) until Spencer left for work. They used a small recorder Buck could replay at will.   I brought Buck his laptop and he kept his medicine to a minimum so he had a clear head and could continue to write, hunting and pecking with the fingers of his free hand.

The book thus proceeded, but Buck still strained to remember the "ask me about" name. He finally remembered that when he had gone to Spencer's desk at my bidding, he hadn't been able to find the list I wanted but he had intercepted a telephone call from a woman who at one point asked if Spencer might be in her town, Richmond, Virginia.

Two days later he remembered that in Evelyn's apartment, he saw the same name sticking out of a book.

"Do you think that old roué Spencer has another love interest beside Mary Ann?" I (always suspicious) asked Buck. "Think Evelyn learned of it? It fits her 'Partner' letter that Spencer is so eager to tell us couldn't be for him. I'll have to look further into that address book of hers when I'm able to go back there. Do you think Evelyn could have been blackmailing Spencer himself?"

EVELYN: *Blackmailing?!* Even if I'd actually sent the letter, which I hadn't, I don't call it blackmail if you just hint you know something! (Which I wasn't really sure I did.)

BUCK:
"Blackmailing her boss?" I said. "Yes, she could have been. But wait -- you're going back to Evelyn's apartment?"

ADRIANNA, defiantly:
"Sure, when I can do so safely," I said. "My landlady Mildred goes with me. She has a gun, and she knows how to use it." I didn't tell Buck that I also had my own little gun. Mildred had driven me to Virginia, where about all you need to buy a pistol or even an automatic weapon is the money to pay for it.

Meanwhile, Buck was having his jaw wired and a repair of his smashed and twisted nose. Nothing much could be done about cracked ribs, except to keep him quiet while they slowly healed. Ditto for his clavicle, which I told Buck I previously thought was something you play with padded drumsticks. Turns out it's M.D. talk for "collarbone." (Factoid: The two collarbones, the doctor told me, are the only long bones in the human body that are horizontal.)

Being laid up had its pluses for Buck. Without having to go to work and unable to do strenuous exercise, Buck actually had an abundance of time to finish the Spencer book. He worked every day on it but he also, I think, sweated over Evelyn's death, his determination fueled, I think, by the painful, near-fatal attack on him, as well as the attack on me and the earlier stealing of my computer, which he could no longer consider simple theft. (Besides, what else could he do? Even on the weekends he couldn't bar hop, binge drink and pick up women, as he used to. Couldn't even sit on those hard pews at St. Columba's to ogle the choir girls.)

BUCK:

St. C's priest, Ledlie Laughlin, came to visit *me* and sent me weekly communion. I had other visitors, too. Athena's know-all Connie Yeager came by, probably to try to get the skinny on how I fell.

Mary Ann came by and, though she seemed somewhat alarmed at how I looked, she read pages from the Spencer book and had good things to say about them.

She seemed more than a little stressed, partly from having shouldered some of my work I supposed, though she had brought someone in from the field to help.

Maybe there was more to her stress than over-work, however. She pressed me about Adrianna's listing of Evelyn's things in the apartment, harshly ridiculing the idea that "everything that awful woman owned" needed cataloguing.

"I just don't know what Jeffrey was thinking about to offer to get that done," she complained. "There are firms that will buy and sell any good furniture, and charities that will take the rest, while gross stuff, like crude pictures and black negligees could be trashed. Just trashed!"

I was thankful that not once did she ask me to do work at home or pressure me to come back prematurely.

But I wondered: Did she guess or did she know about that negligee and the porn? Had Spencer told her? That seemed unlikely.

Meanwhile, George came by and left a bunch of pictures from my fateful dinner and a smaller packet from the Oldest Customer shoot.

And Lou came by to ask me, as I was on the Credit Union board, about getting a low interest loan so he could pay off a $45,000 debt for the decorators who did over the living room of his home. I wasn't allowed to get involved in the loaning process but suggested he ask the Credit Union to work out a series of quarterly payments with the decorators, so as to get them off his back. Since my apartment was largely furnished from my Mom's and other people's attics, I couldn't imagine how or why the Howards blew $45,000!

ADRIANNA:
Regardless of these interruptions, Buck had plenty of time for the Spencer book and for thinking about the Evelyn conundrum, even as he graduated from the hospital proper to its rehab wing and as his stump toughened up and his prosthesis was repaired.

Part Two: **FLASHBACK TO A SQUIRREL**

Chapter Twelve: HOW IT STARTED

BUCK:

Yep, I had time to think back to the cursed day I first tangled with Evelyn.   It was coincidentally the same day I met the challenging Adrianna and heard her first evidence of fraud at the company. Guess what? That was also the day I discovered that my boss Mary Ann was in an irregular relationship, by Athena standards, with Vice President Spencer.

It was one hell of a load of stuff for this traumatized ex-Marine to process:

Coming out of the service into the Great Recession, I felt lucky to be hired at Athena or anywhere at all – my friend George Brown let me know about the opening -- and my job was hardly high level.

On this particular day my crapola included supervising the caterers, wait staff and so on for a banquet honoring Claims' VP Jeffrey Spencer on his 20th anniversary with the company.

But first off, that day, I had come in almost two hours early to prepare a report on what are known as 409 pensions. My acting boss Mary Ann Howell had promised the report to the Athena board members "in an easy, non-legalistic version," hoping it would help her lose the conditional "acting" in front of her title. Of course, she unloaded the task on me, and I, already over-worked, put it off as long as possible. Up against it now, with my annual job ratings coming up, I hoped to maybe get it done by noon and then devote myself to any last-minute details involving the banquet.

It's funny what I remember of that day, how driving into the dark and empty parking lot, I narrowly missed running over one of Washington's ever-present brown squirrels. It had been chasing an egg-and-sausage muffin wrapper.

Mr. Squirrel froze in terror. I tossed him the rest of my breakfast bar and earned a "chirrup" of thanks.

Totally comfortable with the prosthesis that replaced my lower left leg, I walked briskly into Athena's building, a great glass rectangle reflecting the world around it, including a soft glow where the sun would rise. I was soon at my desk making great progress in the early quiet. My ideas bloomed like roses in a well-manured bed, and the pages flowed.

But when the workday officially began, this Evelyn Robbins person came barreling down the hall to demand last-minute changes in the night's dinner honoring her boss.

"We," she crowed, implying this came from VP Spencer as well as from herself, "wanted a seafood entree, not these common steaks, and *we* wanted an anniversary cake!"

I began explaining that Athena's founders favored the beautiful ribeye steaks I had ordered because they and many others disliked or were allergic to seafood. But Evelyn persisted, screeching her demands while managing to comment on my "bright, floral necktie," by which she seemed to imply I was some kind of personnel pansy she could push around if she just said "we" enough and was nasty enough.

Her yammering went on and on until it set off my PTSD. Announcing that I had work to do, I rose to my full six feet four and finally cussed her and sent her packing. ("Cussing," I'll admit may be minimizing just what I said, for she got an alarmed look on her face and stepped back and quickly bolted, shouting she would "get me" later.)

I had barely returned to the pension report when nine women arrived to complain about their lack of parking space. Their tiny no-nonsense leader was Adrianna Canter, who was also new to me. She said, "This is supposed to be a woman-oriented insurance company, yet most parking is reserved for men. Lower level women employees, who can't afford it, are forced to feed parking meters and risk getting tickets they can't afford. And there is no accommodation for the cleaning women who work at night and must walk long distances through a dark parking lot, if they are lucky enough to find a spot at all."

After Evelyn's tirade, I almost welcomed this relatively reasonable complaint.

I promised the group I would read their petition carefully, see what I could do and report back in three weeks.

"Two weeks?" one of the group said hopefully.

"Nothing worthwhile gets down around here in two weeks," I said. "Three."

They left not exactly smiling but hopeful I meant what I said, that something "worthwhile" would get done in three.

Adrianna returned after a few minutes to tell me she had been reviewing "personal" telephone use by employees (in conjunction with my friend George Brown's look at computer abuses such as game playing, Face Book and Twitter exchanges, and worse). For her study, there was no record of what was said on calls, or even what individual person made a call since our phones are shared by clusters of people, but our telephone contractor could provide her with the outside numbers being called. She could thus sample who was being called – clients and businesses Athena routinely worked with, say, versus schools and homes and hospitals, which might be legitimate personal calls, if not too frequent, but if the numbers called were bookies, or race tracks, stores and home repair firms, they might indicate inappropriate use of the Athena phones.

Adrianna said she hadn't uncovered "anything too awful" until she stumbled on calls made from Claims telephones to outside attorneys whom she knew to have somewhat shady reputations in the two cities where she had worked before coming to Athena. She knew some of these lawyers were suing us over accidents our policy-holders were involved in.

Turns out, she discovered, these same lawyers subsequently won very large judgements against Athena and drivers we insured, which meant Athena paid out a lot of money, from which the lawyers, in most cases, would often get a percentage as high as half in fees. Adrianna said she suspected someone was leaking crucial Athena information to these lawyers.

Since both of us had piles of pressing work, we agreed to talk more about this at the end of the banquet.

By the time the banquet began, Evelyn—the angry *we* woman— appeared to have forgotten our fight and to have relaxed enough to have a shrimp or two and a pre-banquet drink. ("Just the one" she said). As for me, for PTSD-related survival purposes I don't drink at all during the workweek, but this was a Friday. I downed a couple of stiff ones. Bourbons.

The dinner went very well, and Spencer's subsequent speech began in the manner you would expect, with verbal bouquets to the Athena founders, the boards and his fellow officers. However, the speech quickly turned and surprised me and most everyone, I think. Mr. Spencer bluntly announced, "I have concluded that this, my 20th anniversary would be the right time to not only say 'thank you' but 'goodbye.'"

There were gasps and a few shouts of "no." Evelyn remained red-faced and slack-jawed as Spencer continued:

"Some of you may know that when I was young, I lost a beloved wife, Marilyn, in childbirth, along with the beautiful little girl she was carrying. We had planned to name her Abrielle. A pretty name, isn't it? Abrielle.

"I have never truly recovered from those losses. I often think of how much life and love they've missed—and how much I've missed. Now that I have a secure retirement, thanks to the generosity and opportunity provided by this great company and its people, plus a substantial amount of worth in Athena stock I bought early when it was as little as three or four dollars a share, I plan to contribute seed money for a foundation to work alongside the March of Dimes to study several specific birth problems—and hopefully reduce or eliminate some of the deaths and disabilities attendant to them."

Maury gently blew his nose. His wife Stella listened with tears in her eyes.

But Adrianna Canter? The newly prettied-up parking crusader was mouthing, if I lip-read accurately, "Bull-pucky." Her crimson lips clearly, if silently, formed the euphemism again, even as the crowd gave Spencer a standing ovation several minutes long.

Although at the time I had barely met Spencer, I didn't automatically buy Adrianna's view of him. I knew his reputation as a hard-nosed boss, but, hearing his remarks, I thought: *Somebody famous said that, like the moon, each man has a dark side nobody knows. For Spencer, maybe the reverse is true: This seemingly strict, dour businessman has a better, warmer side, now brightly, if briefly, illuminated.*

Yet Adrianna for a third time mouthed her opinion, as she walked aggressively toward me.

Wow! While she was small, her walk, her attitude and the swing of her hips made me feel an enjoyable pre-tumescence. If she was willing, and my size and weight didn't kill her, I was arrogantly sure she would enjoy the big gift I could offer her. I was glad we had a kind of date, even if I'd have to listen to her suspicions of fraud.

So, Adrianna and I headed for Georgetown and, for the moment, I forgot about my guest Sibyl, who was waiting for me at home. At a stoplight, I gave Adrianna a boozy kiss and she gave me an equally boozy kiss back.

Adrianna and I were soon entwined in a dark corner of Chadwick's, my hand on her thigh, her mind on fraud. Over more drinks, Adrianna told me about her discoveries: "This is a case about a rear-ender. That's not too technical for someone in Human Resources? You do know what a rear-ender is?"

"Car gets hit in the tail by another car," I responded, slightly slurring my words. "Automotive corn-holing."

Adrianna ignored that remark. "Braking suddenly, our insured's SUV was hit in the rear by a sports car like your little Miata – is that what it's called? – except this was some kind of sporty discontinued Pontiac. It went out of control and over an embankment. Both occupants were killed. As you know, the driver who rear-ends the other vehicle is likely to be adjudged the guilty party—leaving our policy-holder in the clear." (This is a case that Maury would also mention Athena losing big, so it appeared to have bothered him too.)

Adrianna warmed to her subject. "So, there was apparently no liability, but our insured, the woman driving the SUV, told our Athena adjuster that she had been tailgated by the sports car 'with these two boys who looked like fairies in it.'

"'Why do people tailgate?' our insured driver said. 'I hate that. I pumped the brake, so they would back off, or maybe pass, but I guess the driver didn't react fast enough. They hit me and then they lost control.'

"This was transcribed, as is our standard practice. But the plaintiffs, who were the wives and kids of the sports car victims (who had been brothers, incidentally) and their lawyer ordinarily wouldn't get this information and shouldn't know any of what she told our folks. The families had asked for just $10,000 in each death—hardly enough to go to trial over. Athena offered eight thou per person plus the legal costs to this point. A compromise was all but sure. Might have been a little over $9,000, I expect.

"Instead, the plaintiffs' lawyer withdrew the offer to settle and insisted on a trial."

"And?"

"The jury's verdict was $350,000 per victim -- $700,000 total. That's 35 times what the families originally asked."

I whistled. "Sounds like some Athenan leaked the woman's slur and the deliberate braking to the plaintiffs' lawyer."

"You catch on quick for a Marine in Human Relations," Adrianna said.   "They got inside information, for sure. When the heirs' lawyer examined the SUV driver in court, he reminded her she was under oath and then quickly proposed how the accident happened:

"'You thought these two men in their sporty little car closing in on you were probably homosexuals, didn't you, and you wanted to teach those tail-gating fags a lesson,' he badgered, 'didn't you?'"

"Our lawyer tried to head off our insured's replying in the heat of the moment, but the driver blurted out, 'Well, weren't they?' virtually admitting in three words all the lawyer said.   And Athena paid the price.

"And the plaintiffs' lawyer, who paid maybe a couple of thousand for the information, still made $70,000 to $140,000 easy. Maybe much more. They usually work for a fixed percentage of the settlement, you know, as much as half, which might be $350,000!"

"Quite a 'stimulus package,'" I said.

"This is circumstantial, Buck, but in my telephone-use survey I ran into a telephone call from an Athena Claims line to the very firm where the Plaintiffs' lawyer worked, and the call was just before he ditched any compromise and asked for the trial."

"One call, Adrianna? I don't think even Perry Mason would call that 'proof' though, do you?"

"Right, Buck. It's not proof, perhaps, of who gave out the information, as our units share phones.   But I've found a pattern of such calls before some of our biggest losses, even if I can't be sure what individual made the calls."

 I nodded. "We share lines too in Human Relations, with four or five other people.   Most of us do." I wondered how Adrianna would or could ever narrow the calls down to one person.

But before I could ask that, my jaw dropped, as I spotted Adrianna's boss Spencer and my boss Mary Ann Howell enter the bar and slip into a booth. They looked most cozy together, most cozy. I'm no prude and I'm not a gossip, but it sure looked from the way their faces came close to touching as they talked that they might be intimate — in violation of Athena's "no relationships" rule, antique though it might be.

ADRIANNA:

I spotted them too, and I got the same impression. So, as Buck and I started leaving the bar, I maneuvered us so that we stopped by their table to make sure they knew that we knew.

Putting his own spin on things, Spencer allowed that he was thanking Mary Ann bcause she had helped with his speech — "made me include the personal background and my plans so no one would think I was mad at the company or had any ulterior motive for leaving."

Hmmm, I thought.

Spencer also asked us to join them for a drink, and we foolishly did. We had already had plenty.

BUCK:

"What will you be doing at your new foundation, pre-precisely?" I asked.

"Personally? Administrative work and fund-raising. No research, naturally. I know nothing about that. We'll have a chief scientist or scientific director.   I'll be kind of a dollar-a-year man, which will keep the administrative costs down while at the same time supporting my innate need to boss people around."

Spencer and I talked about the work while Mary Ann and Adrianna put their heads together. Suddenly Adrianna jumped back in, imposing a blunt question for Mr. Spencer:

"You don't advertise your virtues, do you?"

Spencer froze and suddenly looked as stern as ever. "I'm not into 'image,' if that's what you mean."

ADRIANNA:

"Mary Ann was telling me how you helped when her husband died two years ago." I said that with genuine appreciation, though I still suspected he had to be connected to the fraud in some way, if only that he was trying to get out before someone else's leaking came to light.

"So, I was thinking that maybe, like an ice bag, I mean iceberg, you've got a lot beneath the surface." (I was beginning to realize I had drunk too much.)

Spencer said, "Mary Ann has more than repaid me with advice when I needed a sounding board. My administrative assistant Evelyn Robbins is pretty inflexible about listening to anyone else, even me, her so-called boss. That's why it was a pleasure to find a way to 'share' her with my assistant VPs, Lou and Maury! Mary Ann suggested that. She understands personnel. Understands people. A high-quality lady!"

Mary Ann Howell glowed. "Thank you, my dar— Jeffrey. And Buck, that was a good party you wrung out of the caterers."

"Thanks, Mary Ann." Buck turned to Spencer. "I guess we'll be giving you another party soon — for your retirement."

"Absolutely not! Tonight's was more than enough!" Spencer told Buck.

When Buck and I finally reached our parking place, I was emboldened by drink and by a visible increase in that "pleasant tumescence," as Buck had called it.   I quoted the Viagra ads, "If an erection persists for more than four hours, see a doctor."

Buck reacted by pressing me against his car. "Why a Doctor?" he said, spreading that grin of his from left ear to right. "A red-haired lawyer could treat my condition just fine."

It wasn't a "Me too" moment. I welcomed that he was thinking of me that way. He reminded me of my strapping father, whom I loved so much. *Too* much, *some* would say, when I crawled into his bed to comfort him after Mom died.

BUCK:

I drove Adrianna to her place, hoping to be asked in, but instead of erectile me getting treated by the red-haired lawyer, we found somebody had broken her door in!

Somebody had also shot a bullet through her front window. And, just inside, her distraught land-lady was wringing her hands, tears and mascara running down her cheeks.

The landlady expressed relief on seeing Adrianna. "I thought you would be coming home early after that company dinner. I thought when I saw the door broken in that maybe someone had hurt or kidnaped you! I didn't find anything missing. Your big TV's still here. Did you have a computer?" the woman, Mildred, asked.

"Oh my God, yes, a new Mac."

Had someone simply wanted a new Apple computer and broken in to steal it? Or, as seemed more likely, was someone onto Adrianna and wanted to see how far her investigation might have gotten? And did the bullet hole mean someone was trying to scare her into dropping her inquiry or at least not digging further?

If that was the intent, it didn't work. Adrianna doesn't scare easily. And, luckily, she had cloud and paper copies of her findings.

She called the cops in case they could lift some fingerprints, but that proved a dead end. Meanwhile, I discovered her butch landlady was an ex-Marine like me (well, not exactly like me) and we exchanged war stories over a few beers until my head fell back and I was out. Sorry, Adrianna.

So much for the doctor or the lawyer. As Shakespeare observed, "Much drink… sets him on and takes him off."

Early the next morning, I woke brighter and clearer-headed on the same sofa. The women must have stretched me out, unbuttoned me somewhat, and covered me with a light blanket. I was renewed in spirit and body, you might put it, and I rattled around and tried what I guessed was Adrianna's bedroom door, but it was locked, and she didn't stir.

I banged around the bathroom and the kitchen, noisily making myself coffee, but still without waking her, darn it. I started a note of apology and thanks on the back of one of my Athena business cards, meanwhile glancing out the window to where I'd parked kind of carelessly, half up on the curb. *Damn.* I saw my Miata was on the side of the street they ticket and tow to clear an extra lane for morning rush hour, and a meter maid was just four cars from ticketing it for a hefty fine or maybe worse: tagging it for towing.

I got as far as writing, "Thanks for the sofa. A meter maid is threatening. Call me," when Lovely Rita, as the Beatles had forever named her, moved closer to my car and I had to quickly stuff myself into my pants and shoes and dash. Rita had reached the car next to mine when I leapt into my open Miata and drove off with a wave. A good sport, she waved back. She was tall and stacked and reminded me of — Oh my God, Sibyl!

I zoom-zoom-zoomed to Hal's Sporty/Healthy Gym located just under my rooms. I've got my own key to the facility. As quickly as I could, I lifted weights, swam hard, sweated in the sauna, showered and shaved. All the better for it, I hurried up to my apartment.

Surprise! A nice one: Sibyl was there in my bed, and though considerably peeved that I had not come home earlier from my business dinner and reception — "You could at least have used your phone to let me know" — was still glad to see me. I explained that I had had too much to drink and had fallen asleep on a lawyer colleague's couch, which Sibyl decided to accept.

(It was true, too. I just didn't mention the lawyer's gender.)

"You didn't find yourself another willing woman?" Sibyl asked.

"No way," I said, again in truth. "I wish," I added with a wicked smile.

"Well then, come here." She spread her arms, forgivingly.

"Yes, yes!" I said, and we made pleasant work consummating our relationship. I had been looking forward to that ever since I met her two weeks before.

I thought that even my father would approve. He had told me in an email, "With those flashbacks and dark moods, I don't like you living alone."

Perhaps he didn't have Sibyl in mind, but I responded, "No reason to mention this to Mom, but there's a Nice Girl, an English teacher, who is coming to stay with me. She was living with a bunch of other teachers who lost their lease because the condo's rules didn't permit sub-leasing to groups. I told her she could stay here until she moves to California for a job she's angling for out there.

"Sibyl will help keep my head on straight for a while. And I'll do my best to make sure she enjoys the arrangement. You would like her, I think. But not as much as, I hope, I will!"

Indeed, I thought Sibyl was not only the most beautiful but the best, save one, of all the girls I had met since I put on a Marine uniform. (The best was Ramona, but she met, preferred, and married, the steadier, happier George.)

Though Sibyl would prove to be no cook and would leave the bathroom a mess, she swam with me sometimes and would hum off-key or sketch while I played the blues on my electronic piano. And when my thoughts turned to war and death, she would pull me to her and hold me.

Now, enjoying her hand sweeping my chest and abdomen, I said, "You must have gone to one hell of a teachers' college."

Sibyl beamed. "Graduated cum laude."

Despite her having spent the night alone, I hoped she now thought herself well-taken-care-of and appreciated, but to make sure of that I called Café Soleil on Farragut Square and made lunch reservations.

An hour later as we hurried out the door, the phone rang. Sibyl answered with a simple, "Hello."

I said, "Who is it, Sibyl honey?"

ADRIANNA concludes this part of the story:

Having called the home number listed on Buck's business card, I heard a woman's voice answer and then heard Buck call her, "Sibyl honey."

I didn't have to be co-chair of a telephone/computer-use committee to guess what was afoot.

I hung up with a crash.

Then I surprised myself by bursting into tears.

Chapter Thirteen: More Flashback - NOW WE KNOW

EVELYN:

So now we know, even if she didn't know herself, that our Adrianna had an itch that wanted scratching!

About that time, which was right after Mr. Spencer's announcement he was leaving, I was pretty down myself. My mentor, my boss, my very business identity, my "We," was leaving the company.

And Jeff Spencer had made no move to take me with him.

In fact, he said—just matter-of-factly—that he'd miss me. Miss me!

So that's how I started thinking what leverage I could apply to him or to Maury Woodrow or Lou Howard—one of whom was likely to be Mr. Spencer's successor. And that's why I drafted short letters to them, "To My Partner" and "To My Dearest"—not to actually send them but to clarify in my head the leverage I might exert ont those guys, in case it should be worth my while to dangle something in their faces or, say, lean on them. Spelling out their pressure points kind of made me feel better.

I still had to make a living. And I didn't want to get pushed of into some nothing job in the bowels of Athena, which would be a possibility if I didn't keep my wits about me.

Oh, how I hated being in limbo — like I am now, come to think of it: Held here in my ghostly state, waiting my final disposition, ya might say. But then was worse, as I would have to make a living.   Maybe the best outcome would be that some outsider gets Jeff Spencer's job – someone who'll need an insider like me to tell him where the bodies are buried – and where the Men's Room is.

Chapter Fourteen: Flashback

HORMONES, TEARS

BUCK:

Blissfully unaware of Adrianna's aborted phone call (as well as Evelyn's draft letters to Dearest and Partner, which we found much later) I enjoyed Saturday with Sibyl. The pleasures continued on Sunday morning in our now-shared bed. Afterward, I scrambled eggs and bacon for us. Then off we went to St. Columba's Episcopal Church (where Sibyl sang in the choir and I listened.)

We had a Bloody Mary or two and lunch in a favorite Connecticut Avenue bar. We strolled hand-in-hand around the zoo enjoying the monkeys and snakes and elephants and inhaling their various earthy odors. I don't think I thought once about Athena, or Evelyn's anger, or Adrianna's evidence of fraud. (Sorry.)

In the evening, Sibyl and I ate cold chicken and half-watched "60 Minutes" like old married folks and went early to bed and to sleep.

At about 3 a.m., I'm having my war dream: *The boy on his bike, his backpack almost surely holding a home-made bomb, pedals toward our Humvee and I can't shout out a warning to our driver fast enough!* I awoke shaking, but Sibyl's smooth, warm body stirred beside me and comforted me.

Monday, the bad dream was all-but-forgotten but Sibyl's kindness was not. Nevertheless, I was up before dawn and in Hal's gym (I have a key) for my exercise and a shower, a combination that dissipated my slight hangover and got me fully awake.

Hal found me shaving while balancing on my one good leg and using my stump to brace myself against the low sink. "You haven't grown that mother of a leg back yet?" he said in a loud voice. The volume reflected the officer in him wanting the Marine in the very back row to hear every word.

"Not yet," I said. "Maybe I better try some of your hormones."

A veteran of both Iraq wars, his shaved head a stubble of grey, Hal had retired as a Major and started the gym. Already big, he had built himself such massive arms, shoulders and legs that I kidded him that the muscles were formed as much by chemistry as by weight-lifting. When no one else was around, I called him "Hormone."

"How's work?" he said.

"A lawyer-woman wants me to help her look into possible fraud at the company. Get us killed," I mumbled, "or fired."

"Is there a third choice?" Hormone asked. "Prove the fraud and be heroes?"

"Humph. That's what she says."

I finished shaving, strapped on my leg, returned to my place and fed Sibyl and then dropped her off with a warm kiss at her current school.   Sibyl liked to get to work early, before the chaos.

I hope that worked for her. But, for me at Athena, chaos was already forming. And lots of it had Jeffrey Spencer's stamp on it.

Before I was two blocks away from where I had dropped Sibyl, Mary Ann was calling to tell me Spencer had refused to recommend Lou over Maury or Maury over Lou as his replacement. "He said, 'They are both deserving and superior candidates.'"

So, board members wanted to go through the motions of taking a "discrete" look at the field, Mary Ann said.   She set a time for us to see Joe Pelican, the man who wrote Athena's recruitment ads and placed them in the appropriate newspapers.

Soon after I reached my office Jeffrey Spencer himself appeared at my office door. "Have you got a minute?"

He didn't wait for me to answer.

"Regardless of who gets my job, I want to provide him or her with a personal administrative manual with stories about things that have worked for me and about those that have not worked."

"'Lessons Learned?'" I asked. "Something well beyond your Claims Policy and Procedures Manual?"

"Yes. I already see you're the right person to help. You listen. You got it when I said 'personal' and 'administrative' manual.

"Even in your own short time here, young man, you may have found that there are some important things that you don't learn from manuals or advanced management courses but only from painful experience. I want to put some of those situations on paper so that my successor won't make the same kind of fool of himself, or herself, that I often came close to doing.

"I'm not a facile writer, Buck, so I'll need help. Mary Ann recommended you. Joked that if you could make 409 pension data as interesting as you seem to have for the Athena boards that you could probably make my ideas something less than boring. Also, you're pretty new, so you could use a bit of gravitas in this conservative company. I believe working with me on this manual would give you that.

"If we do a really good job, the book might even gain some circulation beyond Athena and the insurance field," he said.

Not having enough time to get my current work done, I started to decline: "Danyel Lemon is in charge of –"

"She's cute, and I enjoy looking at her, but I need some brains here. Are you going to help me, or not?"

There was no way to say no. Hoping I sounded sincere, I said, "I'll be glad to. You're right. It could be a good opportunity." *And if it doesn't guarantee me a top job rating from Mary Ann, nothing will.*

Also, I'll be watching to see if Adrianna is right about you and the frauds.

Aloud I said: "Mary Ann and others think I have a knack for straight-forward, informal writing. Maybe it's inherited from my Dad; he's a reporter, who taught me not to use unnecessary, fancy words like 'existential.' That simple skill will be the best thing I can bring to a writing partnership. As for me, I'm sure I'll learn a lot about good organization and management. That'll be a clear plus for me."

"Good. I also like that you're an early bird. Meet me in my office at 7 a.m. tomorrow and we'll get started."

We shook hands on it.

Mary Ann and I then met with Joe Pelican on the recruitment ad. Mary Ann emphasized the "discrete" approach ad nauseam to Pelican. "Let the reader think the ad could be recruiting for GEICO or Erie or any of the mid-Eastern auto insurance companies." She explained why the approach was important.

Pelican nodded. We added that he should not even use our usual box number for replies to the ad.

Mary Ann then invited me to lunch at Moby Dick, "that noisy Greek place you like. My treat." The restaurant was Persian, but that wasn't what worried me. *What is it that can't be talked about in one of our offices?* I wondered.

But off we went.

Mary Ann and I waited in line at the crowded counter to order a dish of lamb, rice and fava beans for her and lamb shish kebab with a small salad for me. When our numbers were called, we collected our lunches, and soon were eating and talking in the privacy afforded by the din around us.

"Jeff has tentatively set his retirement for the twenty-ninth of the month after next," Mary Ann began. "The Smiths feel the party you organized for Jeffrey's anniversary with the company was sufficient, especially given his statement that he wanted nothing more. Instead of a second dinner, Wilma Smith suggested that the company present him with a contribution: money for the birth-related medical research."

"He'll appreciate that," I said.

"Yes. And did you agree to work with him on his business memoir, as I call it? I recommended you."

"Thanks, I guess. It won't be easy. I'll have to let some other work slide. But in the end, we might produce something worthwhile."

"Buck, you'll be working with Jeff and I'd like you to give him a small, private dinner party. I can't give it because some would see that as confirming we've become more friendly than Athena regulations permit."

The idea made me boil, but I counted to ten, snapped my fingers and said, "The regs won't mean that much, now that he's retiring."

But then, angrily, stupidly, maybe even inappropriately, I said, "You're out of order. You're my boss and you're telling me to suck up to you and do this irregular, non-business favor to hide your relationship! Even if you fire me, I'm not going to be your—your—your—toady!"

I stood up to leave.   I doubted I had a job left.

But Mary Ann surprised me. "Please," she said, taking my hand. "Please sit down.

"I guess I was wrong to ask it but I thought we were friends as well as co-workers, and I was hoping you'd want to do it and get any and all the credit that comes from hosting one or more of the Founders and the others who will attend. It could be where Athena gives Jeff the contribution to his new foundation. I especially don't want the founders or Pulsudski or that Evelyn person to know about me and Jeff. I'd be a guest of yours, not the hostess. You, as co-author of the book, would be the host. I would buy everything. You'd basically just need to provide the place—and the 'cover story.' Please." There were tears in her eyes.

"Your place is quite presentable, overlooking the park, with even some art by that famous grandmother of yours. Adrianna Canter and I could add a few touches. She might be hostess. Jeff kind of thinks of her as the daughter he never had. His Abrielle."

"Adrianna?" I asked, while thinking, *a 'daughter' who's trying to send him to jail?*

"Jeff has heard that your Adrianna is a fine cook of bouillabaisse, a great favorite of his. And I've asked her to cook it for your party."

'You've already asked her to cook for my party?" I was coming to a boil again.

Mary Ann said, "I've gone about this all wrong again." The tears were back. "But please, please: Say you'll do it? Say it's settled?"

Grrr, I thought. I looked away from Mary Ann and stared at the passsers-by on Wisconsin Avenue. I said nothing for a good while.

But finally I nodded.

"And by the time of the dinner, you and Jeff may really be close," Mary Ann speculated.

Sure, I thought, without buying any part of that.

Back in my office, my anger resurged, as it would a couple more times before that deadly dinner would be served. I banged my desk and cursed. I thought I had fallen as low as possible—*coerced into giving a party for my boss' secret lover.*

I hadn't yet fully studied Adrianna's parking issues but, to spite Mary Ann's overloading me with work and this dinner "favor," I found a way for the people who clean the offices at night, mostly minority women, to park in the lighted, empty spots close by the building that had been vacated by then by the executives. *That will appeal*, I thought.

And, best of all, I got together with an ex-Marine friend at Macy's and we drew up an agreement: Their customers could spill over to part of Athena's parking on the retailer's busy weekends and nights, while Athena employees would use some Macy spaces in a designated area on weekdays, when store customers were few.

Pleased with myself, I telephoned Ms. Canter to set up a meeting with her. Her brisk recorded voice announced she was "out of town on business," but said, "Leave a message. I check my voicemail regularly."

I left a message saying I hoped she saw my note "about my abrupt departure Saturday morning because of the meter maid.   But speaking of parking, I've had several ideas I'd like your views on."

Two hours later, Adrianna called back and left a voice message that she would be back from the West Coast in time to meet at 3 p.m. Thursday "in your office." Her voice remained brisk and business-like, whereas, I was hoping for some "See ya!" or "It'll be nice to talk with you again."

I found myself thinking about Adrianna over the next couple of days, and of her evidence of fraud as well, even though I was now becoming consumed in work on the Spencer book.

For my sessions with Mr. Spencer, Evelyn Robbins was out of the way. She hadn't died yet, of course, but she didn't come to work until 8:30. In the daily hour and a half before that, Spencer and I covered a lot of ground. The Claims Vice President organized his ideas so well that, immediately after we talked, I could rough-draft a chapter or section and get it back to him that afternoon so he could read it and approve or change it before our session the next morning. He didn't change much. He generally liked my popularizations of his ideas. He appreciated I would need anecdotes that helped illustrate the ideas. He generally was ready with an apt tale.

His first points, which I decided to make chapter topics, were:

Learn All You Can about the Issues and, even more important, About the People Involved. (I'd call that chapter "PREPARE LIKE A BOY SCOUT working for the CIA.")

Plan Big, Set Your Goals High. (I'd call that "GO FOR BIGGER AND BETTER. Why fail small?")

And where Jeffrey said, "Persuade your friends and co-workers to join your team and take up your goals, while adding their ideas to yours– and making use of *their* special skills, I wrote, "GET BUY IN— BUT LISTEN, TOO. As granny said, "There's more than one way to skin a cat."

We made quick progress.

He told me thinly disguised stories that involved Evelyn, the head of the Richmond office, and even the Founders, but there was no self-glorying "I won!" tone. No lauding it over "losers." There were, instead, humility, as when he mentioned there were no pictures of him before he was ten or eleven because his parents were too poor to own a camera. And gratitude: For a chapter that I titled, Learn to Accept and Be Grateful for Gifts, he told me how the parents of a friend let him sleep on their boat one summer when he was working nearby. On his own, he made sure the boat was clean and ever-ready. He said he did everything he could to make sure they knew he appreciated their kindness.

He got asked back, so for two summers he didn't have to spend money renting a room and could keep most of what he earned for extras at college.

I began to realize that our book could be more than a guide for management. It could also tell a heart-warming Horatio Alger story.   I had begun to feel a grudging admiration for Spencer. I knew he was smart. I learned he could be daring, helpful to others, sometimes almost charming.

And, although his parents were "dirt poor," they had gumption and good sense. They encouraged all five of their kids to get good educations and sometimes fudged their home address to get them into better schools in another neighborhood.   In Jeff's case, his Baptist parents recognized he had a good voice and arranged for him to try out for the Catholic cathedral's choir. His subsequent selection provided him with a scholarship to the cathedral's excellent school. He did well and college scholarships followed. Increasingly I felt Adrianna was dead wrong to make this choir boy her Villain.

Chapter Fifteen: Flashback
NOT SO DISCRETE

BUCK:

Villain? Suddenly, I found myself to be the Villain, at least where Lou Howard was concerned.

I found him in my office wildly waving a copy of the *Wall Street Journal* open to the boxed ads for executive jobs.

"Discrete!" he stormed, wide-eyed with agitation, 'This is in no way the 'discrete' search I was led by you and your Mary Ann Howell to expect!

"Everyone will know from the wording that it's Spencer's job at Athena you're advertising for. And that Athena, at least from this, is eager to find an outsider!

"How could you guys do this to me?

"I see 'we' behind this" Lou continued, 'Jeffrey and Evelyn, that is, but why didn't you stop them?!"

He slumped into a chair. "Everybody figured I had that frigging job, and that includes my wife and kids and my outside creditors and Athena's own Credit Union!   I thought so too," he said.

"Now it will look from this" —Lou waved the paper under my nose — "as if I'm just 'in the running.' Buck, you could at least have warned me!"

I snatched the newspaper and read aloud, "'Claims VP at top-rated D.C. insurance firm… excellent challenge and attractive compensation package for the outstanding candidate. For consideration please forward full resume including current salary…'" And the address was a box number that many, inside and out of the company, would know was Athena's.

"This is every bit as bad as you say," I said. "This isn't how Pelican was supposed to do the ad. I'm totally blind-sided too."

Lou hardly heard. "But it's not your career and your kids' futures that are being destroyed!" He was shaking. "I've been fucked, Buck," he wailed, "fucked by the king of fuckers and his bitch queen."

He crumpled the paper in his fists. Then he dropped it on my desk. "I do see the hand of Evelyn the Awful, in this. She often acts as if she's the vice president herself. She might have signed off on the damned ad for Jeffrey without even showing it to him.

"I can't face either of them now – I'd like to size them up for concrete boots and drop them off our boat into the Chesapeake! The deep part." He smiled slightly, recognizing how crazy he must sound.

"Not you I should be beating up on, though, I guess. Nice of you, really, to let me blow up like this without calling the cops. I do have a temper.

"I definitely think I'll go home, and then maybe run down and work in the Richmond office for a few days. Enjoy myself at the Commonwealth Club there with Ernie Bell and his pretty secretary pool. Keep out of trouble — and think about my options.

"I need that job and that money. I've been operating on the premise that Jeff would retire and 'turn over,' as he had put it to me, his well-compensated position. I know claims experience has worsened, but that's not my fault. As long as juries continue to give away money just because it comes 'free' from the defendant's insurance company instead of the defendant—as long as that happens, we're going to experience more and more claims costs."

I tried to interrupt. I had heard this rant about claims losses before (and I had also heard Adrianna's alternate facts.)

Finally exhausting his tirade, Lou slunk out of my office.

I kind of laughed at Lou's over-the-top anger—though I was mad enough myself to draft a memo to Pelican that said, "We emphasized that any Athena advertising for Mr. Spencer's position should be discrete. To that end, our notes from the meeting show we specifically said the ad should describe the company not as headquartered in Washington but as mid-Atlantic and that our usual box number should not be used. You appear to have deliberately or sloppily gone against all we wanted, and then failed to provide the ad text for us to review. We want to know why, as our internal candidates have been potentially embarrassed and are angry. In addition, we want to be sure the ad is not run again."

The note's "we" required that I get Mary Ann to also sign on, and as she was "acting" in her position, she might ordinarily have been reluctant, but I had some clout with her now—the Spencer dinner party. And, after she signed the note I added a list of blind cc's to it—so everyone of importance would know exactly what had happened.

The note alone would not get Pelican fired but if anyone else had a similar experience with him in the past or in the future, he would be on his way out. Good riddance.

As soon as I emailed the complaint, I called Lou to alert him to look for his cc of it. But he had indeed gone home. He was "in quite a state," a staffer I knew whispered.

The more I thought about that, the more I worried. Having PTSD had taught me that extreme anger can turn quickly to self-hatred and despair.   Even suicide.

I tried Lou's cell phone. No answer.

Chapter Sixteen: Flashback

ONE SHOT, NOT TWO

BUCK:

I looked up Lou's home address, dropped everything and hurried out. I punched the address into my Miata's GPS and was off. I had an excuse to drive fast and slip through yellow lights, to hotshot my way through the city – and I made the best of it. Soon I was on 301 in Southern Maryland, a highway once known for slot machines but now—after do-gooders got rid of them—just a crowded strip of Washington exurbia that looked like many another, just a bit tackier. I passed La Plata in less than an hour and my GPS (I call her Marge) instructed me to take the next exit and stay to the left.

I was immediately winding through fields with the beginnings of corn and some kind of bean plants. That sunny openness gave way to trees arching over the narrow road, letting only dappled sunlight reach me as I approached a riverside area of wide-apart homes. Before I knew it, Marge announced, "You have arrived."

I parked out of sight and slipped from behind the wheel.

That's when I heard the gunshot.

I ran toward Lou's house.

Another shot.

Whew, I thought, *he hasn't killed himself. That seldom takes a second shot.*

From behind a tree, I looked round the back yard, a partially wooded area which sloped off to the river. A beautiful spot, usually.

Lou was shooting pistols, one in each hand, at a set of targets set up in his woods and doubtless labeled, in his mind, "Jeffrey Spencer" and "Evelyn Robbins." Even firing free-hand, without bracing himself, he hit almost every time.

"Take that you, bastard scum!" he shouted, as he fired at "Spencer."

"And that's for you, you bitch-whore!" he shouted in an even uglier tone, at "Evelyn."

After firing six rounds at each target, he reloaded and fired six more, by my count. It also looked to me that only two rounds, fired by his left hand, missed Spencer and embedded in an adjacent tree. Only one round missed Evelyn. Most hit pretty near center.

EVELYN:

To think: Shooting at targets Lou thought of as Jeffrey and me! I never knew!

Lou must have been loony!

If he had ever found out it really was me, when Jeff was out of the office, who approved the ad, he'd have killed me for real!

Oh yeah! I've *been* killed.

In my defense, nobody'd told me about this "discrete" business! I swear!

BUCK:

Lou, finished with the targets, pointed the guns at his left and right temples. I had seen a marine in Afghanistan kill himself in just this way. I gasped and fell to my knees.

EVELYN:
No, no, no!

BUCK:

 Lou pulled both triggers simultaneously.
Click. Click.

My lungs and heart stopped. But Lou still stood. We had both counted the rounds as they had been shot at the targets —and we had counted right, thank God!

I remained hidden as Lou put the still-warm weapons inside the house and returned, kicking off his shoes, and tossing aside shirt and pants as he neared the water. He was hardly athletic, just a bulky figure pared down to his undershorts, but he waded into the river and began to swim.

The Wicomico is more than a mile wide at this point, but he began to swim for the other side. He swam too hard and too fast, quickly exhausting himself. He began to flounder. I wasn't in shape for heroism but I quickly removed my clothes and artificial leg, hopped to the river and plunged in after him.

I was maybe a third of the way across, and pretty darn exhausted myself, when Lou went under.

God, I thought, *I don't think I can reach him in time.*

But Lou seemed to rise from the dead. The river there was so shallow he stood in water just up to his chest.

As he waded to the far shore and lay on the opposite bank warming himself in the sun, I swam slowly back to his house and was standing there breathing hard and shaking myself dry. I cussed Lou and I cussed myself, for not only was I achy and water-logged but in my rush, I had forgotten to remove my Timex.

I got myself fully dried in the warm air, had my leg back on and was dressed, while Lou swam slowly back.

From behind a big boxwood, I watched him a minute or two and then headed for my car, passing by the home-made swimming pool adjacent to the boathouse. Curious, I looked inside and was surprised to see a huge glass tank crawling with crabs and other saltwater creatures.

The tank there was impressive, and the contents amazing: Besides crabs skittering back and forth, there were sea snails (I guessed) and a variety of other fauna and flora.   It was like looking at a cross-section of the Chesapeake Bay at a depth of five to ten feet.

Suddenly, in a sweet-smelling cloud of marijuana, a young man I guessed must be Lou Jr. appeared, wielding a baseball bat. He looked dangerous, swinging the bat too close to my head for comfort.

Junior said, "If you mess with my project, I'll kill you: I've already had one set-back and I need that living model of the Chesapeake Bay to graduate from the Marine Biology Institute. Mess it up and I'll bang you on the head with this" – he raised the bat – "and dump you in the channel in the middle of the Bay.

"It would be one of those perfect murders. If they ever recovered our body, everyone would think you lost your footing, maybe hit your head and drowned."

I laughed. "This tank is great. I drove out to check on your father. I glimpsed the tank as I was leaving and had to take a closer look. It's amazing!" I pointed to the joint he was holding. "Can I have a drag on that?" Junior handed it over.

Smoking, handing the joint back and forth, I gave Junior a version of why I had gotten worried about his father and had driven down to check on him. "Don't tell him I was here," I said.

Junior nodded.

I slipped away, but not before hearing Lou slam the kitchen's screen door behind him as he returned. Meanwhile, Junior had been joined by a girl of beautiful proportions. Together they headed for the kitchen where I could imagine that they found a soaked Lou drinking Maryland rye straight from the bottle.

I could hear Lou explain loudly: "Problem at work. Effed by Spencer and Evelyn."

"Fired?" Junior asked.

"Oh no. Just deeply, deeply fucked."

"Deeply?" Junior laughed wickedly. "Fucked? But not fired. Could be worse then. Put on something dry and less embarrassing to my innocent friend here than those soggy, drooping drawers and we'll fix some sandwiches and go sailing and figure out how we can fuck them back— Mr. Spencer it was and your administrative assistant Evelyn? Let's plan a pay-back they won't forget for as long as they live."

The two guys sounded about as bonded as a father and son can get. Like each would kill for the other.

Although I thought they might just be jiving loud and strong, and impressing Junior's girl—I wondered if it might not be dangerous to have them as enemies.

Chapter Seventeen:

Flashback

MURDEROUS DAY

BUCK continues:

Back from Lou's, I found more crap piled in my In Box. In frustration I banged my fist on my desk, just as old friend George popped in. "Bad day?" he asked.

"An epic advertising screw-up. Do I understand you're about to head off to West Virginia to photograph Athena's oldest policyholder?"

"Tomorrow," he said grandly, "I'll capture the ancient woman's essence for posterity – and very likely for a public relations or ad campaign. I'll also make photos as promised for the *Herald.*"

"How's Ramona?" I asked. "Think she's ever going to wise up and come back to me?"

"You frigging bastard. Your being 'best man' was only a formality for our wedding ceremony, you know. Matter of fact, I'm here to tell you Ramona's pregnant," which would become concerning after my deadly dinner.

"Congratulations!" I came from behind my desk and gave the man a bro-hug. I thought to ask George who the father might be. But being a nice guy, I held back.

George said, "How's Sibyl? You ever think of marrying her—or any of the others?"

"Wouldn't that be ungrateful," I said, "like throwing their generosity back in their faces? Besides, not one of them could put up with me for more than a month."

"That's probably true," George too readily conceded, "but that little Adrianna in Claims might make that month a pretty sweet four weeks, Buck."

"Sweet? I don't know if that's the adjective I would use."

Nor was it the word I thought of when my meeting with Adrianna rolled around the following Friday and she brought most of her parking agitators along.

But when I told them my parking ideas, Adrianna agreed they "aren't bad—if you can get them implemented." Her group left on a cordial note. Adrianna remained to thank me for "not writing us off as a bunch of kooks and trouble-makers."

I managed to apologize again about my abrupt departure. And, taking George's advice, I responded positively when she said, "Can we get a drink somewhere private—even my place—and talk fraud? I have bourbon, your drink isn't it?"

"I won't be a second." I shuffled my remaining papers into a pile and steered Adrianna to my car. I took a scenic route to her place, the breeze and the late sun making the drive feel special.

She got some crackers out and cut some slices of cheese while I mixed drinks, putting too much liquor in them, Adrianna thought.

"There's a jigger over there," she gently admonished. Then: "Can I really trust you?"

"You can trust me to make the drinks too strong. To make a pass at you. To give you a really good time. Is that trust enough?"

"Seriously. Regarding Athena. Fraud."

"Yes, that way too," I said.

"Good," Adrianna said. "I've combed through the data provided by our communications contractor and found more questionable calls, these to Pittsburgh and New York law firms and one firm in Richmond that all have reputations—at least some of their lawyers do—for shady doings such as subornation of perjury. Excuse the lawyer talk, that means encouraging a witness to lie."

"Hmmm. Not a nice thing to do," I said. "But wouldn't our defense people and the plaintiff's attorneys have to stay in contact?"

"No. That would be through the local claim's representative or attorney, who would keep the Home Office apprised. Otherwise the Home Office should not be involved or in contact. This looks highly irregular.

"And another thing," she continued, "there were a couple of calls made from our Richmond Branch Office to the same trial firms that had been called from here."

Where Lou likes to escape to.   "And you can at least tell what unit made each call – which office group?" I asked. I downed my drink and put together another.

"Could you slow down?" Adrianna said, nodding at my glass.

Then she answered my question: "Yes. I can tell what unit made the calls. The office group is what's so interesting. The calls from here all came from the same area – the Claims executive area – telephone numbers used by Jeffrey Spencer and Evelyn and the rest of the executive group, and at least potentially a few more people. Also, the calls from the Richmond office and the other offices also were made on lines these Claims executive types would be likely to use when visiting there."

I said, "So you think that Spencer or Evelyn or someone around them with access to this information has been swelling his or her bank account from kick-backs they got for tipping outside lawyers off to weaknesses in our cases. Like if a client who wasn't tested for DUI by the cops, so there's nothing on the official record, but he did volunteer to our people that he had a couple beers—"

"Exactly!" Now she handed me her glass for a modest half-refill. "Wondering if I really had stumbled on something, I then went through some dead but expensive Bodily Injury case files – you know what a dead file is?"

"I better know," I said, "if I'm ever going to do more than coordinate parking. It means the case has been settled and filed."

"Good for you," Adrianna said.   She went on:

"I found that soon after Claims' phone calls to them, they won BIG!"

"How much are you talking about?" I asked.

"From $175,000, the smallest, to four at about half a million and one approaching a million dollars. And what's more – "

"More?"

"All the information about these cases," said Adrianna as she finished her drink, "that is, all the hard copies of these files had been signed out to Jeffrey Spencer before they were settled or came to trial."

"But Adrianna," I said, "wouldn't Spencer, as chief honcho, naturally examine cases that had a big loss potential?"

"If a big loss was deemed possible, Spencer might be consulted. But he wouldn't ordinarily hang onto the files. It would be more natural for Lou Howard or Maury Woodrow to spend time on them—seeing if the reserve estimates are correct, for example. Lou handles the day-to-day stuff. Maury is responsible for technical claims handling, and for keeping Spencer informed of possible bombs—big losses.   But Evelyn's personal memo sheets were used to sign out the case files to Spencer."

"Evelyn again," I said.

EVELYN:

Humph. Isn't this what they call blaming the victim?

BUCK:

"Everything bad comes back to Evelyn," I said, "meaning she might have been in on the deal or, more likely, was threatening to blow it up and put somebody in jail. What can we do about it?"

Adrianna said, "I can keep looking for more proof, and for who the mole is. And you can tell the authorities my suspicions if I'm found dead in an alley."

"Whoa—you dead in an alley, Adrianna?" I said. But it did seem a possibility. "Maybe you need me at your side at all times—to protect your lovely flank." I swept my hand down that flank.

"I may take you up on that," Adrianna said. "This may be crazy, but ever since my break-in, I've been scared by odd noises, backfires, strangers in parking garages. Something outside, a catfight or a conversation on the street, can wake me – and I just lie awake shaking."

I said, "Join the club. You've got something like my post-traumatic stress disorder. But don't worry. You get better with time. Or you get worse and go out and shoot someone, or yourself. I've been to the edge."

"Oh, my, I seem to step right into it, don't I? I'm sorry to have even mentioned my little problem —"

"There's nothing so 'little' about it, babe. Yours or mine. Over the past year and a half, I've talked to five shrinks — one psychiatrist, two psychologists, and two counselors, whatever their creds may be.   None helped much. I still wake up with a jolt, sweating, beginning to relive it all, though I do have my tinkling fountains by my desk and in my apartment, and my calming music, and other distractions – exercise, alcohol, sex." I laughed wickedly and twirled my non-existent mustache. "If you want to try my therapies, I can help you with all three, especially sex." I kissed her. I thought she took pleasure in the kiss but suddenly she pulled away.

"I've talked to one of your distractions. She answered the phone at your place the day after my break-in," Adrianna said with the thinnest of smiles.

I guess I looked like a dog caught peeing on the carpet. I couldn't deny. I decided to confess. "Ah, that would be Sibyl. Teacher and choirgirl. Better help than the shrinks—and I've helped her over some hard spots, too. We're not serious."

"'Not serious!' You two have been living together—having sexual intercourse, haven't you?" Adrianna blurted out.

"You do get right to the point, don't you?" I said. I added, "She needed a place to stay until she moves to California, and she does keep me from being lonely. I don't want to make excuses but otherwise I can get in a stew, living alone." I hoped I looked like a little boy about to burst into tears and needing a hug. "I've never required sex as a prerequisite for her staying with me."

I kind of believed that but I thought Adrianna seemed skeptical.

But, whatever she thought, she totally surprised me by reaching over and almost absent-mindedly — as if she was merely picking lint from my lapel — pinching the edge of my fly!

Whee! Her touch aroused me, as she must have known it would, especially as she was saying, "I don't take sex casually, but, if I did, some night when I'm scared of burglars and you're reliving your war, we might say what the hell and have a go, Athena regulations be damned.

"I do like breaking stupid regulations sometimes, don't you?" she said. She paused and then, as if waking up, damn it, took her hand away from my fly, stiffened her back and no longer purred like a sex kitten.

Adrianna counted on her fingers: "Exercise, Alcohol, Sex, eh? —you forget there's a fourth distraction we might employ together, Action. Catch Spencer red-handed, or maybe Maury. Lou. Disgruntled Clifford, maybe. I'll keep my eyes open for any more of the big losses and then check back on who the trial attorneys were. As soon as the June lists come out, I'm going to take a couple of claims numbers, find the files, make notes on them, and then sit tight and watch for developments."

"Sounds sensible," I said. "But I got to tell you, working with Spencer lately, I'm beginning to doubt there's any connection between these crimes you've uncovered and him or with his retiring."

"You mean he hasn't said, 'Gosh Buck, recently I've been making extra money by tipping off plaintiff's lawyers?'"

"I get your point there," I said, "and no, I don't think I have him all figured out. But I once thought him a stiff-necked SOB, and now I know he's not, and that makes me less sure of anything else about him."

"'Everyone is a moon and has a dark side he never shows to anybody,'" Adrianna quoted. "Mark Twain."

I said, "That's the quote that's been churning through my brain ever since Spencer made that unexpectedly moving retirement announcement! Though what was meant was the far side, the side that always faces away from the earth. There is no dark side that's never illuminated and never seen."

"The far side of the moon then," Adrianna mused. "I suppose," she continued, "that you're not totally what you seem yourself—all girls 'n' booze. There's some bitterness on the far side about your twin dying in the war, isn't there?" she said -- "unavoidably, like my Dad felt when Mom died young."

I said, "I guess he would. It's tough losing someone you love! And yes, you've probably seen more than enough of that bitterness."

Something about this conversation unnerved me. Maybe it was this look into what some people call a soul. Mine. I stood up to leave.

Adrianna, seeming to perceive my change in mood, did not try to stop me. She simply said, "I'll come by Friday afternoon the day of your Spencer dinner to cook, if you still want me to. Mary Ann made me promise."

I stopped by the door. "Yes, thank you. Nice of you. Very. I'll definitely need you." I lurched out and got into my Miata, pulling quickly away from the curb.

Home.

No lights were on.

Sibyl was not there.

Her clothes were gone as well.

A note said, "It's been fun but all good things come to an end, don't they? And it's time—for you and for me. I've heard about your friend at work and I guess I'm going to have to be okay with that, if she'll be good to you and for you. If not, see you around the singles bars, here or in California. Regards, S."

"'Regards,'" I repeated.

I looked at the photo of my dead brother on the mantle and addressed him: "This is the way my world ends, eh, Jens, yes this is the way, isn't it, Brother?—not banging Sibyl, but whimpering, whimpering about a life turned so damn gloomy, so fucking lonely--"

What good am I if I can't maintain a relationship with Sibyl or even do a good job of helping Adrianna track down a simple crime?

I swallowed several antihistamines with two big tumblers of straight bourbon and plunged into bed, hoping for Hamlet's dreamless sleep. Instead, awake and distraught, I pressed my face into my pillows and, as best I can remember, asked Something or Someone quietly or help. And then shouted for it. Twisting and turning and beating my chest and my head with my fists—I think I begged, at one point, for my mother's womb to resorb me and relieve me of this wretched life—and of my inability to escape memory's pain or to be useful.

"'I had seen birth and death but had thought they were different.'" I remembered the line and screamed it.

Bad signs and unfortunately familiar ones – talking to my dead brother, feeling useless, seeking the comfort of my mother's womb, and spouting T.S. Eliot or something like it. Not good. Not good at all.

I knew I was experiencing a PTSD and alcohol-related crying jag, and not for the first time. I needed to stop. I needed to exercise some control. But I drained the rest of the bourbon straight from the bottle as fast as I could. I wanted the alcohol to kill me.

Instead, vomit shot up my throat and into my mouth, and I just reached the edge of the toilet before it all came out, explosively, my bowels erupting simultaneously.

Fouled by sweat and vomit and excrement, I crawled back from the bathroom toilet to my bed feeling degraded. And ashamed.

Weak and exhausted, I finally slept. I believe I dreamt of Lou raising the two unloaded guns to his head, but I was Lou and the guns were not empty.

At about 3 or 4 a.m., I awoke.

Screaming.

I reached for Sibyl, but she was not there.

Once again arrayed around me were the dead I believed I would re-visit the rest of my life—even Evelyn and the child suicide bomber, duped and damned and killed, I felt, by his own people. I wept for them all.

Beside my bed sat my twin's photo. I said to him, "Jens, I'm so sorry you didn't live and I did!"   Not entirely coherently, as I was still very drunk, I continued talking to him for nearly an hour about all he had missed, including even Adrianna and her evidence of fraud.

I expected Jens would have had it all this fraud stuff solved by now.

EVELYN:
Too bad he's the brother that died then. With him around, instead of you, Buck, I might still be alive.

BUCK:
At length I slept again, not waking until about 9 a.m., already late for work. I downed half a cold beer, the hair-of-the-dog "cure" that never quite works, does it?

I called my boss-lady Mary Ann Howell. "I've had a bad night, a flashback. Not much sleep. Is it okay if I take a few hours leave and don't come in until afternoon?"

"No need to come in today, Grand. Not much going on. You've been working overtime. Those early mornings with Spencer. Take a long weekend," she said.

"'Those early mornings! Aw, shit, Mary Ann! I was supposed to meet with Spencer this morning at seven!"

Under other circumstances, Mary Ann might have upbraided me for cussing, as well as missing an appointment, but she said, "Don't worry. I'll call Jeffrey and explain."

She added, after a pause, "And please get some more help, Buck. I say that as a friend—as well as your boss."

George came by at noon with two Big Macs. In contrast to my body and the apartment, they smelled wonderful—the beef and the hot cheese—and I almost finished mine by the time George got his unwrapped.

"Mary Ann send you?" I said.

"She said you had a particularly bad night. Nice woman. Wants to help."

"I know," I said, a bit sorry that I'd been such a bastard about giving the dinner for Jeffrey Spencer. And a little happier that I was doing it.

George stripped my bed and replaced the sheets, mopped up the worst of the bathroom, and carried the soiled sheets, towels and bathroom rug to the pay laundromat in the building. He suggested I spend the afternoon in Hal's weight room, pool and sauna downstairs and then, when I felt better, come over to his and Ramona's place for dinner. "No drinks, I'm afraid. You know what Ramona thinks of you and alcohol. And I know she's right."

I did as instructed, with Hal spotting me on the weights and joining me in the pool and then the sauna, the last for a rough-tongued but fatherly pep talk: "You were a damn good Marine, Buck, and if you could make it through Afghanistan and Jens' death, you can manage a bad dream or two – and get on with your life." Hal didn't make a whole of sense, but I appreciated his effort. I was damned lucky, I realized, to have such friends.

At the Browns', Ramona gave me a worried look, and a hug and a quick kiss, plus roast beef, potatoes and gravy, string beans and strong glasses of whole milk. These were comfort foods she knew I liked. As advertised, no wine or beer or other alcohol was offered, and I knew not to ask for any.

Early next morning, Saturday, I was back in the gym under Hal's watchful eye. After a strenuous hour and a half, I fixed a mess of eggs and bacon, took it down to the gym and split it with him. I then biked through Rock Creek Park, envying the couples who biked or ran together, and the older couples who strolled hand in hand. *Will I ever have that kind of enduring love?* I doubted it.

Returning hot and sweaty, I was overjoyed to find Adrianna at my door. She had a picnic hamper. "George said you were under the weather," she said.

"You might say that." I kissed her and took her into my apartment, where I showered, leaving the bathroom door open so we could yell back and forth. And, if she wanted, so she might glimpse my one-legged body, and maybe get used to it.

We drove, top down, to Hains Point where we ate her fried chicken and potato salad beside the Potomac. Under a tree, snuggled close, I fell asleep in the gentle mix of sun and shade and the sweet smells of woman and new-mown grass.

Sunday, awaking alone (damn) without a hangover (ah) after a good sleep (ah again), I had another swim and a big breakfast, and was back at St. Columba's eyeing the girls in the choir. Sibyl was not among them.

There was a moment during communion when people who were ill or needed special help could get a personal prayer in a back corner of the church. Reflecting on my meltdown, I joined the short line. I bent down, whispered a few words about my brother's death and my condition, and was enfolded, cushioned, in the big arms of the short, plump black woman who had preached. This felt good. This felt motherly. This felt like God She might forgive me, after all, for living.

After the service, I called Jeffrey Spencer and confessed to having thoroughly screwed up my life and thereby missed our Friday session. He had heard from Mary Ann on Friday, of course, and sounded sympathetic. But he didn't say, "Forget it." He wanted us to make up for the lost work time. "Can you meet me at my apartment at, say, 1 p.m. today?"

We worked until 7 p.m., with a short break for Cokes and sandwiches Jeffrey made. They were a very good ham on rye with lettuce, tomato and a good mustard he had combined with mayonnaise.

While he put the sandwiches together I glanced over his books: Histories by Commager, Low, Sorenson, Crenshaw and Catton, some books and novels related to sailing, and two books on the theater, a reminder to me that Spencer in college had been quite an actor and had hoped to act professionally. And here amidst the mix of books was an odd surprise: A tome on toxins—natural and man-made poisons. At that time, weeks before Evelyn's death, I thought nothing of it.

Part Three, Real Time Again

Chapter Eighteen: REWRITE, RECOVER

ADRIANNA:

Buck's intense work on the book had continued when he was able to leave rehab for his apartment, from which George and I, without asking, had removed everything alcoholic. By then, Buck, in hospital and rehab, had not had a drink in weeks,

Spencer still came by for early morning "polishing" sessions before heading to Athena. In bed, or increasingly at a small desk nearby, Buck soon finished the draft. He also began limping down to Hal's for light exercise designed to get him back in shape. Hal kept a close eye on him.

Buck's stump was healthy again, but his exercise routine had to be limited. However, the whirlpool, he said, felt glorious. Several times I joined him, and he joked about our getting naked in the warm bubbling water. But sex was not in the picture. He was as celibate as any monk or priest.

BUCK:

More celibate than many, I'd say. But I did have a kind of social life, i.e., company. Curious Connie came by with lunch; she wanted the real scoop on my fall, I think. But I still couldn't say if I was shoved down those stairs or not. (But I had formed an idea for finding out who might have bopped Adrianna.)

George came by with his pictures from my deadly party, as I thought of it, and of his photos of the policy-holder in West Virginia. He left them for me to look over at my leisure. And Lou looked at them the next day, when he visited with some home-made frozen dinners for me to heat up as needed.

Keeping me fed was on a lot of minds. Hal often brought Big Macs for lunch—so much for health food—and ate with me. Stella made me a casserole big enough for eight. Maury dropped it by, along with an apple pie, my favorite. Danyel and Ramona also cooked me dishes I warmed up.

Danyel was keen on my idea for a feature on Maury's steins and ornamental fish but said Maury had told her that *I* must write them up.   Would I?

"When I can get around again, I'll be glad to," I said. It's hard to say no to a pretty girl — especially when she's planning an Athena food services article telling, in effect, how good I am at my job.

George came by to ask me what I had thought about his photos of the party and of the ancient policy-holder from West Virginia.

I gave my friend a blank stare. "Funny, you did bring me the pictures, I know, and Lou rifled through them when he visited, but I haven't seen them since. Maybe Adrianna took them to look at, hoping they would provide a clue to the murderer," I said.

I called her. No, she hadn't even seen them. But she too was intrigued by their disappearance.

She said, "The person who has been to your place the most, maybe even more than me, is Jeffrey Spencer. He might have decided to take the shots for a closer look to make sure they didn't implicate him. Or, of course, he took them because he saw that they did."

Lou visited again, this time looking un-typically uptight. "You're on the credit union board, Buck. Can you help me get a loan? The bastards claim I am already over-extended. Hell, isn't everybody? I need the loan because I'm being dunned for $45,000 that we owe for the re-decoration of our living room."

I whistled at the amount.   "Unfortunately, as a member of the board I can't interfere in the loans, but try asking the credit union for a smaller loan and some debt counseling—they like that. That way you could make a small good faith payment to the decorator and work out a deal to pay the rest over the next year or two."

Brightening, Lou looked a bit more like himself as he got up to go. "I'll try it! Thanks," he said. "Incidentally, that adman Pelican has been pushed out of the company. Thanks for writing that complaint and for copying it to the world. I like a man who fights back." He shook my hand.

"My pleasure," I said. I asked Lou what he thought of the pictures.

"They pretty nearly made me throw up. Seeing other people—even Maury—vomit always does that to me. (Always have had to turn my own sick-at-their-stomachs kids right over to their Mother.) And the photos of Evelyn collapsing, they are worse than awful.   You can see bits of regurgitated food all over Spencer's suit!"

"I can't find the pictures anymore," I said. "I think somebody stole them."

"Good riddance," Lou said, "but it wasn't me. I wouldn't want 'em."

I guess I believed Lou, but *somebody* took the pictures. I brightened: *Wasn't that a clue? by damn! Yes! Something to sink my teeth into! I'd better see what someone might have seen in the pictures that made them steal them.*

ADRIANNA:
That evening—I think Buck was eating a frozen dinner he had warmed up—I called him from Evelyn's.

"You may have lost the pictures," I said, "but I think I've belatedly found the name of the mystery person. As I said I would, I went through Evelyn's address book and found several slips tucked into it. One said, 'P. Gyraud.' And when I unfolded it, there was an address: The Jefferson Davis, Richmond, with three question marks at the end. No phone number, though."

Buck said, "That's the name I was trying to remember! Yes! Remind me to kiss you! We have another clue! What jumped out at me was that it was the same name as the woman who called for Spencer from Richmond. She had talked about him rather mysteriously. I wondered what their relationship might be. The Jefferson Davis's an old, very fancy hotel in downtown Richmond, I think, but maybe there is an apartment building with the same name. Or maybe the hotel has some residential suites. Some hotels do."

I smiled. "This woman could be a secret lover, don't you think? — and, if so, the noose around Spencer's neck tightens!"

"Yeah, maybe," Buck said, "but what about your own pretty neck? Are you back at Evelyn's?!"

"Mildred came with me," I said, not mentioning that she had already gotten bored and gone for a drink.

Buck said, "I guess Mildred is probably tougher and stronger than I am at this point, but I'm getting better. Maybe I can go along soon.

"And, speaking of going along, Adrianna, I feel healthy enough to go write up Maury Woodrow's hobbies, as I promised Danyel. And do a little spying. Want to go? Maury said to swim and to bring a friend, if I liked. I'd like."

"Sure," I agreed. "Maybe Maury knows something he doesn't even know he knows, about Spencer or the poisonings, or these big judgments against the company."

"Worth trying to find out," Buck said.

These days, his nose still sported a bandage, but it was now just a small strip, not the bulbous gauze that had made him look like a circus clown. However, braking and shifting gears still seemed to cause him some trouble occasionally, so I had learned to shift and now I drove him in his Miata to the Woodrows' house.

BUCK:

For her part, Adrianna was wearing one of those short-short dresses that you can't help but stare at because it barely covers her, uh, p-word. She wore a black bathing suit under the dress. *It would be deliciously obscene without it. It looked pretty delicious as it was!*

I enjoyed watching her legs rise and fall as she applied the clutch and brakes. Glad I hadn't bought an automatic.

ADRIANNA:

The Woodrows lived in the exclusive Village of Chevy Chase in a Tudor-style home so big that Buck let out a low whistle as he scrambled out of his little car. Maury, casually but elegantly dressed for the photos, ushered us in. "George Brown not with you?"

"My car can't handle three," Buck said. "He's coming on his own and will be 25 minutes late; you can set your watch on it."

"As you're early, we have some welcome free time," Maury said.

In the big central hall that we entered, a portrait of an eighteenth-century gentleman looked down his nose at us and there were other rich, white male ancestors on the walls and along the curving staircase that swept up to another level. To the right, a grand parlor – too full of antiques and art to be considered a "living room," commanded attention.

"Awesome," Buck said.

EVELYN:

Snooty ancestors! What's this got to do with my death? Oh, I get it. It's because the Spencer management book says to learn all you can about the principal players. Dumb Buck is trying to solve my murder with a management book!

ADRIANNA:

Maury was welcoming and said, "While we wait for George, let's have a coffee." He poured from a silver coffee pot into delicate china cups. Probably Waterford.

"Do these portraits go back as far as they look?" I asked. "To Colonial times?"

Maury said, "Oh yes, and I'm much too proud of them, I suppose. My ancestor that you saw in the foyer was a 'neighbor' of Thomas Jefferson, meaning that his spread was within an hour on horseback from TJ's, and they were friends. I like to think my ancestor was a lot like Mr. Jefferson — land-owner, collector, architect, and creative, experimental farmer and naturalist, early biologist too. Unfortunately, they were also slave-owners. Nothing good can be said of that – and I think they knew it!"

Perhaps sensing that ancestors weren't the kind of "hobby" Buck and the Athena *Herald* were looking for, Spencer said, "You wanted to see my steins. They are a level below, in the recreation room."

"Some of my other ancestors were among the first Germans to settle in Virginia, along the Shenandoah Valley. Germans, you know, fought in the American Revolutionary War on both sides. I inherited six steins from some of them, which whetted my appetite to collect a few more. Now I have more than 50, most made for its original owner to highlight his trade or profession. Here's one with a picture painted on it of bakers making bread. The owner, whose name in written here, was, of course, a baker. He may have had the stein made to drink from at home or, more likely, it was kept at his favorite tavern or biergarten for his use."

Buck was picking up Maury's comments on a small recorder but he also scribbled notes.

Maury then took us to a huge, bright room in which two large glass tanks presented a dazzling variety of multi-colored fish, some of them six inches or longer. Maury pointed to a spectacular, varicolored animal the size of a flounder, I guessed. "She's a Calico Fantail that Stella found for me. I call her 'Jaws'—the fish that is, not Stella."

Moving to a display on the opposite wall, Maury said, "Stella also is as keen as I am for these beautiful shells, such as this rare blue queen conch." Maury proudly pointed it out within a wall of glass shelves lighted to show the vivid reds, pinks, oranges and subtle blues a large number of small and large shells. Their labels gave them such lovely names as Baby's Ear Moon.

Maury said, "The Matchless Cone here is the most valuable and, I think, the most beautiful: It looks to me like a cone made of tiny, bright mosaics worthy of the richest mosque in all Islam."

I was entranced by all its bright bits of intense color. "I'm in heaven," I gushed.

At that moment, George arrived, let himself in and followed the sound of our voices. He started taking photos at once, especially of the Calico Fantail, which seemed to recognize Maury and almost seemed to communicate with him. In trying to capture this friendly relationship, George had Buck and me hold lights over, beside and below the tanks until he got the shot he wanted without reflections on the glass. George seemed to love the challenge, Maury the attention.

After 30 more minutes or so, Stella swept in wearing a cloud of yellow chiffon draping her model-thin body. In contrast, buxom Connie Yeager (who seemed to know everyone of any importance at Athena) followed in a simple bathing suit and denim cover-up.

"I think our fish," Stella said, "have personalities. They seem to talk to you. And the shells on the other wall are so universally sunny and cheerful, I think they're my favorite out of all our collections. I bought that Matchless Cone for Maury."

"You certainly did!" Maury said, smiling at his wife.

"If you aren't needed," Stella said to me, "we could leave the men to their work and go out to the gardens and pool.

Along the way, she pointed out a shiny red, toy-like sports car. "Have you seen this old beauty? Maury's MG. I forget the year but it's an antique. Maury keeps it running himself, too. He can read a manual and do just what it says. He's a genius at everything he touches, I believe, though he does get quite greasy working on his autos. I love that. It's so masculine."

The pool was nestled in greenery and adjacent to a small house with dressing rooms and a bar. Stella gestured expansively. "It's almost big enough to be a neighborhood pool, isn't it? Indeed, one or two weekends each summer we invite the whole neighborhood in to swim and party! And when my extended family comes up from Charleston and Savannah, we have another big bash. We're just about 30 folks, and we have the bestest time here." As she talked, Stella topped half glasses of orange juice at the bar with large amounts of Grey Goose. She thrust the screwdrivers on Connie and me. "I try not to drink alone," she said.

She laughed, downed half her drink, and swept off her dress to reveal a flattering pink-and blue-flowered bathing suit and a well-cared for body. I gaped as she plunged clean as can be into the clear blue pool. I followed, making a bit more of a splash, while Connie waded in from the shallow end.

After a half hour, Buck appeared. He said George was photographing the steins, which Buck had already taken notes about, so he wasn't needed inside at the moment. He changed in the pool house and, while we all stared impolitely at his battered physique, he walked to poolside, removed his artificial leg and the large, condom-like protective wrap that he wore between his stump and the appliance. He eased himself into the water. So as to go easy on his shoulder and ribs, he swam a slow sidestroke for a few laps.

Stella said, "Maury told me you had a near thing down some stairs. He said somebody may have tripped or pushed you! How awful!"

Connie swam up to look at his remaining discolorations and bumps. "Oh, my!" she said.

"The collar bone has knitted back together, and the ribs are mending nicely too but I'm still forced to take it easy," Buck said. "I usually could swim a whole lot faster. But I shouldn't complain; I'm still here."

"I'll drink to that," Stella said, and got the rest of her drink and finished it.

After we dried off and changed or covered up, Stella topped our drinks with more Grey Goose and took us into what she called the "second living room," a room incorporating stunning modern furniture and what I recognized as a David Hockney and other contemporary art. Over the fireplace there was a large pastel portrait of a boy who looked to be about three. The boy held a Pooh bear.

"That is Thomas Jefferson Woodrow, our son," Stella said, surprising me. I didn't know the Woodrows had any children.

"Charming," I said. Connie covered her mouth in an apprehensive gesture; I didn't quite know why.

Stella said, "Tommy loved his bear. I had the portrait done from his last photograph."

"Last?" I stupidly murmured.

"He died two weeks after the photo."

"Oh, my God, I'm so sorry," I said, gasping. I took Stella's hand.

Connie blinked back tears. Buck seemed stunned.

"Maury doesn't talk about it," Stella said. "Doesn't like me to either. He was terribly distraught, but he says it is foolish to dwell on life's might-have-beens."

She rushed on: "I'm so grateful he never blamed me for Tommy's death, though I couldn't help but blame myself. I was quite young, 18, and my parents had died before I was 17, and I knew so little! I got pregnant while engaged but not yet quite married to Maury. He was in hot pursuit though, and I said yes to an early, moderate-sized wedding amidst dear friends. Tommy was born six months later, and Maury doted on him, as did I. Then three years later, when we had just moved to Richmond, little Tommy got measles.

"Few children get measles any longer; there are vaccines. But back then the vaccine, was new, and lots of parents and doctors too thought the disease wasn't serious enough to risk the vaccine's alleged side effects. Our thermometer had been broken in the move to Richmond, so I didn't know how high Tommy's fever was getting. And I didn't know any local pediatricians.

"Suddenly Tommy went into convulsions. I was so frightened! I called Maury's office. He was at lunch. So I got a cab driver to take us right to the nearest hospital, which turned out to be the best, the Medical College of Virginia hospital. MCV, the driver called it. They said Tommy's measles had resulted in encephalitis, an inflammation of the brain.

"Tommy couldn't be saved. Might have been severely retarded by the brain damage if he had beaten the odds and lived, they said.

"I went out of my head! I couldn't have survived another little one's death, I just knew, so I had my tubes tied, fixed, permanently, you know, so I couldn't have another no matter how much sex we have."

She sobbed a sort of one-time hiccup, but fierce, and the three of us reached out and gripped her around the shoulders in a group hug. She kissed us all, then drained her drink. "Oh, how I hated Richmond after that – and so Maury quit Life of Virginia and got the job here. He was so good to do that." She opened a small mosaic box and took out a cigarette and looked around for a light.

Buck spotted a silver Ronson lighter on a side table and pressed it. It worked!

"Thank you." Stella pulled the cigarette smoke deep into her lungs.

"So here we are!" Maury's voice cut in. He took in the cigarette, the drinks, and the portrait, I'm sure, but simply said, "George and I need Buck again to take more notes." Was he angry? If so, he covered it with a smile and a half-laugh. He led Buck off.

By the time I drove Buck home, I had new perspectives on a man I had previously looked on as brilliant but almost obsolescent gentleman — and on a woman I used to think "liked" to drink too much. Maybe she had to.

Chapter Nineteen:

FRUSTRATION

ADRIANNA continues:

Buck seemed very disappointed that while he and George got plenty of good material for a feature for the company magazine, none of this information seemed relevant to the frauds or Evelyn's death.

I had enjoyed the swim and the posh circumstances, but I didn't think I learned anything either. When I asked Maury if he had any after-effects from his poisoning, he simply reprised his smooth line about never again looking a mussel "in the face" with quite the same enthusiasm.

All told, we had discovered Spencer's Mrs. Gyraud, Lou's debts and vindictiveness, and Maury and Stella's family fortunes and terrible misfortune, but none of this seemed to tell us any more about the frauds or the murder.

As we made our way back to Buck's place from the Woodrow palace, Buck was quiet and I grew afraid one of his black moods was about to descend. But it turned out Buck was just dead tired, so I helped him out of his shoes and shirt and into bed fairly early, as we had accepted an invitation to the Howards' the following day.

I started to tell him I was going to spend the night on his couch in the living room but he had already fallen dead asleep on one side of his big bed! Impulsively, without fully undressing, I slipped in on the other side. I woke in the night to find him still in dreamland but gently cuddling me. Did that feel good, like when my Dad and I cuddled!

I smiled as I counted off the nights Buck and I had slept together, Buck in a recliner beside my bed or me in a recliner beside his bed, in the two hospital rooms, in rehab, and now, in his own bed. During all these times, Buck had not had an episode, nor had we made love! Was that a tie? Or would a cuddly dog have helped him just as much?

As dawn approached, I slid guiltily out of Buck's bed, curled up on the couch like a good girl, and dozed.

Buck found me there. He had put on his leg and now brought me coffee and OJ and a microwaved sausage-egg-cheese breakfast biscuit. He gently woke me. He said, "Apologies! To think, we didn't share my bed! This will seriously damage my reputation."

I promised not to tell a soul.

Right after breakfast, I borrowed Buck's car to go to my place to change for our spy-visit to the Howards later in the day.

BUCK:
Meanwhile, George Brown made a surprise visit with contact sheets he'd already made from the Woodrow hobby shoot the day before. He also brought a magnifying glass as the prints were tiny, 36 to the contact sheet. Under the glass, however, they bloomed as banks of flowers, handsomely bound books, large shells of various tints and contortions, and rocks and crystals of considerable beauty. I laughed at close-ups of colorful and exotic fish that seemed to be in conversation with Maury.

In still another group of photos, there were the steins, and the other collections. George wanted help selecting from them. "The big problem is finding a way to connect all these hobbies. Maybe we could run a variety under the rubric, 'With all these pursuits, when the heck does he find time to get any work done?'

"Or should we maybe concentrate on one hobby, like the gorgeous shells?" George asked.

"I think that might make the *Herald* look like a poor man's *Scientific American*. Hmm. Maybe your 'when the heck does he' idea is best. 'A Gentleman of Many Passions' might be a better way to put it. You could use one or two of the best photos from each of Maury's hobbies."

"That could work," George said. "You think you can write a story and captions that will tie it all together?"

I nodded.

"Say, "George said, "what did you think of the photos I brought you before – the ones from your fatal party? Pardon the expression," he said with a smile.

"They're gone, George. I think maybe somebody saw something in them he didn't want others to see, so he or she swiped them."

"You're kidding."

"I'm not kidding at all. Look, can you make me another print of every negative from the party – in order?"

"Sure, but what's going on? You getting as suspicious as Adrianna Canter?"

"Well, you sicced her on me, didn't you?! I'll bet you told her I couldn't turn down anyone in skirts and that I would help her review the information and protect her, too." George looked sheepish, so I knew I was right. "Well, I'm finding out there is something very strange going on," I said. "Sit down." I quickly told George the gist of what Adrianna and I knew and/or believed. *She may kill me for telling George so much of this stufft but it's necessary to get him involved. ("Keep your trusted associates informed," Spencer had said and I wrote it in his book-in-progress.)*

"Man!" George said, when he had heard me out. "Man!" he repeated. "She hasn't told me all that! Fraud! And now Murder!"

George shook his head as he absorbed all I told him. "Well, look, if we want to look for a murderer in my pictures, the quickest way to get every shot of the party in a reasonable size, say 3x5, is to take the negatives to Ritz Camera for their one-hour automated service. I'll do that in the morning and bring them by with sandwiches for your lunch tomorrow. You can then go over them in detail with this magnifying glass."

"Great," I said, "But listen, I've got plenty of food here. Bring Danyel along. Don't talk about this poison-dinner stuff while she's around but you can slip me the photos and we can feed Danyel the 'Gentleman and His Passions' theme along with lunch. She's miffed I got to go with you to Maury's, I expect, and an invitation to lunch will smooth her feathers a bit. I need her happy so that she'll do a good job on that puff piece on Athena food services."

Next day, Danyel not only allowed her feathers to be smoothed but liked our "Passions" theme for the Maury Woodrow feature and announced she already had brainstormed the food services feature she would do as a favor for me. She said she liked what the staff—all volunteers—came up with:

"Each of my writers will review one of the food services, including your planned new computers-and-coffee shoppe and even the Eat-O-Matic.

"We'll write the reviews in the style of *The Post*'s restaurant critic Tom Sietsema and the other restaurant reviewers in the area, at the *Washington Times* and *The Washingtonian*. It'll be funny and draw readers in – and then we'll have a serious side-by-side story on food safety and the excellent record at Athena. You're not planning to kill any other people any time soon, are you?"

"Very funny. I might kill the *Herald* editor just for practice," I said, handing her another half-sandwich, "but not just yet, as you've come up with a great gimmick. Really good!"

George nodded. "Very creative!"

EVELYN:

While you're at it, ya want me to review your damn deadly bouillabaisse for the *Herald*? It won't get Five Stars for wholesomeness, I'll tell ya.

BUCK:

Surreptitiously, George slipped me one set of the photos while he kept another, along with the negatives, for safekeeping, "and I'll look at them under magnification too," he whispered.

I thumbed through them quickly and stopped at a couple showing Evelyn in the background with her hand to her mouth. Guess she was just starting to feel bad. No one else in the photos appeared to notice or be concerned except possibly Jeff Spencer and Lou Howard, at her table.

There were many more: People having coffee… that good dessert… Evelyn apparently excusing herself from her seat next to Spencer. Lou, Maury and Jeffrey's eyes appear to follow her, but still no real concern.

Next, George took semi-posed pictures—Say "Cheese" everyone—of each table.

But, in the next shots, the posing is over. The guests are shown getting their food, and then there is an apparent gap. George must have put down his camera to eat his own meal. Then: Some go for seconds and, after another gap, people are looking up from their tables in surprise and concern as Evelyn makes her noisy return. The camera then turns toward her, and the next three photographs show her stagger forward, pained and frightened. These pictures are hard to look at, and I set them aside.

 I turned back to the first pictures: There I was playing host to the Athena wheels and looking as obsequious – fawning -- as could be... Stella Woodrow looking up startled to be caught sneaking a stiff drink while holding a water bottle in the other hand… Lou Howard looking up from a plate piled with seafood, smiling… Mary Ann Howell gazing lovingly at Jeffrey Spencer and other shots in which she seems to be looking angry.

There are several equally admiring shots of Evelyn gazing at her Great Man. In several photos, the Newells are laughing at remarks from George's pregnant Ramona. Here is Adrianna's cleavage, sans apron. More of them... George seems to have a hang-up, a common one. And here's Adrianna covered up – not so many of these. And what's in the backgrounds? I used the magnifying glass.

Evelyn talking with Lou Howard, who looks distressed... Also, several of Evelyn looking pleased with him... *Could they have been working with each other to carry out Adrianna's Claims frauds?* I remembered Lou's secretive phone call.

Adrianna waving people out of the kitchen, with Spencer in the background stirring the stew...

Scenes at the dining tables... with figures half visible in the kitchen in the background dishing bouillabaisse, passing the bowls along... Spencer carrying two bowls to the kitchen counter and placing one (in a later shot) before Evelyn...

I continued to study the photos with a magnifying glass. *There has to be something someone doesn't want us to see!* But I just couldn't find anything compromising.

I marked all the shots in which the kitchen was visible, even deep in the background, even though the damn flower arrangement on the counter blocked a lot of the serving area.

ADRIANNA:

We've gotten a little out of order time-wise.
Between Buck and George discovering the party pictures
were missing and George coming by the next day with
duplicates, I had driven Buck's Miata to my place and then
back to pick up Buck to go to Lou's.

"You look good enough to eat," he said to me. "A
peach ice cream cone." I was wearing both a lipstick and a
sports outfit of that color, accentuated with a white trim.
Very crisp, very cool-looking, and very right, I thought.

BUCK:

Soon, just as on the day I sped out to Lou's house to
keep him from killing himself, Adrianna drove along tacky,
over-crowded 301 and onto a Maryland state roadway that
was narrow, arched over by trees and restfully "country."

ADRIANNA:

The Howards' stone house was "country," too.
With its incorporated log cabin, it sat close to the road, and
looked old and comfortable. We found Lou on a riding
mower in a skimpy pair of running shorts. He didn't look
like God's gift to women, as some friends claimed he
thought of himself. His chest and his paunch, which he
initially made no effort to suck in, were a mass of black
curls turning grey.

"Welcome, welcome, welcome," Lou yelled as he hopped off the mower. "Damn. Thought I'd have this finished before you got here!" He mopped his head and padded barefoot towards us. Suddenly remembering to pull his stomach in, he kissed me, then shook Buck's hand vigorously.

"Your advice on how to work with the credit union," he told Buck, "was right on the money. We quickly worked out a plan for paying the debt on our living room redecoration. It's all working out."

I poked my nose in. "How did you run up such a debt?" I asked. "I heard it was $45,000!"

Lou threw up his hands. "More! That's what we still owe, nearly. But did you think we were just prettying up? No. The living room was flooded. Lou Jr. wrecked it. He and some buddies and their girls got to horsing around on our beloved waterbed in our bedroom upstairs, and it burst(!) causing great damage below. Donna and I were at the Cape at the time, unfortunately. Donna's mother has a fishing hut up there that's been converted into a wee house with low ceilings and doorways. I call it Chez Concussion! But the big headache was when we got home and saw the mess, even after the kids had tried to clean up."

Donna Howard appeared wearing an eyelet blouse over a pleated bathing suit, neither in the latest style, but attractive. Donna took up the redecoration narrative: "The downstairs ceiling collapsed, of course, and the living room furnishings were ruined."

"Even worse than the destruction of our living room," Lou said, "was that Lou Junior had a beautiful marine display tank right here in which he had a range of Chesapeake Bay creatures—crabs, fish, sea flora. It wasn't broken but the collapsing ceiling plaster fell into the tank, changing the crucial chemical balance of the water. The salinity level and the acidity have to be just so, you know. So, everything was on the way to being killed and most of it did die. Junior could only save a few specimens.

"'Hoist on his own petard,'" Lou quoted. "In today's lingo that might be 'blown up by one's own bomb.'"

BUCK:

I cringed to hear him say that, but Lou didn't know about my war experiences and was already continuing: "Anyway it was a terrible set-back to Junior's effort to graduate as a marine biologist. The tank, you see, was kind of his thesis. I've helped restore it, and we've moved it."

I almost slipped and said I'd already seen it in the boathouse, but I stopped myself in time.

Lou said, "We've moved the tank to an insulated part of the boathouse, where Junior also sleeps on the second floor.   He's re-populating the tank and is working part-time to help pay off our remaining $45,000 redecoration debt.   I hope he's learned a lesson."

"What an expensive one," Adrianna said.

"We should see our 'pride and joy' soon," Lou said in a tone of both sarcasm and love, "and maybe he'll take us sailing. He's a good kid, really. Just a tad wild. I'm afraid he takes after his old man."

As if on cue, Lou Jr. appeared and did invite us to go sailing. The 30-foot craft was old but well maintained. With Junior taking pleasure in shouting commands at Lou and me as his crew, we traveled smoothly down to the mouth of the river and back while enjoying a few cans of Schlitz along with open-face sandwiches mounded with crab that Lou and Lou Jr. had trapped earlier.

On our return, Lou Jr. and I grilled sweet potatoes and hamburgers. ("Rare ok with everybody?" young Lou asked.) Indoors, the women fixed a big salad. I think Big Lou went off to shower and shave.

While we grilled, Lou Jr. pressed me for "the dirt" on Evelyn's death. I told him what I could about the purchase and cooking of the shellfish, about the hospital's treatment of the cases as PSP, Adrianna's suspicion that other, similar-acting poisons were involved, and finally about the CDC's conclusion that no other poison was involved.

Lou Jr. said, "One of my professors, Dr. Prentice Gorse, devoted a whole lecture to shellfish poisoning cases and red tides. Fascinating stuff. Deaths are rare, but they do happen."

ADRIANNA:

As we women made salad, Donna told me of her "escape" into real estate. "It helps when you have six kids. That is, it provides a bit of extra income, helps get me out of the house, and helps show the kids that their mother isn't their indentured servant; they can pour themselves some cereal and milk, make themselves a sandwich – or go hungry. Sometimes they even remember to put the dishes in the dishwasher and when one of them takes the garbage out I say alleluia, there is a God!"

We all pronounced Buck and Junior's rare burgers "juicy and perfect." There were no left-overs. "You work together well," I told them.

Lou grinned but said to Buck, "She doesn't know I once was gonna kill you!"

I was going to ask about the details but the two of them, without asking me along, went off to look at some new specimens in Junior's tank. And even more rudely, I overheard Junior say to Buck, "She's got the hots for you, guess you know. After your fall and all, you in shape to be getting any?"

I didn't hear how Buck answered. But "no" was the answer, I could have told Junior.

On their return, I admitted to Buck, "I'm getting tired. We had better start back."

Nobody tried to stop us. In fact, Lou Sr. said, "I have an early day tomorrow—I sometimes help with the 7 a.m. Monday Mass at St. Mary's before I go into work. Junior and I alternate."

"Also, Donna, needs her rest," I whispered, as we got back in the car. "She's pregnant."

"Pregnant? I didn't see – "

"Very early. It was just the way she held herself—so I asked her," I said.

"In debt and pregnant again.   That will make seven. I'm glad I was raised Episcopalian," Buck said.

"And you remember I told you Lou played around?" I asked as I drove.

"Yes."

"Well, in the bar when we were alone together, he grabbed me—but not, luckily where Donald Trump talked about grabbing women—and he kissed me. Lou, that is. Not Trump."

BUCK:

"Did you defend yourself?" I asked with a bit of sarcasm.

"Didn't have to." Adrianna laughed. "Lou's big watch got caught on that netting around the bar, part of the nautical décor, and it pulled away and that decorative ship's wheel came down with a crash and a clatter. He seemed so scared Donna would come in to investigate and put two and two together that I helped him rig it all up again. So, I give him a bit of credit for being one of those womanizers who is also in love with his wife and doesn't want to hurt or upset her."

In spite of the incident, Adrianna said she enjoyed herself. "Thanks for taking me."

"Nightcap?" I asked.

"We're both pretty tired," she said, "so I'll say no, but I do have some more claims cases to tell you about, maybe tomorrow."

At Adrianna's place, I switched into the driver's seat, drove the rest of the way home and spent the balance of the evening with George's party pictures and the magnifying glass, looking for a possible murderer in them. The magnifying glass helped me probe the many photos that were not directly of the kitchen but included it incidentally in the background. I found a couple of shots where Spencer is there with two bowls and there's someone behind the counter whose face is not visible.

Adrianna would suspect that Spencer took the opportunity to poison Evelyn's bowl or to drop something in the pot. *But who is behind the counter? If ever we rule out Spencer as the murderer, we could ask him who served and handed him the bowls. Lou was back there for part of the time.*

But almost anyone could have poisoned Evelyn's bowl – and gone un-photographed while doing it.

There were also the shots George was famous for – the funny candid shots of people doing odd things when they think no one's looking: *An abashed Maury, caught licking a serving spoon! Adrianna signaling with a thumb up how delicious she thought her stew was.*

BUCK continues:

Spencer and I had no book meetings pending in the next couple days but on Thursday evening I pulled up his number and called him.

Caller ID let him know it was me, so he answered his phone with a question:

"Are you calling about our book?"

"Nope, that's coming along nicely, just polishing it 'til it shines. It's Mary Ann. She's not there is she?"

"No. What about her?"

"I want to talk about the change that has come over her. She's given me lots of time off to heal and work on the book, but she seems, well, distracted. Moody. Short –"

"Hostile?"

"Well, yes, you might say that."

"I've got a busy day or two but come by about 2 Saturday." Spencer gave his apartment number in case I didn't remember it. Without repeating the rest of the address, he hung up.

I headed for Dulles. By luck, Adrianna was attending her brother's marriage ceremony in Maine on the same weekend good old Sibyl was back, so, using our phones to coordinate, I pulled up just as Sibyl stepped out with her wheeled suitcase and a bottle of California bubbly for me. "I'm glad you are still ready to take in an old friend, as you darn well should be, considering all the good times we've had together, all the depressions I've pulled you out of, and all the hangovers we've recovered from together." Her smile blazed.

I grinned mightily back. "It's so damn good to see you!"

I took her to Le Diplomate for dinner and then to my apartment for a bit of reunion dalliance. Beside me, Sibyl said, "If I ever come back to live with you again, I'll learn to cook for you and make you cut down on your drinking, and I'll fall in love with you big time."

"Sounds like a plan," I replied, kissing the nape of her neck.

Early the next morning, I took her by her storage company. As she planned, two students home from UCLA were there with a rental van. As best I could, I helped them load it. The kids were on their way by early afternoon.

Opening the door to us at 2, Jeffrey Spencer was amused (he told me later) at how Sibyl leaned into me "like a Golden Retriever leans into its beloved master."

I introduced them. "I brought along this friend," I told Jeff, "who's never seen the inside of the famous Watergate apartments. Okay if she looks around while we talk?"

Spencer smiled and took Sibyl's hand and led her in. His manner announced that he liked her looks. I thought, *He's probably wishing he were 20 years younger. I'm beginning to see that Spencer has a strong weakness for the ladies, plural.*

He led us to a big window overlooking the slow-moving Potomac River. There were lightly clad people, mostly in their 20s and 30s, strolling, bicycling, and jogging along the river bank, and not a few older people sitting on benches in the sun, while mostly young men and boys stood or sat on the river wall and fished. Beyond them, slowly cruising was a veery large motor-yacht.

I wondered aloud if that was the Sequoia. Keen on the subject, Spencer told Sibyl that I was referring to a 104-foot yacht that had borne many Presidents.

Spencer said, "Even in the Great Depression, Hoover managed to sneak off in it and pursue his love of fishing as far away as Florida.

"He managed to keep the trip secret," Spencer said. "He knew that a nation standing in bread lines would not want to see its President at leisure, fishing, especially on a luxurious boat that taxpayers paid for.

"After Hoover, the yacht was used by Presidents Roosevelt through Kennedy, Nixon and Ford. Their many guests included Winston Churchill and Queen Elizabeth. I tell you, few people applauded when Jimmy Carter sold that ship into private hands as an economy measure.

"She continued to be seen on the Potomac for a time, and I've been a guest at parties on her twice, but there seems to have been a dispute over the payment for some work the ship needed, and the Sequoia ended up in storage and probably is beyond repair now. A great pity."

Spencer's apartment was not large, but it was handsome. Over a carved marble fireplace was an original Andrew Wyeth. Spencer said, "I bought it before Wyeths commanded such high prices. I probably couldn't afford it—or any Wyeth—today, but there are good prints available. I have a print of his famous picture of the white dog on his master's bed. It is in my bedroom there."

Spencer cleared his throat. "Now that you've had a look around, Sibyl, maybe you can poke around in my little kitchen and find us some soft drinks and whatnot while Buck tells me what he wanted to see me about."

Sibyl slipped into the kitchen.   Cast photos that were hung around the breakfast nook probably gave her a sense of Spencer's love of singing and acting in his college days and of his one small part on Broadway before his father's death brought him home and into a steadier profession.

"I'm worried about your friend, my boss Mary Ann," I told him.   "She's given me all kinds of time to work with you and recover from my fall yet she's acting as if she's angry and upset about something.   I don't want to discuss this with anybody in our department or Vice President Pulsudski so I thought I'd speak to you."

"Good.   You think Mary Ann's hostility is directed at you personally?"

I answered, "You said once I was a good listener.   Well, you said 'hostile' on the phone, Jeffrey, and now again.   How did you know that was part of it?"

"You're not alone in observing some, er, behavior changes.   I, too, have felt this negativism," Spencer said.

"And," I said, "Mary Ann seems to resent that Adrianna is cleaning out Evelyn's apartment.   I think she's been there herself."

Spencer scowled.   "Why would Mary Ann want anything to do with that place?"

"She might want to find out if there's anything about you in there.   It's none of my business, but you indicated you were going to talk to Mary Ann about your fling with Evelyn.   I wonder.   Did you?"

"It seems Evelyn beat me to it. That woman was poison."

"Why do you figure she ratted you out to Mary Ann? And when?"

"I'm not sure," Spencer said. "I suppose she resented my attention to someone new, so she told Evelyn about our long-ago fling — probably without indicating just how long ago it had been." He paused. "I believe Evelyn told Mary Ann all this just before the dinner you gave."

"That could explain why Mary Ann was so uptight," I said. "In these photos from my dinner, look, here Mary Ann is looking adoringly at you one moment but here she is looking off into space, tense, maybe mad. Here she is frowning at something. Maybe at you or maybe at Evelyn—hard to tell.   How did Evelyn tell Mary Ann, do you think? Over lunch? With a note?"

"No idea," Spencer said. "But when I belatedly started to bring Evelyn up, I—don't shoot me for stupidity—I foolishly mentioned this will of Evelyn's giving me whatever money Evelyn had. That may well have made Mary Ann think my fling with Evelyn was more important than it was and that it lasted much longer—even up until very recently."

"Wow. That's too bad. One more question, Jeff: Did you ever describe to Mary Ann what Evelyn's apartment looked like, or what was in it—the black negligee and the sexy books etc?"

"I'm not *that* stupid. You think I'd say, 'Mary Ann, Evelyn had this erotic poster of two women licking each other, and, heh, you should see the photograph of a penis that's hanging in the bathroom — maybe it's of me? I admit to stupidity but I'm not crazy!'"

At mention of the photo possibly being of his pecker, I must have looked surprised.

"Yes, you heard me right: That penis," Spencer confided, in a moment of sheepish pride, "may be an enlargement of a part of a nude snapshot Evelyn got of me in a romantic moment that week we spent at the Tides!"

"Well, I hope you didn't want it as a souvenir," I said with a snicker, "because it's no more—I got it out of there, along with the posters and the Mapplethorpe book, even before Adrianna got more than a glance at them. They have been trashed.

"But Mary Ann let slip something about a 'black negligee' being there," I said.

"That makes me suspect she saw Evelyn's place at some point, probably before Adrianna started sorting things out.

I think she used the key that you meant for Adrianna and saw the negligee, the poster and the penis picture, etc.—though not recognizing it was you, I hope, " I said with another chuckle. "Having seen those various things could certainly account for her mood, especially since she doesn't know that Lou and maybe a battalion of others followed you into Evelyn's bed. Or, it could be just her imagining of you amidst all that, er, filth, as she would surely consider it. She also may be suffering some guilt for bashing Adrianna in the head—and the remote possibility she came back after a few hours and pitched me down the stairs as well."

"Buck! You think she did that?"

"No, not regarding me and the staircase, really; we're friends of sorts and she was probably long gone from the apartment building by then, anyway, and no longer in a panic.   But Adrianna's arrival at the apartment, when Mary Ann may have thought she had the only key, must have scared the constipated shit out of her! And maybe there's more. Maybe Evelyn told Mary Ann something more about you."

"What more could Evelyn tell her?"

"Maybe she could have alleged that you have had other women besides either of them," I said carefully. "Maybe Evelyn alleged there had been someone very recently even, while Mary Ann thought you and she were a faithful pair—something nasty like that. The name of that same Richmond woman who called you, a Mrs. Gyraud, was on a slip we found at Evelyn's. Maybe it was a kind of memo to herself to check that woman and you out. Maybe she jumped to conclusions and flat out told Mary Ann that you were double-timing her with this Gyraud woman.

"That could enrage anyone in Mary Ann's position," I said. "You know, 'Hell hath no fury like a woman scorned.'"

"That's Congreve," said Sibyl, coming in with the Diet Cokes, some crackers, and some hard cheese. "It really goes, 'Heav'n has no rage, like love to hatred turn'd, Nor Hell a fury, like a woman scorned.'

"But," Sibyl added, "I see you've not finished your business." Taking her Diet Coke and a napkin with some of the snacks she had brought out, Sibyl retreated onto the apartment's balcony, sliding closed the glass door behind her.

"I think we need a real drink," Spencer said, heading toward the kitchen, but I noted that he hadn't directly denied he knew a Mrs. Gyraud.

"Bourbon ok, Buck?"

"Fine. With rocks and just a touch of water, please," I called back. "Or just pour some bourbon in my Coke."

Alone for the moment, scanning the room, I again spotted the scholarly tome on poisons I had seen before. But now it took on greater significance. *Uh oh,* I thought. *This may be more important than Mrs. Gyraud.* There in the bookcase amidst leather and gold bindings, a nineteenth-century edition of Shakespeare's plays and an 1853 travel journal – there, big as life, was that thick book on poisoning.

Pulling it out, my breath left me as I saw that a slip of paper marked a page that read, "Saxitoxin (STX) -- neurotoxin produced by certain species of marine dinoflagellates, it is responsible, usually through shellfish contaminated by toxic algal blooms, for the human illness known as paralytic shellfish poisoning and resulting deaths. Various sea mammals may also eat contaminated shellfish, sicken and die. The term saxitoxin comes from the species name of the butter clam (*Saxidomus giganteus*) in which the poison, one of the most potent of natural toxins, was first seen.   The toxin halts normal cellular function and can thereby lead to paralysis, most dangerously that of the lungs. "

Spencer returned with the drinks, saw me with the book, and quickly sought to explain why he had it annotated: "I don't remember how I happened to have that book in the first place but I had never read it until after Evelyn's death. I got interested then because Mary Ann had purchased the seafood for your dinner."

Spencer downed most of his drink.

I tried to sound casual: "Speaking of women, in particular that Mrs. Gyraud I just mentioned, the phone rang in your office area and I picked it up, and this Mrs. Gyraud, as I think she pronounced it, was phoning for you and sounded mysterious. I left a message form for you. Did you call her back? I believe the name is spelled G-y-r-a-u-d."

"Humph. I never saw your message. Where did you put it?"

"On your desk chair."

"Oh, well, somebody else probably picked it up and handled it. That was one of Evelyn's better ideas. She got us into the habit of acting on each other's messages like that, when appropriate." Spencer seemed completely unconcerned – *but then,* I reflected, *he was an actor.*

Spencer continued: "And this pile of pictures you brought over– they're all of the party?" He flipped through them and began to frown and sputter. His face reddened as he saw himself and Mary Ann embracing in the kitchen. "Has George never heard of saying 'cheese' before he shoots? He's too sneaky by half.

"I'd say toss these, all of them, or burn them, shred them. Don't show them around. Let people forget that damnable dinner disaster of yours – much," he hastened to add, "as I appreciate what you were trying to do for Mary Ann and for me!

"You know you can read all kinds of thing into pictures," Spencer continued, "if you have a mind to."

Sibyl, seeing liquor being served, came in from the balcony. She accepted a light Scotch and soda. Spencer addressed her: "I can see Buck shows better judgment in women than in his photo-happy war buddy George."

In a firm voice, he added to me, "I owe Adrianna my thanks, and you too, Buck, for your work at Evelyn's apartment, which I understand is nearly completed. But I think I'll do the remaining part myself. I have meetings Monday, but I'll go there Tuesday. I have a handyman I've already lined up to come along to do any heavy work.

"Please thank Adrianna but tell her she's relieved of the chore." Spencer stressed: "Keep her away from there." It wasn't a suggestion. It sounded very much like an order.

The next morning, Sunday, I took Sibyl to her plane, kissed her, and saw her to the security line. I said I was thankful that we "had shared an oasis of such pleasure, in this cruel and transient world." With that last phrase I was thinking of Evelyn's death and Jen's, but Sibyl looked surprised by my sudden loquaciousness. I was a bit surprised myself.

"You're a good woman," I said more plainly. "I hope you find a good man out West."

"Oh, I'm pretty lucky that way," Sibyl said. "I've had a good one here, and I'm not talking about Hormone Hal, though he helped me out too. I mean you. I've just gritted my teeth and tolerated the worst of you sometimes, so it's kind of like the song says, I can't stand you sometimes, but I'll always love you.

"Take care of yourself, please? Go easy on the drinking. Go back to your shrink." She looked at me unblinkingly. "Get serious with a woman and stick with her. If it's this Adrianna, fine. Maybe marry her and do stay faithful. Go to church for a better reason than bedding one of the sopranos in the choir."

"Your advice would be more persuasive," I said, "if I hadn't found you there."

"At least listen to the sermons. God loves you, Buck." Sibyl was beginning to cry. "You didn't kill your brother. When you get those attacks, remember it was never your fault Jens died—and that it's not just me who loves you, and not just Adrianna, assuming she does. It's many people—George and Ramona and your dad and mom, Hal, probably, and God. And your brother too, wherever he may be. Rely on them.

"End of lecture." She touched my face affectionately.

"Anyway, Buck, when I haven't wanted to kill you for being a jackass, it's been fun."

"You got that right, the fun part," I said, kissing her salty cheek, "and if you ever need –"

But a TSA agent motioned Sibyl to go through the pulse induction metal detector.

I watched and waved as she disappeared beyond the device. I moved to a window and waited for forty minutes until her brightly painted plane taxied down the runway and flew her west.

Chapter Twenty: KNOW THAT JOB YOU DON'T LIKE?

BUCK:

Monday, though I was still officially recuperating at home, my mobile phone rang, and it was Mary Ann Howell.

"Jeff says you have photos of your dinner party. Come in first thing tomorrow morning and let me see them." There was no "Can you?" But she did add: "You won't need to stay long."

"Sure. I think I can manage that." I also had an idea.

Next day, when I handed Mary Ann the photos, she studied them one by one in the stack and then said, "I want these all destroyed, pronto."

"They could be evidence."

"Evidence," Mary Ann snarled, "of what? Paralytic shellfish poisoning is a perfectly natural phenomenon— there's no crime—and Evelyn, well, she was—"

Mary Ann thought better of whatever she was going to say. She just began tearing the pictures up.

"Stop!" I yelled. "Have you gone out of your mind?"

But Mary Ann continued to rip them. With increasing fervor. "Don't say that! It will be worth your job to say that again! There is nothing the matter with me! – not if you and Jeff and everybody else will just stop harping on that immoral Evelyn woman and that ghastly party!" She swept the balance of the photos into the trash. "It will also be worth your job to show copies of these photos to anybody else!"

"That's some threat!" I said.

"That's a promise!" Mary Ann shot back.

Standing there in some remaining physical pain as well as new anger, I took a big gamble, thinking I didn't have much left to lose. "Is this your own guilt talking? You want to cover up and forget you burglarized Evelyn's, struck Adrianna and maybe even sent me headfirst down a staircase? I nearly died, broke my nose, a shoulder and a few other bones and I had a concussion, and, damn it, it ruined my artificial leg—that still isn't working like it did before—and you want me to forget it?"

As I said this, knowing it might well mean the end of my employment at Athena, I punched the number of Adrianna's stolen phone into mine: "Maybe you didn't intend to more than get her out of the way so you could escape, but you know you might have hurt her seriously. And well, as for me, I didn't pitch down that stairway for my health! I know you could have just been trying to get away but—"

And then I heard the characteristic Beethoven Fifth Symphony-like ring of Adrianna's stolen phone, muffled, but almost surely coming from a drawer in Mary Ann's desk. Mary Ann heard it too and knew I had her dead on. The jig was up.

With a heavy breath, she pulled the phone out of her drawer and handed it to me. "Please give it to Adrianna," she said and added, rapid as a machine gun, "but I didn't intend—it was a spur of the minute thing that in my haste to get out of there, I knocked her down and, without thinking, grabbed her phone so she couldn't call and have me caught. As for your fall, I didn't—I'm not a killer—I didn't push—you must believe me—"

There was a pause and I thought Mary Ann was about to tell me more but instead the color drained from her face and she began to breathe heavily and quickly like she was having a stroke or a heart attack. She sank onto her knees.

She gasped for breath. "Bag – bag," she mouthed.

"Pills? In your bag?" I pulled open Mary Ann's pocketbook and handed it to her. She shook her head violently, and then sank the rest of the way to the floor. I cradled her in my arms and shouted to her assistant. "Betty! Mary Ann isn't breathing right." I was fearfully remained of Evelyn's collapse. "Call the clinic! Get someone up here. I'll call Mr. Spencer." I could reach Mary Ann's desk phone.

Spencer was in a meeting, his temp said.

"Get him the hell out! This is an emergency. Tell him Buck says Mary Ann can't breathe." (I hoped I wasn't blowing the secrecy about their relationship, but this *was* an emergency.)

Spencer was right on the phone. "She's hyperventilating," he said. "She's done it once when I was with her. Hold a brown paper bag over her nose and mouth right away! And I'll be right there!"

So that's what she meant by 'Bag!'

The company nurse rounded the corner with a wheelchair and defibrillator, just as I grabbed Betty's lunch bag, emptied it and put if over Mary Ann's mouth and nose – and just before Spencer appeared with another bag. Mary Ann was quickly okay.

"Did I ruin your lunch, tossing it out of the bag like that?" I asked Betty.

"No, no. It's no worse for wear." She added with a wink, "And I'll have lots to tell the other girls at lunch."

The desk phone I had used now rang. It was Adrianna. "Spencer went running out, and I knew you were at Mary Ann's. What's up?

Whispering so the others couldn't hear, I told Adrianna the whole story, ending with my fear that Mary Ann was having a stroke or attack because of my accusation "and was going to die like Evelyn."

"And you thought getting blamed for killing one Athena woman was enough?!"Adrianna said with an abrupt laugh, "but with over-breathing, you don't die. You just think you're going to. The solution is a brown paper bag over nose and mouth so the carbon dioxide builds up and the oxygen is reduced. I think that's the way it goes."

"That's what Spencer said, and I did put a bag in place. She was soon okay."

Just then, Dr. Michael Vinson, the company doctor, dashed in. "Ah, things look in hand." Like Adrianna, he said, "You don't usually die from hyperventilating, but you often feel like you're going to. I was with an employee who had a heart attack – but she's in an ambulance now on her way to Suburban Hospital and I've alerted them that she's coming. I'll get over there now." He left.

By now Spencer had spotted the remaining photos on Mary Ann's desk. "Did you show her those? That's all she would need." He gave me a hard, angry look.

"She asked – ordered – me to show them to her, then started ripping them up. She said you had told her about them," I said pointedly.

Spencer looked more than faintly abashed. "I only told her she should tell you not to make a practice of showing George's pictures to every Tom, Dick and Harry.

"But you know, Buck?" he said, "I think this episode proves Mary Ann needs some time off after all this Evelyn-related stress."

"S-s-sorry," I stammered. I confessed how I'd rung Adrianna's phone and proved she had been Adrianna's assailant in Evelyn's apartment.

Spencer cursed. Not at me, I hoped, but at this new turn of events.

I was relieved when Spencer said, "I can't blame you for this; it was good detective work, but just get out of here! Scram!" Spencer said. "I'll see she gets to her doctor, if she needs anything more. And I'll talk to Pulsudski about the time off."

I was glad to leave. I took the remaining pictures and walked awkwardly and painfully away.

I was stopped in the hall by Tom Tennial, the employment director. "What was that fuss all about?"

"Ms. Howell had a hyperventilation attack, but it's all over." I'd done a project or two with Tennial and he asked me how the Spencer book was coming along. Then he whispered his news: "Keep this under your chapeau but I have a very good candidate for Spencer's job coming in. I'd like Spencer to meet him."

"Not now," I said. "Jeff was upset by Ms. Howell's attack and is in with her. I'd let him cool down awhile before you talk to him about meeting the new man—or woman." I didn't ask who the candidate was because Tennial wouldn't have told me, but I knew it would be bad news for Lou and Maury.

I stopped by Frederica Pulsudski's office to tell her about Mary Ann's hyperventilating, but found her to be in a meeting, so I left a long message—also mentioning the stress Mary Ann had been under and taking some of the blame for it, as a result of my dinner and my injuries and my absence. "Mary Ann is a capable and generous boss and I hope I'll be able to do more to help her very soon."

Stopping briefly at my office, I called my chief caterer Burt, who admitted, "That key to the kitchen is still missing." He sounded sheepish, as it was standard operating procedure in such circumstances to get the locks changed right away.

"Still missing?" I boiled over Marine-style: "You simple fuck up! I reminded you weeks ago to get the damn locks changed. Any food been missing or any that looks like it's been messed with?"

"No," Burt said. "I mean, how can I be sure? I mean, well, it does look like someone might have been disturbing things in here. But Ms. Howell and her temporary assistant didn't seem worried. You sound awfully upset!"

"You'll find out just how upset I can get—you'll know because you'll have a grossly enlarged ass-hole. Shut the kitchen NOW and get the locks changed before Close of Business. Remind Maintenance of the death we've had and if they still have any hesitation, give them my mobile number. DO IT NOW, meanwhile tossing out any food not in an intact, unopened package – anything that might have been contaminated." I slammed down the phone. I was exhausted.

I went to the infirmary and swallowed a double dose of Tylenol and flopped down on a cot. After an hour, I pushed myself up and started to my car. On the way, Maury Woodrow stopped me to ask if the photos George took of his hobbies would be ready any time soon. I said I thought I'd be able to write the captions in a day or two. "Then you can see the pictures and check the captions' accuracy at the same time." I didn't say anything about the "very good" candidate for the job Maury so badly wanted.

"What are those photos you're holding now?" he asked.

In spite of Mary Ann's injunction, I handed them over. "If you have to, take a look. I warn you, though, Mary Ann got to hyperventilating when she looked at them."

"That's a terribly scary feeling. I've hyperventilated myself, most recently when I tried snorkeling, swimming with a mask and a mouth tube, you know, and I thought I'd die!" Maury admitted. "I surfaced and pulled off the gear and just gasped and gasped for breath!"

He shook his head as if he had indeed been badly frightened. He quickly changed the subject. "How's Adrianna coming with the organizing of Evelyn's place?" he asked.

"It's about wrapped up." I didn't know the cleanup was common knowledge.

Reading my thoughts, Maury said, "She mentioned she was doing that for Spencer and the family. Nice of her." He looked at some more pictures. "Ugh! What prompted you to have some of these photos printed up at all?"

"It's a mechanical process," I explained, "and cheaper and quicker to get them all done than to pick and choose. And after George made all those pictures, I thought I should at least look at them."

"Well, I guess I'd say, 'Look at them if you must but then get rid of them.' Even Danyel isn't dumb enough to want to run them as a photo feature! Well, is she?" Maury laughed. He shoved the pictures back in my hands and left, thank God.

I felt like hell and went home and got into Hal's whirlpool, where I fell asleep(!) and slipped under the water. I came up wide awake and sputtering, choking. *That must feel a bit like hyperventilating,* I figured. *Like dying.*

The next day, I proofed pages of the Spencer book and then, although I didn't want to make a habit of it just yet, I returned to Athena. I had decided I had better see George before anyone else told him or me to pitch his pictures.

I told him what people were saying but, instead of asking him to get rid of the pictures I asked him to blow up and improve, if possible, the backgrounds in fourteen photos taken with all or part of the kitchen in the background.

"Great minds," he said. "After you filled me in on what may have gone on, I started on some enlargements myself. Are these some you had in mind?"

I nodded. "Though none of these specifically show someone dumping anything in the stew, I hope we can find some clues in them as to who might have done it."

Leaving George to finish enlarging portions of the selected pictures, I forced myself to walk slowly over to see Lou Howard and thank him for his hospitality.

Lou's remorseful reply surprised me: "I've apologized to your Adrianna for, uh, getting a little fresh. I got a little bombed—mowing in the hot sun got me dehydrated and then I drank several beers too fast, I guess. Anyway, as she probably told you, I patted her fanny and, well, kissed her."

"Well, Lou, as the women say, I'll have to say, 'Me Too,' and Adrianna is not likely to make trouble, as you stopped when she said stop, didn't you?"

Lou's phone rang. "Whoops. That's a line I usually answer myself." He pressed the appropriate button and said, "Can you hold a minute, please?" he said. There was a reply I couldn't hear.

"Oh, it's you. I have someone in my office, but he'll be leaving in a moment. I'll be right with you. I'll just put you on hold for a second."

Lou turned back to me. "I better take this call." He appeared somewhat flustered.

"I'm just going," I said.

Lou picked up. "Yes, Jim… I'm afraid I can't give you that, er, information right now, but soon; it should be soon." He turned to me as I reached the door. "See you. Thanks for dropping by."

As I closed the office door, I looked back and saw Lou Howard huddled over the phone. I thought I heard something that sounded like. "Didn't I give you the number to my iPhone? It's more private."

My imagination, maybe. Adrianna has me thinking that a hushed call means fraud, guilt and murder, I guess. I laughed. *But something is going on.*

(I told Adrianna about the call but she couldn't link it to a shady opposition lawyer.)

I was home by mid-afternoon and rested up because I had long-ago agreed to help out at a personnel dinner that night. Adrianna called. "You were right. Spencer told me he wants the key back and that I'm not to go there again. I said I had the key at home but could bring it in tomorrow morning. That means that tonight's our last chance, if you feel up to it."

"Last chance for what?" I asked. I knew it wasn't romance she was talking about.

"A last look at Evelyn's apartment, of course," she said. "Virtually everything there, I'm proud to say, is organized and listed as well as anyone on earth could have done it, but there remains one pile of papers to go through thoroughly and there's the kitchen, where I've sometimes prepared a snack. It needs cleaning."

I thought a last look around was a good idea too, but I told her about the Washington Personnel meeting. "As all I need do is sit at the door collecting dinner tickets or money, I figured it would be no problem. Can we go a little later? It's dangerous for you to go alone."

"You're being silly. I've got my gun. Just come along after the dinner."

Chapter Twenty-one:
SOMEBODY TRIES AGAIN

BUCK:

Beginning at 6:30, as I had stupidly promised, I sat at the "will call" desk handling tickets for the city-wide personnel event, which involved cocktails, dinner and a talk on what a company can legally demand of its employees – and what it can't. I figured I wouldn't stay for the talk. *I'll ask someone later whether Athena's relationship rule came up.*

There was supposed to be a second person out front with me, but whoever it was didn't show, so I was stuck with it all. Cursing under my breath, I managed alone.

Someone brought me a red wine to drink while I worked. I don't like wine much without food but "any port in a storm." I sipped the wine and watched the clock.

At 7:30, a nicely rare roast beef dinner was brought to me. With the other guy being a no-show, I knew that if I was a "good guy" I would remain at my post until 8:15 in case there were late-comers.

To Hell with that! I was worried about Adrianna being alone in Evelyn's apartment — and knowing her to be as dumb as a post when it came to keeping safe or to using that pistol she bought, I scarfed down the dinner in ten minutes and was running, as best I could, to my car by 7:45.

I got to the apartment house by a little after eight. I could have called Adrianna or the super to buzz me in. Instead, I just sauntered through the apartment house door behind a cluster of residents and got on the elevator with them and punched the top (eleventh) floor. Everybody else got off earlier.

As the elevator door opened at Evelyn's floor, I found myself face-to-face with Adrianna herself, her gun in her hand. She jumped into the elevator with me and pushed L for Lobby.

"What's going on? Fill me in, lady!" I demanded. "Fill me in!"

"Somebody tried to get into the apartment again!" Adrianna explained as we descended. "I heard them at the door and opened it and found someone in a hoodie – a man, I think – running down the hall. He got away down the same steps you were pitched down. I had my little gun and rushed to this elevator to get down to the lobby before whoever it was can get out and away. Can't you make this thing move faster?" she said with her usual knowledge of machinery.

"You were running after a possible murderer alone?" I said. "Woman, you have a lot more guts than brains. But now that there are two of us, one of whom actually knows how to shoot a gun, let's go for the brass ring." I put out my hand and, with some relief, I think, Adrianna relinquished her firearm, as I said, "We may be about to solve this thing, nab the baddie."

But the elevator stopped at the sixth floor. A large woman got on. We hurriedly told her we were in a hurry trying to catch "a criminal," Adrianna blurted out, "before he gets out of the building." Nevertheless, the woman took her time exiting on four, all the while telling us who she was going to visit, and why.

EVELYN:
C'mon. Get moving!

BUCK:
I immediately punched the button to close the door and we moved down again, but the delay cost us. The elevator opened to the shiny bright, white-marble lobby. Empty as a bottle of gin after a night of boozing,
The lobby door was swinging. We dashed out and looked up and down the street, which was almost empty. I ran half a block to the only figure I saw and was growled at and nearly bitten by the Pekinese the woman was walking.

I returned. "Lady dog-walker," I said. "Your intruder probably jumped into a car or ran down an alley."

"Are you limping again?" Adrianna asked, looking at my artificial leg.

"Just from kicking myself that I ever let you come here alone. Well, truthfully, maybe the stump is sore again. But I have an idea for something that won't require standing or walking (and isn't sex.) Let's go back up and use our phones to 'round up the usual suspects,' as they said in 'Casablanca,' or at least phone them on their landlines to see who's home and who's not. Those who are home, we can eliminate as the person in the hall."

Adrianna nodded. "You've got a good idea there," she said and speed-dialed her boss at his home, while I speed-dialed mine.

"He's out," Adrianna said.

"Same here," I said, and dialed a few other potential perps and got no answer. "Doesn't narrow things, after all. Busy people. Guess my idea wasn't so damn hot after all."

Indeed, the only answer either of us got was at the Howards' where Junior told me Donna was with a real estate client and his dad was at Rotary.

"Say," Lou Jr. said, "isn't this the one-legged mother who was down here checking my tank?"

"Yeah," I said, "I'm the snoop you wanted to bash in the head and drown for good measure. But I thought we ended up friends. You smokin' weed again?"

"Matter of fact, I am," Junior said, "I grow the good shit myself, as you noted, alongside my PSP-polluted shellfish. Ha, ha. Hope I didn't scare you too much that first day, man. I just thought you ought to know that somebody could really kill someone and get away with it. I mean, if you don't believe me, ask Mr. Woodrow."

"Maury? Why would I need him to tell me how you could knock me on the head and drown me?" I asked.

"No, motherfucker," Junior said, "I was just joking about drowning you. I'm talking about how to poison your bouillabaisse. I thought Maury (who got poisoned, didn't he?) might already have told you. Like the rest of us, the old gent gets his rocks off over marine life, and I don't mean sailor boys. He drives down here and audits lots of classes at the Institute. He's probably at the Institute as much as Dad.

"Mr. Woodrow's rich and stuffy but, under it all, he's a nice guy. I've taken him out on my boat now and then, and he's good crew. Knew what he was doing, you know? Helped me get my tank re-stocked, too, after the water bed puncture ruined so much that was in it. Suggested where I could get a part-time job, too.

"And I'm pretty sure he attended the class on the Perfect Murder. That's why I thought maybe he would've told you how shellfish can hold onto a poison without being hurt by it, and how a person could keep these tainted shellfish alive in water of the same salt balance and temperature. It's work, but it doesn't require an Einstein; I could do it. Then, when you're ready to kill someone you just stick them baddies in your seafood stew whenever you get the inclination—and watch folks eat, fall on their faces, and die." He cackled.

"You have a strange sense of humor, Junior," I said. "Must be pretty good weed."

"I'll roll some for you, you like? Cure what ails you. That post-traumatic whatsis I hear you got."

"Post-Traumatic Stress Disorder," I said. "PTSD."

"Don't tell me," Junior said, "that what I'm saying to you hasn't occurred to you or that woman lawyer. You didn't sneak into the boathouse to look at my set-up out of purely scientific interest, Mr. one-legged Marine Sergeant, did you? (Or maybe you're not as smart as I thought.)

"My tank looks pretty primitive compared to those of the National Aquarium in Baltimore's Inner Harbor—but I believe I could keep tainted mussels alive plenty long enough to do the dirty deed on a few bitches like Evelyn. But," Lou Jr. cackled again, "as I got A-plus on the course final. Ironically the test was the same evening your Evelyn was poisoned. That's a pretty good alibi, don't you think?

"You'll have to pin the murder on Dad or Mr. Woodrow, I guess, and Dad doesn't have a tank, and I'll swear by the great god Neptune that he didn't use mine."

"Mr. Woodrow has two or more. Not that he'd ever kill anyone or poison himself, wouldn't be proper or prudent, would it? -- but he could."

"Interesting," I said after a pause. "Hmm. If I can get down to La Plata, do you think we could talk a bit more about this 'Perfect Murder' stuff sometime? -- sometime convenient for you, maybe at Casey Jones, on the main drag near the old railroad?"

"You mean sometime when I'm sober? I almost never smoke before 7 p.m. or later, as I want to graduate. But tomorrow I'm taking my girl to look at St. Mary's College. She's been out of high school three years and is stuck waitressing and we both think she should get some college so she can do a lot better. She has the brains."

As well as a non-stop body, I thought. "I'm going to Richmond, maybe as soon as tomorrow. I could stop in La Plata on the day I drive back."

Junior said, "We could do late afternoon sandwiches and beer at The Charles, which has replaced Casey Jones. They have an awesome crab cake-cheesemelt-with-bacon sandwich."

"Sounds great," I said.

As to our telephone calls to the "usual suspects," Adrianna summed up what she thought we had discovered: "Nothing.

"Everyone was out, so any of them could have been the person in the hall."

I started to tell her about what Junior claimed, but Adrianna was off on her own kick:

"When are we going to do something about 'P. Gyraud'? We've got to determine how deep her connection is with Spencer, don't we? She lives in Richmond and some of the fraud calls came from our branch office lines there."

"You'll be glad to know that now that I'm driving again I'm planning to go to Richmond soonest. Gyraud may be the kind of "key minutia" Spencer's book says managers overlook at their peril. And I think I'm well enough and can butter up Frederica Pulsudski by offering to check the rumors she's heard that there is an effort at union organization there. While I'm there, I'll track down this Gyraud woman, if I can. I'm also going to take pictures along from the official 20th anniversary dinner and my dinner as well. I'll keep studying the pictures from my dinner for clues but I'll use the pictures from the formal dinner as an excuse to see the woman."

EVELYN:

While Spencer was a good boss, I never thought he was an angel, especially after I taught him a few tricks. So, when I learned of Gyraud trying to call him at the office I thought I better check her out. I always like to know who is doing what to whom!

But how's it figure into my murder? Doesn't.
Probably one of those red herrings, Buck.

BUCK, as usual not hearing Evelyn:
"I can drive a couple hours to Richmond, easy," I
said to Adrianna

"A good idea, heading down there," she said. She
was so happy about it, she kissed me. But then she quickly
got busy on a note to Spencer spelling out all that we (her,
mostly) had done in straightening and cataloguing Evelyn's
things. Adrianna listed what items had been discarded, and
where to find everything else.

"Done at last," she said. "Home, Sherlock."

"That's a good idea. Your place or mine?"

"Drop me off at mine and make your own way
home and pack. Frederica will like your plan and want you
to go to Richmond asap. She might say, 'Why not go this
afternoon?' so we need you bright if possible, awake if
possible, and ready with an overnight bag for sure, which is
entirely possible if you go home now and pack it. Don't
forget your toothbrush, razor and hairbrush."

"You're saying you would like me to be ready," I
said.

Adrianna gave me a hug and another kiss on the
cheek. "I'm excited you're going! Gyraud may well be
the missing link in the case against the departing Jeffrey
Spencer."

As Adrianna and I hoped, Frederica Pulsudski was indeed happy for me to head for Richmond to check on union activity "as soon as you feel able," as she put it.

She may also have wanted me out of Washington because she had just listened to a voicemail from Burt about the missing kitchen key and my order to throw out anything that might possibly have been spoiled or tampered with.

"I don't blame you for being cautious," Frederica said, "especially after what happened at your dinner. Burt volunteered that you had told him, when the key first went missing, to change the lock, but he hadn't been able to get Building Maintenance around to it right away. Nevertheless, with this poisoning idea possibly stirred up again, it's an ideal time to get the locks changed and get you out of town."

So, Burt was half-way covering his ass, I thought, *and half-way covering mine.*

ADRIANNA:
Before Buck could start for Richmond, I corralled him for an early lunch at Brick's Grill and confessed, "I'm in trouble. I think I'm may lose my job." Tears must have welled in my eyes, because Buck took my hand and squeezed it.

"You can always come live with me if you're fired," he said. "Then we wouldn't be violating Athena regulations when we decide to hook up."

That sounded like a pretty pleasant idea, I started to say. Instead I said, "Humph. Mildred would make me the same offer, you know, and for the same reason: A little bit o' sumpin'."

"You wouldn't enjoy her nearly as much, I guarantee you," Buck said, "and I wouldn't enjoy it at all. But get to the point: What's happened? Why is the most fearless woman I ever met suddenly scared down to her toes?"

I told him: "When I gave Spencer the key to Evelyn's and my note listing all we had done, Spencer said, 'You went back, didn't you, against my strict orders not to?'"

"How did he know?" I asked Adrianna.

"Maybe he just guessed," Adrianna said. "Or maybe that was him in the hoodie in the hall? — our villain, as I've suspected from the first. Too bad I've never learned to lie convincingly. It's my one great failure as a lawyer. I admitted I had been there to finalize my inventory. 'Just to wrap things up,' I said.

"But Spencer said I deliberately disobeyed his orders, so he 'had to' put me on probation."

"'Had to?' Ridiculous?" Buck said.

"Spencer told me I'd been spending too much time in areas that are none of my business and not enough time on my own job.

"'Time in process is above average in your unit, reserve estimates are way off, and absenteeism is high,' he said."

"None of which is your fault. Where's your manager in all this?"

"She wasn't in today." Adrianna took a big gulp of wine and squared her shoulders. "Maybe he's right, Buck. I thought I had the answers to everything. I knew our reserves were off, but we were fixing that. We have a guy out with cancer, and I thought Spencer would realize that's what pulls down our attendance rate. And we do have a couple of old dogs that are pulling down our time-in-process."

"'Old dogs?'" Buck asked.

"Claims that have been around for a time without resolution," I explained.

"So," Buck said, "does this action of Spencer's further convince you he's the leaker and the killer, or is he just overdoing his inner disciplinarian?"

"I suppose I'm still not sure," I admitted. "But it may not make any difference in terms of keeping my job. I thought my manager liked my work, but I suspect she probably doesn't like trouble. If Spencer is eager to get rid of me, she'll probably go along with that, even with Spencer retiring." I smiled at Buck sadly.

He squeezed my shoulder. "Don't give up, Adrianna. As you've said, we may be closer to proving something that will knock everyone's socks off."

"Then you better get the facts on P. Gyraud of Richmond ASAP!" I said. "First we knock their socks off. Then," I half-promised as an incentive, "maybe we'll get naked."

"Okay, Adrianna, I'll 'do or die.' Just remember what you just promised," Buck said, flashing me that big I'm-ready-for-anything-you-want-to-give-me grin.

Then he turned serious. "Can you take some advice from your friendly personnel adviser?" he said. "Do just like Comey, the special investigator Trump fired: Document everything. Write down and date what you've told me Spencer said. And if you have a further run-in with the man, jot it all down as soon as you can. Keep a record in case he does fire you. At the least, that'll assure you collect unemployment insurance—and you might then have a law suit as well."

I gasped.

"But here's to tenure," Buck said, raising his water glass and drinking deep. "And to Mrs. Gyraud."

Off he went to Richmond, via Interstate 95.

BUCK:
On the way to the car, I felt a little queasy.

Too much talk from Burt and Adrianna of food poisoning and firings! I decided. *This ballsy woman lawyer I've gotten to like is suddenly scared — and promising me sex. That last part's good, but she probably wants intimacy. Love. Not sure if I can provide that, or fake that, or even handle that.*

I drove race-car style to Richmond, with the Miata's top down. The air and the sun improved my disposition, and as I approached the city, I got a call from Burt that made my stomach feel much better: "The lost key probably wasn't used for messing with the food," Burt said, "but for thievery. Ten frozen steaks are missing. And we were short some steaks before. I think some employee has been having friends and family over for some really good cook-outs, at our expense. But stealing is so much better than tampering."

So right! "Thanks, Burt. Yep, stealing *is* a helluva lot better than tampering, but let's get the stealing stopped too."

Chapter Twenty-two:
THEES IS SHEE-UH

BUCK:

I also had a text from Adrianna. The good news was she wasn't being fired. The bad news was, "I'm being sent 4 cross-training at Chicago Branch. So, Spencer gets me out of way!!!"

All this has happened during a two-hour drive to Richmond!

And here, requiring my attention in the Richmond branch's parking lot was the branch manager, Ernie Bell, a man known as a happy host. He was living up to his reputation. He grabbed my hand with both of his and said with sincere-sounding vigor, "Great you could visit, Buck. I've set up an office you can use if you want to make calls or talk privately to people. Then, how about drinks and dinner at the Commonwealth Club, my treat? Can't say no to that, can you? We can leave from here about 6 p.m. – or earlier, or later. Your call."

I allowed that I was recovering from a fall and better not stay out too late but that I couldn't turn down such generosity and 6 p.m. would be fine. "I'll just get my messages etc. and see you then."

In my assigned office, I closed the door and looked around for a telephone book. These are not often found any more, and the one here was four years old. But there was a P. Gyraud in the book. I punched in the number.

"Hello," answered the feminine voice, slightly breathy and very Southern, just as I remembered it.

"Ms. Gyraud?"

"Thees is shee-uh."

EVELYN:

Can you put a lid on that accent you're aping, Buck? It's making me si-yick.

BUCK:

I said, "This is Buck Grand from Athena, Ms. Gyraud – you may remember I took a message for Jeffrey Spencer when you called him here in Washington some weeks past."

"Ah do remember, and Ah thank you for getting the message to him. He called right back—though, to tell the truth, he wasn't real pleased I called his office." *Called right back?* I thought. *He claimed he didn't get the message. Why would he lie about that?*

"How is he?" the lady asked. "Such a gentleman and a cutie."

While I had a hard time envisioning Jeffrey Spencer either as a "cutie" or that much of a "gentleman," after a pause I said, "Mr. Spencer is fine. And you? Since I was coming to Richmond on business, I thought I would call you and see if I could show you some pictures of a company dinner where Jeffrey was honored for his service, but I don't want to intrude –"

"Aren't you jus' the sweetest thing," she said. "I'd love it. Why don't we have lunch here at the Jefferson – it's not far from the Athena office. Shall I make a reservation for noon tomorrow? On me, of course. Can you sneak away long enough? Jeff usually can. Just ask for the table reserved for Gyraud."

"I'll be there!"

"Ah look forward to meeting you, Mr. Grand." She made my name sound as if it had two syllables.

But before the next day's lunch, there was the Commonwealth Club dinner that night with Ernie. It was not only delicious but enlivened by a woman friend of his of great charm. She patted my arm and leaned in and laughed the way some women do who are saying, "Yes," before you even ask. I liked her. However, tired and still not completely over my encounter with the staircase, I managed to have just one bourbon and one glass of wine and went to bed early and alone. (Who knows? I might have been wrong about the lady anyway. Guess I'll never know.)

When Ernie proposed lunch the next day, I begged off, saying that a friend was in town and I had already agreed to meet her.

Ernie said, "I understand," and winked.

I found Mrs. Gyraud in a vaulted dining room that looked most palatial and smelled of old bourbon, fine wine, broiled steaks and crab meat. The lady was handsomely turned out and quite composed as she toyed with a martini straight-up at a table for two covered in a crisp white cloth with a vase containing a single yellow and pink rose. Behind the vase and the martini, Mrs. Gyraud sat tall. She was a mighty handsome woman—no surprise as I was beginning to know Spencer's taste. Her eyelashes were long and dark, and she batted them as she took my hand and greeted me. "This is such a pleasure," she said, making me feel quite comfortable.

"They make a fine martini here," she said. "That is, if Athena allows such things during working hours, as I believe Jeff said the company did." Athena's policy was no drinking at lunch, but the edict was largely ignored, so I ignored it now. "I'll have bourbon," I told the waiter, "neat with a twist."

Mrs. Gyraud and I made small talk for a while, as if we were on a first date, but soon we found Jeffrey Spencer a comfortable subject. "I've known him for over a year," Mrs. Gyraud said. "Have you worked with him long?"

"No, but at his request I'm helping him write a personal manual – that's 'personal,' not 'personnel' – a book of heartfelt business wisdom." I found myself speaking excitedly about the work. "It's a great idea. I've learned a lot helping on it. It's helping me plan and organize. I'd say anyone who reads it will learn a lot. For the company, I think it will be worth its weight in gold, to coin a phrase."

"Jeffrey's pretty particular. I know you must be special to have been chosen by him."

I smiled: "I'm emboldened to say the same about you!"

Her eyes fluttered again. "I do-o-o thank you for that fine compliment."

"Have you been to Washington to see Jeff lately?"

"Oh, no, Buck, not lately, not ever. Under the circumstances, as Jeff explained them to me, it would be awkwahd to the nth degree. Ah respect that."

I nodded. *Awkward? I'll say!* "He explained why it would pose a problem?"

"Yes, Buck, he certainly did, but it's a very private matter."

I decided I might blow my cover if I probed further so I changed the subject. "How did you meet?"

She gave a girlish laugh. "We bumped into each other at the Virginia Museum – lookin' at the eggs."

"Eggs?"

"Those famously beautiful Faberge-made eggs from Russia. They were made for the Romanovs before the Revolution, you know. The museum has a most marvelous collection. You must see it if you haven't."

"I'll make a point of it," I said. *Eggs!* I thought. *Never!*

Mrs. Gyraud said, "The museum is notable for the way it displays its items, often with music of the period playing in the background. That first occasion Jeff and I got to talking about the Faberge artistry and just hit it off. He suggested dinner, and we came here, and sat right hereabouts, as I recall. Jeff was in town for a conference and had arrived early. Wasn't that lucky for Mrs. Phyllis Gyraud?! I think it was the first time since I was widowed that life seemed really worth living again."

"Having a soul-mate," I said. "That is important."

"It makes one feel more complete," the lady said. "I've been a much happier person. I'm so glad I didn't upset the applecart, so to speak, when I called Jeff at his office."

"And got me."

"That was lucky. He called back without anyone else being the wiser, I guess. He was just a wee bit angry, as I mentioned, but he's such a courtly and easy-going soul."

"I almost blurted, 'Called you back?" but I did say, "Easy going?" I almost choked on my delicious trout.

"Why, yes, he has to have an easy-going manner to put up with his horrible personal life, don't you know?"

A widow in every port? That's a horrible personal life? Aloud, I said, "I guess there is a lot about Jeff I still don't know."

"Well, it's just tragic that he's stuck with that odious woman."

"Odious?" I said. *That hardly describes Mary Ann,* I thought, *but—*

"Well yes, that's what I'd call his wife – not in love with him but refusing him a divorce after all these strained years. Just bleeding him dry. Ah thought everyone would know about that!"

Wife! I thought, and my expression may have changed.

Then the lady gasped. "Oh, no! That's probably what he'd like kept secret! Oh, Ah'm so sorry. Please don't let on to Jeffrey that I let his cat out of the bag, so to speak. No wonder he was upset when I called him at work. I knew he wouldn't want *her* to find out, but I didn't realize it was such a secret from everyone."

Pretty odd of Spencer to claim he was married, I thought. "'Everyone is a moon and has a dark side he doesn't show to anybody,'" I quoted once again, now able to add, with a flourish, "Mark Twain."

"Oh, I wouldn't say Jeffrey has a dark side, just that he has that sad situation."

I was puzzled. I didn't see the point of Spencer's lies. However, I was sure that Adrianna would be excited that I had confirmed that Spencer had this additional love interest that Evelyn might have threatened to expose.

Over desert and coffee, Mrs. Gyraud admitted, "I don't always understand Jeffrey, but we do have a wonderful time. Not that I don't have other friends. And there's my job. John left me so awfully well off, many of my friends wonder why I still do the old 9 to 5, but I do enjoy working.   It's kind of a validation for living!"

I really didn't hear her description of her job. I was abuzz with Mark Twain and Jeffrey Spencer. *A side nobody knows? That was putting it mildly, Mr. Twain!*

Despite Mrs. Gyraud's protests, I paid the bill. Then I focused again on Mrs. Gyraud, who was saying, "Of course I look forward to his occasionally calling me, whether he gets down to Richmond or not. I'll certainly tell him when we talk how much I enjoyed having this nice lunch with you!"

Oh, God! That's all I need! I hadn't thought how easy it would be for Spencer to discover my spying. "Oh, Mrs. Gyraud, I do hope we have occasion to see each other again soon. But I wouldn't want Mr. Spencer to think I drew you out on that point we won't talk more about, so I'd say it might be best if neither of us mentions this meeting."

"Oh, I hate not to be open with him, but I guess I see." she said.   "I even think I agree." I breathed a sigh of relief.

I said, "Oh, I almost forgot, here are some of the pictures, as promised, of the dinner party Athena gave Mr. Spencer.

"The short, white-haired older man and the two tiny women in some of them are Athena's founders. Others include Mr. Spencer's assistants and other employees.

Mrs. Gyraud picked out several. "May I keep these?"

"Any that you like," I said.

And I left well-fed and entertained but puzzled. What had I learned that would help me solve Evelyn's murder?

EVELYN:

Damn little. What difference does it make that Spencer may like women, plural. If every man who played around also killed somebody, we wouldn't be worrying about a population explosion, now would we?!

BUCK:

When I got back to the Richmond office, Ernie Bell asked about my lunch and handed me the *Athena Herald* "hot off the presses." Putting it aside to read later, I brought up the "rumor" that headquarters had heard about a possible effort to have a vote for a union.

"That's really what I was sent down here to find out about," I admitted.

"I figured," Ernie said. "Truthfully, I think unionism is mostly big talk by a very, very few. My people are paid well and treated well, and are pretty happy and content, and this is Richmond, capital of the Commonwealth of Virginia, home of Robert E. Lee and Stonewall Jackson, who were not for the Union," he joked. "Pretty conservative place."

In case Ernie was painting too rosy a picture, I talked to a couple of fellow ex-Marines I knew in the Richmond office who I could trust for straight answers. Both knew there was some agitation among the low-paid clerks. One of the ex-Marines was quite opposed, but the other was somewhat sympathetic. He said a union might be just what Athena's employees, and the company itself, needed: "Stir things up a bit. Bring in some new ideas." Both men gave me the names of several people they thought might know more or be pro-union. I spent the next two hours talking with these people over a coffee or two. I doubted they had much of a following.

Ernie Bell came by at closing time with a plan – a visit to a road-house that wasn't far from my motel. "We'll have some drinks with a couple of friendly ladies, enjoy a good dinner, listen to the music, and then get you to bed early." He winked again.

Ernie, as usual, knew his man; I was sorely tempted. But I had to say I wasn't quite up to it "just yet, on this visit." I had a pizza brought to my motel room, ate it while I watched the PBS news, and was in my own bed asleep and alone by 9.

Early the next morning, I walked on the treadmill in the motel's modestly equipped exercise room, swam quietly in the small pool, and went to the lobby for the motel's free breakfast of cereal, coffee and a watery orange juice. The motel didn't supply the local *Times-Dispatch,* so I opened the copy of the *Athena Herald* that Ernie had given me.

There was the beautiful double-page color spread on the Woodrow's fish tanks, shells, pool and greenhouse, under the headline, "A Tropical Paradise"—which I had to admit was a better headline than my "A Gentlemen and His Passions." The photos were some of George's best— clear, bright, and colorful. The shot of Maury seeming to talk with his big fish Jaws was stunning.

But I suddenly burst out laughing, spluttered and nearly spilled my coffee! The caption under Jaws and Maury read, "Ms. Randall, 91, says she got her auto policy shortly after Athena was founded because it looked like 'a good value.'" That's what I assumed Danyel had written – but not for that picture! I quickly turned to the article on "Our Oldest Policy-Holder, young at heart."

There was a picture of the old lady with her insurance policy and, underneath it, as I expected, I read what I had written for the Woodrow photo: "Dubbed Jaws by Mr. Woodrow, this orange and white mottled Calico Fantail is a valuable type of goldfish."

I could just imagine what old Ms. Randall said when she found that she had been captioned as a mottled fish, valuable or not! But having a newspaperman as a father, I knew how easy it is to reverse captions of similar length when making last-minute changes. Both captions probably had a typo.   In removing the similarly sized captions to correct their two typos, Danyel or her assistant had simply reversed the two.

Such reversals weren't the end of the world, especially since a reader could easily tell the caption was a mistake. *But if both pictures had been of people,* I thought, *and their identities been reversed, people would accept that Joe was John and John was Joe. Those were the most confusing and embarrassing mix-ups.*

Suddenly I sat up straight. Spencer and a bunch of other people had been in the pictures I showed Mrs. Gyraud, but was the person I knew as Spencer the same person Mrs. Gyraud was looking at and knew as Spencer? If not, that might explain the "odious wife" and "easy-going" manner of *her* Spencer.

I reached for the phone. "Hello, Mrs. Gyraud, this is Buck Grand again," I said. "And we've got to stop meeting like this, I guess, but I have a few more really good photos of the party honoring Mr. Spencer. Can I just take ten minutes more of your time to show them to you and let you take your pick?"

"Of course, you may—my pleasure!" was the gracious response. I showed up about an hour later and, over coffee, handed Mrs. Gyraud a few photos I thought she would like, but she reached over and took the whole pile and began leafing through them. "What a party! You'll have to tell me who all these other people are.

"But here's Jeff with you, Buck – a good photograph of you both. May I keep it?"

Though I nodded, I was curious what photo that might be.

"And here he is with an attractive woman. Should I be jealous? Who is this slender woman beaming at Jeff?"

And with that, Phyllis Gyraud handed me a photo that was not of Jeffrey Spencer at all. Nor was the photo of Lou, the womanizer I might have guessed, or Ernie Bell.

It was Maury Woodrow and his wife, Stella.

I then looked at the picture she had said was me with "Spencer" and saw it was really of me and Maury. Gentleman Maury Woodrow!

I hardly could keep from blurting out the truth! However, for once, my PTSD-ed brain worked quickly and smoothly and I said, quite truthfully, "That's just the wife of Maurice Woodrow, one of Jeff's assistants."   Fearing I might easily become entangled in lies, or—worse still— give the game away before I'd thought it out sufficiently, I hurriedly finished my coffee and made my escape.

"My guess is that the reason Maury Woodrow posed as you," I would soon be telling an incredulous Jeffrey Spencer, "and the reason he dreamed up this unhinged wife who won't divorce him/you was to minimize the risk of anything getting back to Stella. Also, the story helped isolate him and reduced the chance of Phyllis Gyraud coming here and meeting Stella or otherwise screwing up his plans, whatever those were."

But before I would see Spencer with this strange information, I had something else to do that had suddenly increased in importance. I immediately finalized my appointment for that late snack with Lou Jr., and it wasn't just because I craved the crab cake sandwich at The Charles!

I said my goodbyes to Ernie, assuring him that I would report to headquarters that the union effort was weak and not likely to take over. Then, after driving a few miles on 95, I took Route 301 north to La Plata. It was a little out of the way, but I was pretty sure it would be worth it. Junior was right on time, neatly outfitted for a student, and, for good measure, sober.

I wasted no time telling him what I wanted: "You said Maury Woodrow probably attended that Perfect Murder class. I want to know for sure. I need proof. For $15 an hour, can you find out if any other students saw him at that particular class? Can you get me sworn statements? Can you do this without arousing suspicion or any of this getting back to Maury — or to your parents, who might spill the beans?

"Can you do that?"

Junior smiled and said, "For fifteen an hour this will be more money and more fun than working at McD's, and it's important, isn't it? It has something to do with that woman's murder?"

"Maybe, but don't press me. It gets out, I don't pay. I'll ask again: Can you persuade your fellow students to keep mum about it? Can you keep it all from even your folks?"

Lou Jr. said he thought his fellow students would be quiet about it — "there being no media around this berg to get wind of it, anyway."

As to his folks, he pulled out his phone and thrust it in my face. It showed a sunny selfie of himself and his girl in the Wicomico. They were naked, both of them, at least down to their belly buttons, which is where the river water rose to. "They don't know about us and how we grow pot in the woods and do other enjoyable things together, so yes, you can be sure I can keep this quiet."

"You may be a girl-crazy pothead," I said quietly, "but I believe you'll do a good job."

Junior said, "You got me pegged, all right. As I said, I don't smoke the stuff until night after all my schoolwork is done. And my girl and me," he said, smiling, "are not at it every minute of every day. I just wish. If Mr. Woodrow was in the class, and I'm pretty sure he was, I'll get you the proof you want."

We shook hands. I went to the restaurant's ATM and withdrew $200, which was nearly all that I had in my account at the moment. I gave him $120 of it as a down payment.

Back in Washington, I told George what I had found out and done. I also contacted Adrianna by phone. She slowly came around to the idea that Maury, not Jeff Spencer, was our most likely defrauder and killer but she was leery of our telling Spencer what we knew. "If you tip Spencer off and he does turn out to be the perpetrator, he'll be able to quickly cover his tracks and get away with it," she argued.

She also seemed a bit pissed that I had so readily brought my ex-Marine friend George into full partnership with us, though I was sure we would need his particular combination of skills down the road. And I knew I could count on him.

ADRIANNA:

As to bringing Spencer in on it, Buck argued—using the Spencer book(!) unfairly, I thought—that we needed a major ally: "Without Spencer, we can't move a whole lot further. We need the man's power and status. Without that, who will listen to us? We can't even get you back from Chicago without him." I had no argument against that.

So, an hour or so later, Buck and George found Spencer working late in his office and laid it all out.

BUCK:

I started with the suspected leaks that were hurting Athena's bottom line. Spencer was familiar with the big losses and I briefly explained how Adrianna's telephone review had found that these losses all followed calls to the plaintiffs' lawyers from Athena's Claims offices. I said Evelyn might have discovered this same evidence of fraud and may have tried to put the squeeze on "someone." I looked hard at Spencer, remembering Adrianna's old suspicions, but he did not react.

"This someone," I said, "must have seen her as a threat and murdered her to protect himself." I looked at Spencer again. He didn't seem intimidated. He looked incredulous.

EVELYN:

Ya think? I couldn't believe all this either.
Remember, people, I drafted but never sent those two
letters you found. But, maybe, fumbling and stumbling
around, you may be getting closer to the truth.

BUCK:

When I told Spencer what I had found out from Ms.
Gyraud, he was again incredulous, saying, "Why would
Maury do something that crazy? Why would he?"

"We," I said, including Adrianna, "think that
Stella's small fortune long supported Maury's many
hobbies and interests – and may even have provided him
with the painted likenesses of his ancestors. But he must
have managed to squander it, so that what's left can no
longer support Maury's ever-expanding need to acquire
things.   So, he turned to fraud to get kick-backs and was
stringing along the rich widow Gyraud so as to marry her if
he got rid of Stella, and—"

"Ah, Avarice," Spencer muttered, "as I remember
from my boy choir days, one of the Seven Deadly sins."
That sounded like the stiff-necked Spencer of old, but that
was okay. We were drawing him in.

"And potentially," I said, "Mrs. Gyraud might
provide Maury with the heir that he very probably wants,
that replacement for his lost son Tommy. She's probably
young enough, if he doesn't wait too long.

"Meanwhile, he may have thought that Evelyn somehow threatened exposure or possibly would blackmail him for a share in the rewards, so he found a clever, 'natural' way to kill her. Unfortunately, both the murder and how he did it may be hard to prove. That may be our toughest job in all this."

EVELYN:

You're giving me credit for a lot more guts and brains than I ever had, but I'll take it! I'll take it! — if, right or wrong, it'll lead you to my killer.

BUCK:

"The fraud won't be so easy to prove either," Spencer said to me, "but you know what you say in your book, 'Think and Plan Big.'"

George then laid out enlargements of sections of his party photos. By speakerphone, Adrianna presented her records of phone calls from Claims to the various lawyers who ended up with information that helped them as well as their clients, win big.

I told them all what Lou Jr. was looking for and about some Athena travel records I'd stumbled upon; Maury had visited Athena's smallest field office in Alaska, where there are plenty of tainted butter clams to be harvested, as Spencer probably already also knew from the tome I'd seen in his apartment. I told them my boss Mary Ann had told me about an "odd request" from Maury to take his time and drive rather than fly back from Alaska, probably, I speculated, in a van or SUV carrying the live killer clams in a big glass tank.

"We're hoping," I said, "that you'll be willing to join us in a high-stakes effort to prove all this.   If we succeed, it will clear away any future suspicion that you fled Athena in fear of discovery of the frauds. It will enhance your standing within the business community generally, and it will win you the ever-lasting thanks of your successor. And it may prevent the murder of Stella Woodrow and the ruination of Phyllis Gyraud.

"You realize we can't do it without you," I continued, "as it will take your status and persuasiveness to help us manage and coordinate our effort, find us an arena for our revelations, and do it all in total secrecy. Without you we haven't a snowball's chance in August to see justice done."

ADRIANNA:

I was still in Chicago, but via the speakerphone connection I heard Spencer say, "If you think I don't know you're buttering me up, Buck, you're mistaken. But since someone has posed as me and has come close to destroying all I have built up at Athena, I'm in. And my first step better be to get Adrianna back from Chicago." Whew!

BUCK:

"However," he said to me, "you, Buck Grand, have been ghost-writing my personal business guide—my ideas but your words—so, except where my alleged prestige is needed, *you* must take the lead, *you* must continue to follow my principles, and *you* must succeed at this tricky enterprise, if you can. You know the ideas now as well as I do – and I think you've already started following them:

"Take for example, chapter one, 'PREPARE LIKE A BOY SCOUT who is in the CIA.' You've already amassed a lot of damning and persuasive information. Adrianna has well over a half-dozen very solid examples of the fraud, right? while you, Buck and George, have been going over the party photos with magnifying glasses. A student had been gathering important testimony. I'm confident if there is more to find out, you'll discover it.

"'Plan Big, Set Your Goals High,' I said, and you call that 'GO FOR BIGGER AND BETTER. Why fail small?' You just said you want my help in finding 'an arena.'

"And where I said, 'Persuade your friends and co-workers to join your team and take up your goals, while adding their ideas to yours– and making use of *their* special skills, you wrote, 'GET BUY IN— BUT LISTEN, TOO.'

"Somewhere we say 'Keep Your Opponents in the Dark as Long as Possible. As much as in war or politics, utilize the element of surprise.' And you've echoed that call for secrecy with Lou Jr. and will, I'm sure, with others.

"Especially remember, as you're still not quite up to speed physically: 'Don't Try to Do Everything Yourself but Make Sure *Somebody* Is Doing Everything that you need.' Delegate but remind and check. (That's your main job now, Buck.

"Be Generous in Sharing Credit. People given credit for their help on Plan A will be more willing allies if there has to be a Plan B. (Marines instinctively know that, don't they?)"

We concluded our meeting on a high.

EVELYN:

Not me! I was on no high! So old Maury played fast and loose with this Richmond dame, according to her(!) at least. Did that make him a murderer? Hard to believe Adrianna's idea that Spencer killed me, but wasn't that more likely than that fussy, fastidious Maury would have poisoned himself just to kill me! And isn't it women who poison people? Maybe it was Adrianna herself. Well, I don't know, but I wanted to shout at this team of defective detectives, *"You're going to try to solve my murder with a book? I can't believe that's all it will take."*

BUCK:

Nevertheless, we increasingly lived The Book. I did in particular, but all of us did, really. We were increasingly hopeful that The Book's straight-forward methods would help us manage our complex entrapment plan and nail and publicly expose the killer!

l carried the manuscript of the Spencer book on my laptop, everywhere. I reviewed what I had written as I flew to CDC in Atlanta to enlist still another power player in our effort. It wasn't soft and cuddly, but I would obsess over Spencer's Great Work, doing the final editing over and over until I nodded off and slept with it. Cold comfort, but it was good to have a plan devised on an outline of an organizational genius, Vice President Spencer.

EVELYN:

As much as I had liked and even loved Spencer at one time and as much as I was beginning to appreciate Buck in some ways, I wrote off their use of Spencer's personal management guidebook to solve my murder as ridiculous. I saw no value.

I know how you get things done: You intimidate people. Yes, you make people *fear* you. I figure Buck had gotten wrapped up in that book just like the fool had gotten conned by Mary Ann into having that dinner where I was poisoned.

However, when Buck suddenly flew off to Atlanta and got the Centers for Disease Control back into the picture, I began to have a little hope.

And when the big cheeses at CDC agreed to pay the travel expenses for their Dr. James Aitchison to fly with Buck to Alaska, I got excited and less critical! I even decided it to take up some of the narration and let you know what I was seeing happen.

EVELYN coming forward and now narrating:

CDC's Doc Aitchison was hardly my kind of guy, really.

I have little use for Government people. Know-it-alls. So-called experts.

But he was the CDC scientist who took samples for testing when the hospital doctors pumped my stomach. He took the vomit samples to CDC in Atlanta for testing. He must not have smelled too good on the plane, I'm thinking. Glad I wasn't sitting nearby.

After taking all this trouble, I guess he must have had a stake in the CDC view that my death was a natural result of a red-tide-type poison getting into the shellfish bought and used in the damn bouillabaisse.

Now, unbeknownst to me and the others, Buck had remained in contact with this Aitchison. In particular, he kept him in the picture as the nature of the case shifted in Buck's mind from "natural accident" to "deliberate murder."

The doc was very skeptical, but Buck told him about the "perfect murder" lecture and asked Junior to send Aitchison his notes on what his prof had said. That's when Buck learned Junior took no notes. He *recorded* the lecture, which was his practice. (This new generation, huh? Do they even know what a pencil looks like?)

So, Aitchison was sent the tape of the actual presentation, get me? Aitchison listened to it several times, three or four, I think. Then he called and discussed it with the prof himself, one Prentice Gorse, Ph.D. Gorse stuck to his guns that clams and such from a tainted tide could be harvested, kept alive an indefinite time and used for a perfect murder. He did express regret that anybody might have tried to follow his recipe. (Well, damn! A little regret. That and five dollars might buy me a beer!)

Finally, finally, finally, Aitchison concluded that Dr. Gorse's speculation was what he called "scientifically credible."   That's doc talk meaning, "He might be right."

Furthermore, he finally got it through his bureaucratic head that – what with Buck's reports about the marine skills of the Howards, Maury's possible attendance at the Perfect Murder lecture and Spencer's sailing and reading about clams that could carry paralytic poison for months, any one of them could be the perpetrator of the First Case, or "first *known* case," as he put it, "of PSP murder."

Ta-dah, I thought. Maybe we are getting somewhere.

Bit by bit Aitchison filled in his superiors.   From my all-seeing perch I heard him argue that "CDC should be in on the discovery," if there is a murderer to be caught. "Instead of others laughing at CDC for making a wrong call, and CDC being on the defensive," he said, "we can be a part of the solution to this mystery, this historic first, you might say." Hurrah!

CDC's public information office strongly supported Aitchison's idea. "Otherwise, we'll be known as the agency that missed the boat, so to speak, and our past scientific view might even be used by a good defense lawyer to prevent the conviction of the murderer."

Good for PR! I say.

You don't hear that very often!

Well, that's how the preeminent federal public health agency's director, Dr. Tom Frieden, came to sign off on Aitchison's trip. That was one of his last acts, just before Frieden's nearly eight years as director ended when my man Trump figured that if Obama appointed the guy, Trump didn't want him.

(Caught buying stock in a cigarette company, Frieden's replacement was in and out of CDC so fast that she didn't know about, much less could block, Aitchison's trip.)

Spencer and Mary Ann Howell meanwhile got Athena to pay Buck's expenses for a so-called Human Resources visit to the far-flung two-person-and-a-half Athena office in Alaska, and Spencer personally footed the bill for Lou Jr. out of the money he was getting from me, maybe.

Junior's job was to re-create my murder. Yeah, I know: The kid might smoke pot and have other distracting habits, but he had built a tank in which Chesapeake Bay's crabs thrived, and he had recorded them on tape for presentations at his school, so Buck thought he was much the most able person to do the same for Alaska's butter clams.

And he might be—unless he and his dad are the ones who poisoned me! I noted, didn't you? that Junior *taped* the "perfect murder" lecture. That means that while Big Lou didn't attend the lecture, dollars to doughnuts he could have listened to the lecture tape many times!

BUCK:

Junior was to go to Alaska two days before Doc Aitchison and me. He would work with an Alaskan expert or two to assemble the material for a duplicate tank—an environment of sand and rock and a couple of fish. For our planned duplication of what the killer did, Junior's tank was to keep the clams we would collect in Alaska alive and well on the long trip by van or SUV back to Washington.

Junior had a secondary job, too. Impressed by how Junior had used a video camera to document some of his experiments with Chesapeake Bay critters for his classes, George and I decided that if Junior made a video of the trip to Alaska it would be more persuasive than us just telling what we found and did. George was too busy preparing the gadgetry for the grand finale to make the video himself, but he would work with Buck and Junior on its editing.

EVELYN:

I got to admit, by this time I was getting pretty impressed by how much of my Spencer had rubbed off on our Buckeroo. Even from somewhere between the here-and-now and the here-after, I could see my Spencer's influence in Buck's ability to get and keep all the players involved and doing the necessary work. Maybe writing up Spencer's ideas for The Book did help Buck a bit.

ADRIANNA:

Indeed, talking to me, Buck credited Spencer's book for keeping him focused. (All the days and nights George and I had kept Buck off the booze hadn't hurt him either!) Spencer, for his part, seemed to increasingly admire his protege. But he wasn't blind to Buck's remaining problems.

Considering those, he loaded Junior with still another job, i.e., supporting the still-ailing Buck. I heard from Mr. Spencer that he made it clear to Junior that he should watch out for Buck physically, keep him off the booze "and no pot or womanizing for either one of you."

A tall order.

I think it was important to Spencer personally that Junior succeed in revealing who had done so much harm to Athena (and Evelyn). But beyond that I think Spencer wanted Buck to succeed for Buck's sake as well.

I too felt that Buck needed this. Needed to succeed. George, Junior and all of us on the assembled team wanted Buck to have every chance to do so. But in the back of all our minds there was a fear that if Buck got stretched too far, his PTSD might rise up and overwhelm him. And we could also tell that sometimes he was still in pain from the battering he took in that awful fall.

I didn't hear their conversation, but I can imagine Junior responded to Spencer's directions with something cocky, like, "So you're saying that I shouldn't regard this as an (f-bombing) vacation?" but he probably quickly added, "Seriously, Mr. Spencer, I want Buck to win as much as you do. And I haven't let him down yet."

That was true. Junior was totally part of that team that the Spencer book had urged be created and the job ahead required. Junior had found several fellow students who remembered Maury auditing marine classes including the "perfect murder" session. And he had followed through with them, getting signed statements and taping their testimony.

BUCK:

I thought Dr. Aitchison, with the prestige of CDC behind him, would be the best person to call ahead to the Alaska Fish and Game office so as to pave the way for Junior's arrival. And to ask for any help they could give Junior in his locating the tank we would need and a van or SUV to rent. With me listening in, Dr. Aitchison made the call and described what we hoped to do. After our call was transferred a couple of times, we were talking to a couple of their clamming experts. Aitchison asked what they thought of our chances of success.

"Might pull it off," a female voice said.

'Yup, I guess you might," said a male.

Or might not, I guess they also meant.

But they said they would help.

EVELYN:
Of course, you know by now that I didn't have to buy a ticket to Alaska. We specters have our own ways of getting around, and I'm quickly learning what powers I've got. The moment I thought I should like to be in Atlanta, where CDC is, or in Alaska, I just appeared there, observing Lou Jr.'s arrival at Anchorage's Ted Stevens International Airport!

A woman from the Fish and Game office in Seward and a man from the Anchorage Fish and Game headquarters met Junior's plane. (These were the folks Aitchison had talked to on the phone.)

The Alaskans introduced themselves as Aurora Asangin and Yupik Smith. Both had high, round cheekbones in chubby faces, with brown eyes and thick black hair that showed their Eskimo blood. No mistaking them for Hugh Grant and Meryl Streep, I'll say, but right rugged in Yupik's case and almost cute in Aurora's. Both wore heavy boots and sturdy clothing. I could see they knew their clams from a hole in the ground.

Aurora used her maiden name, Asangin, at work but was a Mrs. Bradley, married to a regular white American, it soon turned out. She looked at Junior in an appraising way. Even I saw it, and I think Junior's antenna was quick to pick it up too.

The three went to two stores and quickly found several glass tanks that could accommodate the live butter clams they planned to collect, plus a couple small saltwater fish, some snails, rocks, sand and so on that Aurora wanted to contribute.

She also had a list of car rental places with SUVs and vans to go to the next day. *This is going to be a cinch,* I thought. Meanwhile:

At the end of the workday, Yupik went home to his wife, while Aurora and Junior had dinner and drinks together, and she whispered in Junior's ear: "My husband Jim and I want a baby.   He hasn't been tested but after two years of marriage with very regular sex but no baby, I figure he must have had mumps or measles or something as a kid and it made him infertile.

"I'm ovulating right now, as a matter of fact, and I wonder if you could do us a favor. Help us out."

I've seen and heard and done a lot in my lifetime, but my jaw dropped. But Junior knew right off what "help us out" meant.

"Sure," he said, and immediately rose from the table. "Let's go."

Aurora laughed and said, "We had better pay the check first."

Once in Junior's room, Aurora was all business as she undressed matter-of-factly. Junior licked his lips as he watched her and quickly stripped. Both naked, they stood on opposite sides of one of the two beds, pulled down the bedspread and the upper sheet and climbed in, meeting in the middle. From there they slid into a horizontal position, each murmuring a perfunctory compliment about the physical appearance of the other.

I watched, of course. Aurora may have thought there would be no more passion involved than when one airborne plane refuels another, but these were two healthy young people, so they couldn't help but quickly get into it. Aurora seemed embarrassed by how much they enjoyed themselves. The must have felt like they gave $2 to a charity lottery and then won the Cadillac! Afterward, they lay naked, side by side, gently cuddling like newlyweds.

They made me realize how bad it is to be dead: No sex. No romance. I might as well be English.

In the morning, they repeated their altruistic deed rather eagerly, I thought, before hurrying off to meet a grinning, knowing Yupik for breakfast. Yupik raised an eyebrow, got a nod from Aurora in reply, and saluted the couple with a thumbs up. This was no surprise to Junior. On the way to the restaurant, Aurora had mentioned that Yupik himself would have been glad to help but the baby had to look a little something like her husband, a vanilla-flavored "Euro-Amurrican," and round-cheeked Yupik didn't fit that bill.

After breakfast, the three of them measured several of the SUVs available at Anchorage car rental agencies, and found matches for the glass tanks they'd found available for sale. When Buck and Doc Aitchinson arrived, Yupik, Aurora and Junior met them and quickly reported that all had gone well. All thought they had spent their time profitably.

BUCK:
First thing, I went by the Athena field office for 45 minutes and learned I had a message from Mary Ann. *Typical*, I thought, *she can't give me a minute's peace. What could be so important?* I didn't rush to call her back.

When I got to the nearby Fish and Game office, I found the others settled into a conference room with coffee and big sugary buns called bear claws — "this is Alaska after all," Aurora said.   I took one of the pastries and a black coffee and joined them.

"We're glad you wanted to do this collecting while the weather's still warm," Aurora was saying, "as soon our winter will begin, and Yupik and I will both be hunkered down doing reports and other paper work and planning for next spring and summer. This'll give us something to think about — ponder with pleasure, I might say."

Yupik said, "Yep. This should be an interesting end to our season, and I hope you'll let us know how things move along once you leave here. Maybe," he said to Aitchison, "you'll even write something up for CDC's MMWR—*The Morbidity and Mortality Weekly Report*, right? "

Aitchison said, "Very likely, if things go as planned."

Yupik said, "But right now I'm looking forward to what we can help you do in the next few days. Usually, we are steering clam diggers toward the safe shellfish at tested beaches, but we will try to remember that for your experiment, we must find the tainted ones. It isn't going to be hard. We got several beach and waterside areas that are currently far off limits. You won't be wanting to cook and eat the babies we find there, or even drink the clam juice, tasty as it might be.

"And don't forget, even after you drive back with your poison clams, we can help you look up and check facts, if you want."

My mouth was full of a delicious hunk of a sticky, sugared bun so I just nodded. But Dr. Aitchison expressed our abundant gratitude.

"I see you have good, waterproof boots," Yupik said. "We'll loan you the wide-toothed rakes we usually use. The wide-spaced tines leave the little butter clams behind to grow big. The rakes just snare the large ones. We also have plastic buckets to put the ones you want in. We'll take you to the toxic sites and help you rake up a good pile of bad clams to put in a good tank that, with luck, will keep the clams alive. We've got rocks and sand and debris that these clams like to bury themselves in, and we can add a couple of fish—a pretty pair of dwarf angelfish— coral ones, maybe.   That's about it at this end.

"I'm not sure how the clams, or the fish, will take to the movement of the water as you drive along. But if the killer drove his home and the clams lived and worked, you should end up with a load of living killer clams too."

Aurora interjected, "If you have time, we should also dig in a tested and approved area for some tasty and safe clams. We can then have a fine clam bake, so you will not always think of Alaska seafood as deadly."

Aurora had some butter clam shells to show us. "The clams start out tiny, too tiny to harvest for food. As the years pass, they grow up to be these big fellas, four or five inches across sometimes, with a shell that looks something like a flattened version of the classic Shell Oil company symbol.   They tend to bury themselves in the dirt and gravel and other debris, including broken or discarded shells alongside waterways. They filter out their food from the water—and these nutrients are microscopic dinoflagellates for the most part. What makes butter clams especially dangerous is that if some of the dinoflagellates they take in are poison, butter clams don't cleanse themselves of them very quickly. They can hold the poison for months, whereas mussels and some other clams flush the poison out much quicker." She handed two of the big shells around to Junior, Dr. Aitchison and me. Examining these shells, I grew excited. *We are closing in on this mystery,* I felt.

"The clams," Aurora said, "live by filtering nutrients out of the waters around them. They keep their shell partly open to do so

I asked: "These nutrients they get out of the water, these are the same 'dinoflagellates' that can become toxic?"

"I'm afraid PSP has given dinoflagellates a bad name," Aurora said. "Dinoflagellates are life-giving food—the bottom of the food chain—that sustains many animals. They are one-celled creatures with tiny hairs much like the amoeba and paramecia you may have seen through a microscope in high school biology. 'Dino' comes from the Greek for 'swirling' and 'flagella' is the Greek for 'hairs.' They move, to a degree, by the swish of these hairs but mostly, like the much larger jellyfish you're familiar with, they mostly float with the tides and motions of the water they're in. They are among the smallest and simplest of the critters often called Plankton that sustain shellfish and some fish and even whales. And, indirectly, us, too, as we eat the fish and the shellfish. So dinoflagellates are important to life. But like men and like at least one fallen angel, Satin, we are told, dinoflagellates sometimes go 'bad,' you might say.

"These 'bad' dinos don't hurt the shellfish but, unfortunately, affect birds and mammals—that's us—who eat the shellfish. PSP is a neurotoxin, meaning it damages the nerves, at least temporarily. When the nerve damage is at its worst, it stops the muscles that open and shut our lungs. And we can't breathe."

EVELYN:
Damn straight! It was awful!

BUCK:

I knew that butter clams remain dangerous a long time, and Aurora confirmed, "Butter clams can hold the deadly PSP poison for up to two years.

"And they've been killing people for over two *hundred* years. That is, since in 1793, when a man named John Carter was on an expedition headed by Captain George Vancouver, for whom the Canadian city and the bay are named. Carter is generally listed as the first human known to die of PSP, probably from mussels. I should say, 'first white man' or 'first foreigner.' Probably a lot of Aleuts—Native Americans— died in the past without a captain's log to record it.

"Unfortunately, there were no mass media or social media to spread the news of Carter's death, so we were doomed to have more. About six years later Aleuts working for the Russian-American Company stopped to harvest mussels. Within two minutes, according to Aleksandre Baranov of that company who wrote about it in his log, about half the group feasting on the mussels were sick. Maybe two minutes is a slight exaggeration. What's certainly not an exaggeration is that within two hours, nearly a hundred, yes, nearly a hundred otherwise hearty and healthy persons died! This happened near Sitka in an area now called Peril Strait, for obvious reasons."

Aurora clutched her throat. "Death from PSP must be terrible—like drowning."

EVELYN:
Absolutely.

BUCK again:
I remember Aurora saying that even in Alaska, where they can't test every beach because the state has more shoreline than all the other states combined(!) PSP fatalities have greatly declined. "Commercial shellfish growers and harvesters continually test their product," she said, "so it is safe. And also, with modern transport we can get people with breathing difficulties to a hospital quickly.

"It's the amateur clam diggers," she said, "who get in trouble when they harvest from untested, unmarked water, falsely believing that clamming in these areas is safe if done in the 'R' months—JanuaRy, FebruaRy, etc. The algae that explode into visible blooms that taint the shellfish do occur less often in the cool 'R' months, but they still can and do occur other times. And there's no test a recreational clam digger can use to detect the toxins. Even the fact that other people haven't gotten sick from eating clams they dug from just down the beach is no guarantee."

Aurora said, "Okay, now, let's look at how you dig for clams. "She snapped on a TV monitor. A U-Tube segment showed a man raking through grubby layers of old shells beside a waterway until he came to intact shells and picked them up—the man saying, "These are live clams—and, if you don't break their shell, they should stay alive awhile." He rinsed a clam off in the nearby saltwater and tossed it in a plastic bucket.

"As for your plan to keep them alive for weeks or more," Aurora said, "let's see if the tank we located for your purchase can fit in a rental Jeep or four-wheel-drive Toyota you can use to carry it home in. Then you can fill the tank with salt water, sand, gravel, and the toxic clams.

"You guys ready to go kick some tires?"

EVELYN continues the story from her vantage point:
Off they went, me hovering and watching eagerly! Junior, having videoed all the less-than-fascinating (I thought) details about dino-whachacallems, now recorded the group's look at the tank they thought to buy and the rental of their selected vehicle—maybe a Jeep that Aurora had seen.

Routine, right? Boring. I thought it would be. Until:

An extremely out-going salesman showing them the prospective tank (which looked like any old tank: glass with four sides, ya know) stopped half-way through his spiel, and volunteered: "Funny thing, this is the second time in recent months that someone wanted to be sure a tank would fit into a van or SUV to be driven to the contiguous states—the 48."

I'll bet Buck nearly pissed in his pants when he heard that!   I was proud of him though; he was ready for just such a chance development! He showed the salesman pictures of Maury Woodrow, Spencer, Lou and others and asked him to pick out his customer.

The salesman studied the pictures at length and then said, "Sorry, I can't be sure. I see an awful lot of people, a lot of customers." He said, "No offense but all you white folks from the 48 states look alike to me. Just kidding!"

Buck pressed the salesman to look at the pictures again and "search your memory."   He briefly explained to the salesman that the man's identity might be important to a murder case.

"I'll be darned," said the salesman. "Murder case. But then it's also very important that I be sure." He thought for a long minute and said, "Now that I think back on it carefully, I don't think the man I'm thinking of could be your killer because he never completed his purchase. I should have remembered that right off because after spending a lot of time with the man, his cancelling was an inconvenience and, of course, a loss in sales.

"I remember he came back, embarrassed, to tell me he couldn't use the tank after all because no one would rent him a van to carry it in. I was annoyed but it was at least pretty nice of him to come back and tell me. I thought it quite gentlemanly."

Gentlemanly. That fit Maury to a T but any of the others could act gentlemanly too.

But what was slowly sinking in to all of us, one by one, was that the salesman's story threatened Buck's whole scenario for how Maury (or anyone) might have brought tainted clams back and killed me. Even Aitchison, at that point, said, "Damn."

BUCK:

What a downer. We all realized we had better check out the rentals ourselves before buying the tank. Maybe we were up a blind alley, of course, but just maybe Maury had just told the salesman that explanation for not buying his tank, but it wasn't true. I clung to that hope.

We soon found that Anchorage has big-name car rental offices like Avis, Enterprise and Hertz and all had vans, "but we are all franchises," as the Budget clerk said. "That means we can't participate in any of the companies' rent-it-here, turn-it-in-elsewhere schemes, what's called, 'One Way Rentals.'

"Those are just between company-owned facilities. For our van or cars or trucks, you have to bring the rental vehicle back here, nowhere else."

Junior said, "Then how—"

All three of us realized that our (especially my) assumption that Maury had brought the live clams back in a tank in a van could be very, very wrong.

And very stupid.

Thinking out loud, I said that the man canceling the tank purchase might not have been Maury after all, even if he was "gentlemanly."

Or maybe rich Maury, Junior said, had just pulled out a credit card and *bought* a van. He might have then bought his tank elsewhere or just carried the live clams in sand and saltwater in three, four or five plastic buckets for the trip to Washington where he would put the survivors in his own seawater tank.

"We could pool our credit cards and buy an old van ourselves," he suggested.

"We might do that, Junior, yes, and maybe we will," I said, "but, let's face it, we'll have no guarantee we would be duplicating what Maury did. Let's sleep on it."

While the others discussed our situation, I grew more and more dejected. I returned to the Athena branch office, where I could sit alone and think. I mentally kicked myself. I saw nothing ahead but Mr. Doom and Mrs. Gloom.

That's when the part-timer in the Athena office stuck her head in to where I was sitting head in hands. She seemed ridiculously bright and cheery. "Just want to remind you of your boss Mary Ann's call," she chirped. "She called again while you were out."

Feeling that no news could be worse than what I had recently got, I called headquarters in Washington.

Mary Ann said, "Jeff hasn't told me one little thing about what you've been cooking up, except to twist my arm to get your travel approved, but I've guessed it has something to do with my mentioning Maury's trip to Alaska and his unusual application to rent a van and drive back here rather than fly."

"Yes?" I said. "Your deduction is right on," *and a lot superior to mine!* "What of it?"

"So, although nobody asked me to, I looked into it further and—long story short—it seems like Maury decided not to drive home after all. He cancelled his request."

"What? Oh my God. You're sure?" I said. I slumped further into the desk chair. *So much for pooling our credit and buying a van. Instead,* I figured, *I'll buy a whore and quart of bourbon!*

"Yes, I'm sure," Mary Ann said. "He did stay a couple extra days to 'play tourist,' he told someone, but then he flew back after all."

"He flew back," I repeated. *Then what are we doing here?* I thought, but I told Mary Ann, "Thanks. You may have saved us from buying a van and making an initial mistake worse. But look, don't tell a soul about this, not even Spencer, please. Or, if you do tell him, tell him we're 'adjusting.'"

Adjusting?

I adjusted by knocking down two bourbons despite some hard looks from Junior, who put an arm around my shoulders and said, much like the burly guy in the ambulance transporting Evelyn to Sibley Hospital, "This isn't the end of the effing world, you know."

"It's the end of my fucking world," I said. How would I face Adrianna and Spencer and George and tell them that after all our work, and their faith in me, I had come up with zero. Nada. *What's Eskimo for screwed up?* I ordered another bourbon, but Junior must have somehow signaled the waiter not to bring it.

Still, I had dinner with him and Aurora—and was slightly diverted by their leveling with me about their baby-making activities. They thought I should know, since I was supposed to sleep in a king-sized bed in the same room. (Aitchison's CDC had reserved a separate single room for their man.)

"Well, er, what we mean is, will our, er, activity still be okay?" Lou asked.

I looked at my young friend and laughed. "You've never met my old college room-mate have you? Works at Athena now, married and as faithful as the sun rising in the morning, but back in the day George was quite the assman—far luckier or better'n me. If I could lie there in my bed four feet away from his and sleep—and not even suck my thumb and cry, while night after night his black ass rose and fell in ecstacy," I said, "then, tired as I am after this awful day, I won't know you're there."

All that wasn't quite true, maybe, but it put the kids at ease.

EVELYN:
Far from bothering Buck, I think the doings and screwings in that room were all that kept Buck sane, all that kept him from having a PTSD blow-out. It distracted Buck from his panicked worries about his expensive gamble gone awry. The rising and falling, the moaning of the bed and the happy groans and quick breaths of the bed's occupants – these may have been just enough distraction to keep him out of the depths of a PTSD collapse that night. (Watching them sure was a pleasant distraction for me as well, even as my hope for a solution to my death was disappearing.)

BUCK:
I did consider asking for "seconds" but, instead, quietly played with myself and then managed a little sleep.

The next morning, we each took a turn in the bathroom and dressed with our backs to each other, in separate corners of the room. After we shared the motel room's coffee, we were all business. But I'd say the two were a good deal more cheerful than me. Lou Jr. annoyingly whistled.

We all met for an early breakfast in a nearby diner that featured big skillets of hash browns, eggs and ham or steak. Our group also shared a stack of apple pancakes, as if full stomachs would solve everything.

Grim-faced, I ran over the situation in detail and asked if anybody knew what we should do: "Go home now, empty handed and admit failure? Buy a van and continue with the tank plan? Are there other options?" (The Spencer volume I'd ghosted advised sharing ideas, so I was trying. I was trying.)

"Slash our wrists?" Lou Jr. said, capturing the general mood.

Yupik seemed to chew thoughtfully (or maybe hungrily, I don't know) on his steak. Then, after he swallowed, he said, "What about clam juice?"

"Clam juice?" Junior and I said together.

"What about it?" I said. "What is it?"

"Yupik's not a cook," Aurora said. "He means clam *broth*, the liquid created when you boil or steam the clam. He mentioned briefly when you first arrived that many of the records are old, second-hand and/or imprecise but that some folks who got sick or died from PSP may not have actually eaten clams. They may have only drunk, or drank, whichever is correct, the broth produced when the tainted clams or mussels were cooked."

Suddenly, I could see, in my mind, Maury running into all the obstacles we had, and then, like us, discovering the possibility of cooking the clams and carrying a quantity of their broth to Washington in his baggage and then keeping it refrigerated until he wanted to use it.

It was a vision that also explained how he could so easily smuggle the poisonous material into my party and secretly add it to one or more bowls of the stew! He just had to smuggle in a couple of small viols — *about the size of the three-ounce travel bottles allowed in airline luggage.*

With hardly a word said between us, this revelation rose and shone on all our faces like dawn after darkest night.

EVELYN:
They may not have said a word right away, but *I* was silently screaming, Yay! Voila! Hosannah! Damn Right! Maybe you fumbling fools have finally got it figured out!

Their silence finally gave way to cheers. They high-fived. Without much further ado they headed for what Yupik and Aurora agreed was the most likely site for dangerously tainted butter clams. They took a Fish and Game motorboat to this tidal area and raked while the tide was out. "This way," Aurora said, "we can stay dry, if our boots don't leak and it doesn't rain, and we can see what we're raking. "

(*That's if nobody pisses in their panties out of sheer joy,* I thought.)

The gang had gotten quite competitive by this point, and each of them screamed and yelled with delight when they raked up a really large butter clam. They couldn't hear me but I cheered them on. (After all, they were building up evidence that maybe would finally prove how I was killed and, maybe, by whom.) They kept at their work, and I continued to cheer them on, and sometimes I couldn't help but jump up and down. *We were getting somewhere!*

They soon had beaucoup big clams in their buckets—plenty enough, I figured, to have killed off every last guest at Buck's dinner! Each butter clam in its tightly shut shell was rinsed and placed in one of the buckets. About noon, the diggers stopped and ate KFC chicken, biscuits and slaw Yupik's wife had sent along, and they drank beer Yupik had brewed.   After the bourbons Buck had kicked back the night before, Junior didn't think drinking a couple of beers at lunch seriously violated Spencer's no-alcohol rule. Nor did Aurora or Yupik seem to be worried about any Fish and Game harvesting limits since these were deadly clams nobody else would want.

And I wouldn't tell, even if I could. I was as happy as any dead woman has a right to be.

The others puttered around some more, and then, when the tide began to come back in, they pushed their boat and its deadly collection back into deeper water and motored back.

"A good day's work," Buck said as they reached the Fish and Game slot on the pier.   "What's the best place we can have dinner in, say, three hours. My treat, and bring your wife, too, Yupik."

Junior and Aurora went with Yupik to his home to cook the clams and produce the broth. Buck and Aitchison went to find a drug store to buy the little bottles that can get through airport security in the carry-on luggage which Buck, Junior and Aitchison all had brought on the trip. Leaving Atlanta on the outbound leg of the trip, Aitchison's too-large shaving cream had been confiscated by the TSA so he had practically memorized the carry-on rule: "You're allowed to carry 'liquids, gels and aerosols in travel-size containers that are 3.4 ounces or 100 milliliters.' Each passenger is limited to how many of these can fit in one quart-size plastic sack."

"If we checked our bags we could take more, but this should be plenty for our purposes—as we believe it was for Maury's," Buck said.   They took the bottles to Yupik's house to be filled, holding back a couple to put different colored shaving lotion in. "The TSA folks might get suspicious if all the bottle's contents look exactly alike," Buck said.

The poison prepared, the group washed their hands thoroughly and headed for the Kincaid Grill on Jewel Lake road. They had drinks and joked and told stories noisily, but the restaurant was full of folks acting like that. Most ate halibut or wild salmon and ended up with a cheesecake engulfed in blueberries. I'd have loved to have joined in, especially for the cheesecake. They all seemed to like it. (Where I am, we don't seem to eat.)

Aurora decided she had either conceived or she hadn't, so further sex would be an indulgence rather than a gift to her husband. She thanked Junior "for everything, very nicely done, my good friend," kissed him on the cheek and drove home to Seward and Mr. Bradley with the hope there was a fertilized ovum in her belly.

A good couple of days work, I imagine Junior and Buck each thought.

Junior fell onto his bed, and though he probably missed Aurora, he fell quickly asleep.

Buck, for his part, took the final version of the Spencer book to bed with him, along with an illustrated script he had begun. He made revisions in the script in light of the group's altered view of how the murder was organized and carried out. Though undoubtedly still anxious, he too fell asleep, but not for long.

BUCK:

I awoke in Afghanistan, trembling. I again shouted at the Humvee driver to steer away from the boy on the bike but it was too late.

Lou Jr. sat up. I guess he saw a panicked look on my face.

"What?" he said.

"The war," I said. In front of this kid, I tried not to twist in the bed, or shake, or tear at my face and head, as I had done so many times, but Junior recognized I was in crisis.

Junior pulled out two sticks of his home-grown weed, lit them, and handed one to me. I pulled the sweet smoke deep into my lungs, easily ignoring the long-run risk of lung cancer from the stuff as, like Junior, I concentrated on its immediate, relaxing effect.

"Tell me what happened," Junior said, and, as we smoked, I did. All of it. And tears rolled unbidden down my cheeks, soaking my T-shirt.

Junior cried too.

EVELYN:

I know I had told Buck to Man Up, War is Hell and all that, but, hearing him tell about losing his twin brother in the bombing, I wanted to cry too. Buck would have died too, if George hadn't got a tourniquet on his leg. And George, who then passed out, might also have died if Buck hadn't dug around in George's pockets, found his phone and called for help.

The motel room had a little porch and Buck and Junior went out on it. They couldn't see me, but I walked out there with them. We looked up at a billion trillion stars. They smoked another round, while I tried to sniff their second-hand smoke.

Buck's trembling subsided, and they soon returned to their beds and slept quietly.

Despite Jeff Spencer's orders to Junior, I think my old boss would have approved this use of pot. If not, to hell with him.

Chapter Twenty-three: A GALA DUEL

ADRIANNA:

The home of Wilma and Bella Smith – the founding sisters who had established Athena's women-friendly image – is an impressive construct with great white pillars that even a large man like Buck could not embrace. (And I couldn't begin to.) The pillars reach up three stories and they announce, quite clearly, that this is an urban mansion of impressive character.

Neither Buck nor I'd ever been there socially. Most Athenans hadn't. But Spencer had been a frequent guest and George had taken photographs there, and both believed it was the perfect venue for our trap. It included a colossal central hall opening onto several large public rooms, one of which had served as a ballroom, and beyond the biggest room was a theater seating 35.

It took all of Spencer's persuasiveness and his good standing with the Founders, but here we were in this grand house, ready (I surely hoped) to close in on our suspect. It was hardly two months since Buck had clued Spencer in, but I now saw the great value of his participation, for he had gained Wilma and Bella's excited cooperation in hosting this gala party for Athena's A-List without even having to tell the ladies who our suspect was!

Ostensibly the party was to introduce the new head of Athena Claims, Edward Chase, Spencer's replacement. But those who saw the large video screens in every room realized this would be more than a simple meet-and-greet.

From the moment a guest turned his or her car over to the valet parking attendants, that guest felt themselves to be, as a competing insurance company might say, "In good hands." Inside, white-gloved waiters circulated with wine and Perrier. Maids offered canapés from Ridgewell's, plus some specialties the Smith sisters particularly liked by Mrs. Toms of Frederick, Md. There was a full bar in each of the big rooms and large adjacent tables with fancy cheeses, fruit, nuts and snacks, and a whole salmon recreated with sliced-cucumber fins. There were platters of bite-sized quiches, and of individual pizzas and egg rolls.   At two smaller tables, carvers provided turkey and roast beef freshly cut and enclosed in easy-to-handle rolls.

The reception line included the three Smiths (for brother Nod, a bit of a loner, had deigned to come in from his farm for this event) as well as Spencer, and his successor. Chase's forbidding dignity seemed to disappear as he beamed on each man and woman he met and chatted – and asked for their support and help in his new job.

Except for Lou Howard, that is. Lou and Donna were among the first to arrive, and in his case, Chase wished Lou the best of luck in *his new job*. Lou had announced he was leaving to go with a British underwriting outfit that was opening an American bureau in Baltimore. He would run the American end of things.

"That time you were in my office and I got that phone call," Lou told Buck, "and I kind of pushed you along, so I could talk in private? That was a Scot named Jenkins about this new position. It's an amazing jump-start for me, with a salary quite a bit above what stingy Athena has been paying me.

"And to think, I'd never have seen or heard about this new job if it hadn't been advertised in that same *Wall Street Journal* where adman Pelican screwed me by advertising Spencer's job so openly!

"I think Donna and I'll now manage to pay, with a little scholarship help, for seven college degrees and a few years of post-grad for some of the kids as well. Right now, we have six kids, but I guess it's pretty obvious Number Seven is soon to appear!"

BUCK:

I said I was glad for them. Then I gave Lou the "To My Darling!" letter. "I found this at Evelyn's and think it was a draft meant for you."

Lou read the letter silently. "Damn that woman! Thank you, Buck! Thank you! I was afraid there might be something like this among Evelyn's things. I had veiled demands — and not so veiled ones, too — ever since Evelyn took me to her bed one weekend during the month that Donna and I separated. You ever know about that? It was waaay before you joined the company. I thought it was a sympathy fuck on Evelyn's part. "

EVELYN interjected:

To hell! I don't do sympathy! I do pleasure! Or did. And it wasn't just once!

BUCK continues to quote Lou:

"Actually, there was more than one weekend, but I almost forgot about them after Donna and I patched things up.

"You won't be surprised though, Buck, to hear that Evelyn didn't forget. Every six months or a year I'd get a note like this one and I'd have to go to her and say I'd like to buy her a present to thank her for being such an asset to the office, most recently as our administrative assistant – and she was always ready with a suggestion – a flat-screen TV, laptop or once even a bedroom suite. She kept me broke until she found other, presumably richer, fish to fry."

EVELYN:
I realized, as the saying goes, that it's foolish to try to squeeze blood from a turnip. And I felt a little sorry for Lou.

BUCK:
 I told Lou, "Just keep the note in a safe place, like your safety deposit box, for example, because it kind of clears you of worse things." Lou then gave me a funny, puzzled look I hoped was real. I also hoped that by evening's end he would know what I was talking about. "I'll let you know when you can destroy it once and for all – so that Donna need never know."
Lou nodded; he would hide but not destroy the letter for the time being.

ADRIANNA:

Minutes later, Maury and Stella Woodrow went through the line, and Our Suspect was positively glowing. Though he had missed out on Spencer's job, Maury was assured of more money and greater influence now that Lou Howard was leaving.

At the end of the reception line and elsewhere, there were piles of Jeffrey Spencer's book. In keeping with the book's dictum to be "generous in sharing credit," the book cover was emblazoned, "with Buxton Grand" in just slightly smaller type than Spencer's own name.

Maury had already read the volume. He told Spencer it was "a good read, as I knew it would be, with lots of fine advice we'll try to follow."

He was equally effusive when he spotted Buck in the crowd. He shook his hand. "Congratulations. I was surprised how readable the book is, you know—how anecdotal, even humorous, and I give full credit to you for that touch. Stern as Jeff can be, I always thought there might be a hint of humanity in him and I think you extracted every ounce of it. Of course I knew you would do well, especially after your work with George on my many hobbies."

All this praise made Buck a bit nervous, I expect, and me too. Maury was a smooth old devil. *Even with all Buck's preparation, this will be no slam dunk, as Buck would say. Everything must go just right.*

"If George is here," Maury continued, "I'd like to tell him again how much I appreciate the extra prints he made me."   Maury appeared in the best of spirits—as why not?

"Did you say 'George'?" asked George's wife Ramona, appearing with a plate full of good things. "George is here all right.   He's checking the equipment in the Smiths' theater and those big monitors that are here, there and everywhere. Since I don't know a lot of Athenians – excuse me, *Athenans*—and George is too busy to introduce me around, I picked up some of these hors d'oeuvres to share, as a way of meeting folks. Steak tartar, little pigs-in-blankets, clam spread on little toast squares, which I really recommend. Have some."

"Such a variety," Stella said.

"Trying to impress the new man, I guess," Maury said, reaching first for the steak tartar and, after a polite delay, for the clam spread on toast as well. "Yum. This is a tasty way to get over any lingering reluctance to eating shellfish."

Seeing beyond the service tray that Ramona was clearly pregnant, Stella said, "Apparently George doesn't spend all his time behind a camera. Will this be your first?"

"Yes. A boy," Ramona said.

Stella seemed to wince.

BUCK:

I noticed that wince too. I asked Maury, "Shall I get Stella a light Scotch and soda, and I recall you like a martini. Want one of those dirty martinis they're featuring?"

"Dirty?"

"They're delicious," the omnipresent Connie Yeager volunteered. "You include a few drops of olive juice and it makes the drink cloudy – and extra delicious. It's the new thing with the elite 'in' crowd."

"I'll try this 'new thing' then – and, yes, a light Scotch and soda for Stella would be fine." He lowered his voice. "She'll accept 'light' from you or Connie."

I soon returned with the drinks. Maury took the large, straight-up martini glass I presented, sipped at it and, to my relief, pronounced it, "excellent." He added, "I'm a Virginian of the old school. I like the old things – honor, tradition, respect, and gin martinis – but some new variations are good, and this would seem to be one of them." He held the drink carefully by the stem, with his pinky finger out in gentlemanly fashion.

I lifted my own bourbon and water. "To our health."

We drank. We ate. We circulated. I returned at intervals, once to freshen Maury's drink, "but two's my limit," Maury told me, and to refill Stella's.

"Are there more of those toast squares with the clam spread?" Maury asked Ramona. "Try one, Buck."

"I've been a little off seafood," I claimed, "since Evelyn's poisoning, you know—and yours. All in my head, I suppose."

"Water over the dam, so to speak," Maury said. He proved it by taking another piece of clam-spread toast from Ramona.

About 45 minutes into the party, the reception line was abandoned. Abundant food was consumed for another 20 minutes or so, along with more alcohol, which caused the rooms to get noisier and noisier. At that point, Wilma Smith began ushering Chase and Spencer, the Woodrows and the Howards and others into the mansion's multi-media theater. The gigantic monitors around the other public rooms came on, with a flourish of music:

"Ta daaa." No one in the house could miss the sounds and psychedelic images suddenly flashing from the theater stage and every monitor that George had placed around the house. To miss them, you would have to be in a a closet. Even the bathroom had small monitors.

EVELYN:

This event was all about me, really, about nabbing the guy who killed me, so I should have been the guest of honor, right? Couldn't be, though, and while I wished I could eat and drink all this great party stuff, couldn't do that either. *This can't be Heaven yet!* But I watched from my perch with keen interest.

Most guests seemed surprised when the voice that resounded through the rooms was not that of a founder, or of Jeffrey Spencer, or any of the other of Athena's god-like elites, but was "that tall guy from Human Resources with the bad leg," as I overheard someone put it. Buck's handicap, once so well disguised, had become obvious in the days after he pitched down that staircase. Even now his repaired appliance and his banged-up stump did not always move as smoothly as they once had. But standing there, he didn't look too uncomfortable.

He spoke right up, thanking the hostesses and explaining what his role was. Wisely skipping any of his previous mentions of his PTSD and editing out his F-bombs, he explained, "My name is Buxton Grand — Buck — of Athena's Human Relations Department. Some think of me as 'the guy who makes sure the cafeteria donuts have the right size holes.' Sadly, and more seriously, I'm also the person who gave the dinner at which Athena administrative assistant Evelyn Robbins was fatally poisoned." There was a stir among some of the guests at that statement, as a portrait of me, yours truly Evelyn Robbins but from ten years before, appeared on every screen. Good looking shot. I looked hot.

Everyone paid close attention now as Buck told the crowd, "I have obtained the Smiths' approval to introduce a sound-and-light show aimed at clearing the boards for our new Claims Vice President, Edward Chase about the poisonings and about two important reviews of our desk computer and telephone usage that have just been concluded.

"Please, will Assistant Claims Manager Adrianna Canter and Computer Services Director George Brown -- whom many of you know best for his side-line prowess as a photographer – stand up? These two have been co-chairing an ad hoc committee of two looking for indications of inappropriate telephone and computer use at Athena — unnecessary private telephone conversations like calling your bookie or game-playing, for example.

"Did I hear a few gasps?

"The bad news on the computer side of things is that considerable accessing of war games and crossword puzzles and even porn—girly stuff and more—was found, and visits to other inappropriate websites too – and a lot of non-business action on Facebook and other social networks.

"The further bad news," he continued, "is that the committee recommends that the game and porn sites be electronically restricted." A few people in the audience got in the spirit of things and moaned dramatically. "Blocked," Buck said.

"Some additional news for the viewers of these sites: The committee will name… no names.

"Did I hear a general Whew!"

ADRIANNA: Then, in a very flattering way, Buck got to my telephone review and the fraud:

"Ms. Canter, who looked most closely at this, couldn't review the content of calls, of course, but she could obtain from our telephone contractor what telephone number was called. She found almost no evidence that personal use of phones went beyond Athena guidelines. Most non-business calls appeared mostly to be to employees' homes, medical facilities and their children's schools, presumably for home emergencies and such, and that's okay."

"However," as I interrupted Buck, as planned, to say, "our telephone contractor's records showed some outside lawyers representing plaintiffs with cases *against* our policy-holders had been called from some phones possibly used by people in Claims."

"From Claims?" Buck said, to emphasize the point.

"Yes, yes," I confirmed, "the calls were from Claims.

"Some of you," I continued, "may well wonder why Claims people would call lawyers whom Maury Woodrow has called 'the Enemy'—the lawyers of the plaintiffs who are suing us. What business indeed?"

Buck said, "The reason became clearer when Adrianna discovered that the calls were followed by major wins by the firms called, which of course meant major losses to our company. I'm talking millions!"

"For example, Buck," I said, and here the screens lit up in the theater and throughout other parts the house with the first case scenario, "Plaintiff Attorney A is called from an Athena Claims line (202) 386-blah, blah, blah on June 12. Afterward, Attorney A refuses generous settlement of $25,000 offered by Athena and demands a day in court.

"When the case comes to trial, Attorney A is armed with questions that were not hinted at in the police report, or other public documents. Attorney A suddenly questions our Athena client about possible lapses in attention to the road that may have occurred – and that only the client and Athena were privy to."

Attorney A hammers home to the jury the information bought from the Athena leaker, and the jury awards $300,000 – as much as half of which may be Attorney A's fee.

"And who knows how much, as a kick-back, that the grateful Attorney A then sent to our Athena Claims man or woman who leaked the info about the child being in the back?"

"Good work, Ms. Canter," Maury said loudly. "It's an outrage that this could happen at Athena. It borders on the criminal!"

What a smooth character Our Main Suspect is turning out to be! I thought.

As the screens lit up with the details of four more cases, Buck and I alternately described them in brief, one after another, Buck always crediting me. The audience became quite sober and there were cries of, "Oh my God!" and, "Whew, a million bucks — that's real money!" and "Can you believe it?"

BUCK:

I announced, "We may soon know more about the kick-backs because we have this week shared our information with D.C., state and federal authorities. As the government agents may choose to place charges against the three attorneys in these five cases and/or subpoena their telephone, computer and check book records, some may choose to cooperate. And there are at least four more attorneys involved in additional cases, who also may be persuaded to cooperate.

"These leaks were detected by Adrianna Canter while doing her phone survey," Buck repeated. "But Claims administrative assistant Evelyn Robbins may also have overheard or stumbled on what was going on. Or, at least, the man leaking the information may have feared Evelyn had. After all, the person may well have been someone she worked closely with.

"Here on Evelyn's notepaper are the numbers for files reporting the cases I have just outlined," I said, as the notepaper flashed on the screen. As secretary to Claims executives Jeffrey Spencer, Maurice Woodrow, and Lou Howard, she could call these cases up on her own to look at without anyone getting suspicious."

BUCK:

"And here's a draft letter found in her apartment," I said. Evelyn's "To My Partner" envelope and letter now flashed on the screen for all to read in silence. The "To My Darling" envelope and letter were underneath, so that all the group could read of them was "To My D –"

Spencer had read this but now Lou Howard and Maury Woodrow, along with the many others, read the letter for the first time. Lou loosened his tie and looked miserably at me. Maury swallowed the last of his dirty martini, slipped off his coat and folded it across his lap. With all this talk of fraud, Jeffrey Spencer didn't look too comfortable either.

"Evelyn's 'partner' may not have wanted to share," Buck said, "or to be open to blackmail.   So, at a party I gave for Jeffrey Spencer after he announced his retirement, his administrative assistant Evelyn was poisoned." George's awful photo of Evelyn staggering toward Spencer sprang onto every screen, her twisted face in gruesome close-up.

EVELYN:
Awgh!

BUCK:
 Some in the audience stared in horror. Others quickly turned away. Jeffrey Spencer, I saw, was among the latter.

 I quickly covered the back and forth arguments about some artificial poison v. tainted shellfish. "Was it possible that the person who leaked information and defrauded the company could have also put poison into Evelyn's bowl of bouillabaisse? I thought that very far-fetched, especially after the Centers for Disease Control's tests ruled out any other poison except the naturally occurring poison that causes paralytic shellfish poisoning. I thought that meant the killer was Mother Nature, who seems to get away with that sort of now and then. But I learned otherwise.

ADRIANNA:

 Dr. Prentice Gorse's professorial face filled the screens, and key parts of his lecture at the Marine Biology Institute, as recorded by Lou Jr., boomed through the mansion, telling everyone just how to get away with using tainted shellfish to kill:

"First you locate a red tide and collect the seafood tainted by it. You keep the tainted mussels or clams or whatever alive and just serve them up in a tasty dish, perhaps a little seafood stew," Gorse began. He continued in great detail to tell how to get away with using shellfish carrying Paralytic Shellfish Poisoning to kill.

BUCK:
"His lecture, to stir and engage his students, was even called, The Perfect Murder," I said.

"Gorse didn't intend anyone to actually follow his directions – he merely wanted to get his students attention. But now they and you know how to do it!' I said. "All of you could get away with it – oh yes, if you only had the tanks and the skills and the ability to obtain tainted shellfish from a red tide to follow Dr. Gorse' instruction. But while simply making a teaching point dramatically to most of his students, Dr. Gorse seems to have taught someone with an interest in killing Evelyn Robbins exactly how to get away with it. This person listening to that lecture had the skills and the tanks and could get the poisonous shellfish. He could keep the water within the bounds Gorse suggested and get the salt balance right."

Gorse's voice resumed: "The murderer's biggest hurdles might be that he would have to know his or her way around boats and about collecting shellfish just after a red tide, on the East Coast. And also, some shellfish get rid of the poison fairly quickly. You'd have to use them quickly to be effective."

Slightly out of sync with the audio, George's pictures of Maury's tanks and fish, including that classic photo of Maury and Jaws seemingly chatting with each other, flashed on all the monitors. There was general laughter.

Maury's own laugh rang out the loudest. "Too bad Jaws didn't tell me all this stuff," he said, "and too bad I missed the professor's lecture. I wouldn't have eaten that bouillabaisse at your place and gotten sick!"

EVELYN:
Oh, my! Maury was carrying out his innocent act pretty smoothly.

ADRIANNA:
But Buck was not ready to give up:
"Dr. Gorse admitted that his scheme had one problem, that being that red tides and contaminations with the organisms that carry the toxin appear erratically and are not common on the East Coast."

The professor's face and voice returned. "You might have to run up to New England to have even a modest chance to find tainted shellfish in a red tide, and as most shellfish don't hold the toxin for long, as you know, you couldn't wait too long to serve them.

"Alaska's butter clams, however, provide a steadier supply because large parts of Alaska's vast coastline are not routinely monitored for PSP and these clams can hold the poison up to two years."

"'Alaskan butter clams,'" Buck repeated. "Alaskan butter clams. You can see why we became interested when we heard that Mr. Maury Woodrow had gone to Alaska, a few weeks before the poisoning here.

"Presumably on Athena business, as he was doing it with Athena money, Mr. Woodrow flew to our three person branch office in Anchorage, Alaska. He then made an odd request to cancel his return flight, because he wanted to rent a van and drive home, taking vacation time. He asked if he could get full reimbursement for this more expensive return."

"The gall!" someone said.

"I had a lot of 'use it or lose it' vacation time and I wanted to see a bit of the northern USA," Maury said. "And I would have paid the difference, but I found they don't rent vehicles in Anchorage for drop-off elsewhere."

"Right," Buck said. With Junior's video illustrating, Buck showed the crowd how he, Lou Jr. and Dr. Aitchison of the CDC had flown to Alaska to duplicate "the perfect murder" but had been "flummoxed" when they also learned you couldn't rent a van and drop it off in the lower 48 states."

"We thought we had gone down a blind alley," Buck said. The disappointment on the faces of Buck and the others at the rental car office was unmistakable as their videoed faces appeared on the screens.

Maury said, and laughed. "And so you had."

Buck looked pained. I think that he had been standing too long and, worse, that he feared he wasn't getting his message across. *Maybe Maury is too slick for this trap*, I also began to think.

But **BUCK** continued:

"While we talk all the time about victims who *ate* poison clams, by luck we learned from an Alaska Fish and Game expert that some of the long string of Alaskan victims of PSP may have just drank the broth created in the clams' cooking. Suddenly we saw how someone could put enough broth to kill someone in a few small bottles and get them through airport security and to home. No SUV required!"

Lou Jr.'s videos of the cooking of the clams and the bottling of broth appeared on the screens.

"And it worked. That is, we got through the security guards without a single question.

"But was the broth really potent? To make sure, CDC fed a little to some lab rats."

The many screens throughout the mansion lit up with photos of dead—poisoned—rats, on their backs, their feet in the air. Ugh. Gross.

"Thus," I said, "we realized how easily our killer could not only get on a plane with the poisonous broth but could easily smuggle it into my party, under our very noses. Adrianna made things difficult for the would-be killer by making clear that she wanted no help in the kitchen. But a few people managed to squeeze in anyway"— pictures of Lou and Stella and Spencer at the stove or fridge flashed quickly on the screens. "But Adrianna forcefully and quickly made them go."

ADRIANNA: An unattractive shot appeared of me handing soda water to Doug Clifford (for his splattered tie) and shoving him out.

"But when Evelyn and others wanted seconds," Buck said, "our killer got a second chance."

A picture of Jeffrey Spencer filled the screen. His recorded voice announced, "I'm not clear enough about who was serving us to name him, but I know I said to put a big helping in the bowl with the spoon in it because that was Evelyn's and she was crazy about the stew."

The screens showed Spencer at the counter with the two bowls, one with the tell-tale spoon. The face of the person behind the counter, however, was obscured by Mary Ann's big flower arrangement. In a second shot, the head of the server was again obscured but this one did show the server's arm clad in a blue blazer. George's photographic magic now zoomed in on the man's wrist, where a gold cufflink could be seen. The cufflink seemed to have a face in relief on it. An image of Thomas Jefferson? Hard to tell.

But Bella Smith couldn't help volunteering loudly, "I think Maury Woodrow's wearing that blazer and those very cufflinks tonight!"

"Every man in the Free World has a blue blazer," Maury said in an unconcerned tone, "nor are my cufflinks, while I hope they are handsome, unique. Frankly, I don't know if I was behind that counter or not. Maybe I was at some point.

"But remember:

"*I* was one of the people poisoned. And the CDC said it was a naturally occurring toxin that accumulates in shellfish, which we were eating.

"So, I really doubt there was a poisoner among us at all. But even with George taking all these pictures, if there were a maniac there trying to kill us, think of all the *un*-photographed moments during Buck's party when *anyone* could have put something in my food, and Evelyn's, and Adrianna's!"

"Not just anyone, Maury," Buck said, trying to get his presentation back on track. "It's a tricky project to carry out. You would need that instruction on how to proceed, as in that class at the Marine Biology Institute in southern Maryland. Lou Howard Jr.—son of our Lou Howard in Claims—was in that class for this particular discussion, and—"

"Aha," Maury said, passing it off as a joke, "so I guess the kid's the killer!"

EVELYN, back as an involved narrator:
Buck didn't laugh. And I, from my purgatorial position, didn't laugh either. I was afraid Buck's "trap" was becoming a duel he might not win.

But Buck said to Maury in his strongest, sternest voice: "Lou Jr. remembers you auditing many of his classes and specifically remembers you at the one on Paralytic Shellfish Poisoning, or the Perfect Murder, as the professor, to assure the students' attention, had labeled it."

Buck continued, "I questioned whether his single memory would be considered proof —"

"As well you should have," Maury shot back—

"So," Buck continued, "he interviewed every regular student in the class that he could locate. Twenty five of the 40 in the class recognized Mr. Woodrow as attending some classes and eight of them said they had seen him in that particular class."

"Nonsense!" Maury said. "I have sometimes audited a class, but I know nothing about any 'perfect murder' class. Nothing!"

Buck turned to the audience. "You just heard Maury Woodrow say he knew nothing about the class on PSP but here," Buck said, pointing to the nearest screen, "superimposed over their talking heads you see sworn affidavits from the eight who said Maury Woodrow attended the class where paralytic shellfish poisoning was discussed in detail – as was the possibility of using it in a 'perfect murder.'   This class was weeks before Mr. Woodrow's trip to Alaska—time enough to plan Evelyn's 'natural death' for a few weeks later."

"And time enough for the students to have faulty memories," Maury countered. "Eight out of 40 in a class means nothing."

"Eight alert, young memories seem pretty strong to me, but I won't argue with you right at present," Buck said, "because George and Lou Jr. are signaling me wildly. I'll ask Jeffrey Spencer to hold the fort while I talk to them."

Slipping easily into Buck's place in what had rapidly turned into a trial of truth and falsehood, my old boss Spencer added gravitas, I guess you call it, when he said, "I think all of you should know that for many recent hours, I have gone over this tragic situation with the man we are honoring tonight, Ed Chase, my replacement as Vice President of Claims. I have tried to explain how it might be that claims kickbacks were perpetrated under our very noses—kick-backs that have cost Athena millions and have provided wealth to a fraud, a thief, a killer—and a liar." I think that got the crowd impressed with the importance of what they were experiencing.

As if on cue, Buck handed Lou Jr. back the marijuana cigarette he had briefly puffed on. Buck had Mrs. Phyllis Gyraud in tow, the Richmond gal I myself had just started checking on when I was killed. She was carrying a portable microphone, but she remained in the background.

Buck said, "This is where I was to introduce this nice lady from Richmond, Mrs. Gyraud! But I'm going to ask her to wait a moment while I settle a matter of disputed fact. You remember those students who said Maury attended the 'Perfect Murder' class? And you remember Maury's adamant denial? Well, one of the students got worried that he and his friends' words might not be enough, so he found some proof and brought it to Lou Jr. yesterday. It may just appear to be a picture of a pretty girl but it is a particular pretty girl in the class we're talking about. The young man was so attracted to her that he secretly photographed her with his iPhone.

"Lou brought it to George who saw its importance and has been working today to add the picture to our show. And here it is!"

It now appeared on all the screens.

"She is pretty, isn't she? And note the date automatically recorded in the corner—the very date of the 'Perfect Murder' lecture which Maury has been swearing he never attended. Now," Buck said, "look closely at the man absorbed in taking notes in the background."

The crowd began answering among themselvees.

"Why, it's Maury," an employee suddenly shouted.

"It's Mr. Woodrow, all right!" another said.

Buck said, "Yes, yes, yes, it's none other than Maury Woodrow! George is now zooming in on him, so there can be no doubt."

Maury squirmed.

Buck nodded. "Yes, there is no doubt. That's Athena's Assistant Vice President Maurice Woodrow. He was indeed auditing the course for this important lesson. He's been lying to us all this time."

Maury Woodrow started to respond but Mrs. Gyraud jumped in,

"Speakin' of lies," Mrs. Gyraud interjected, "I've been invited up here from Richmond as a surprise to an Athena executive who introduced himself to me and, if I may use such an expression, wooed and romanced me, as *Jeffrey Spencer,"* she said, setting the crowd back on its heels.

"Hello, Jeffrey!" she said, almost gaily, and marched toward the area where Spencer was, but then veered suddenly to Maury Woodrow.

"Surprise! This man, this same Vice President Woodrow that Buck has just caught in one falsehood, also put forth another huge lie as well. He *pretended* to me that he was Mr. Spencer, and said he was suffering in a loveless marriage his wife wouldn't release him from. He asked for my love and patience, which have now been exhausted as I now see that, for reasons of his own, Maury Woodrow was pretending that he was Jeffrey Spencer, for no *good* reason that I can think of, but for several evil reasons I can speculate. Perhaps, when he had gone through his wife's money, he was hoping to have me and my money as a back-up!"

Stella had returned from the bar with a new drink in time to witness Mrs. Gyraud's disclosure. They faced each other.

"I'm so sorry to have to tell you all this," Mrs. Gyraud said to Stella.

"Oh, I am sorry for you, too," Stella said. "But you have discovered in a few months what it has taken years—yes, years!—for me to learn: That the man who has charmed us and made us love him (for yes, I did love him *so* very much) is a fraud from his claims of 'ancestors'—his great, great, great grandfather whatchacallit was hardly even a foreman(!) I've discovered—to his recent misuse of my money, and now his infidelity." Stella began to weep and Mrs. Gyraud embraced her, followed by Connie Yeager, whose arms enclosed them both.

"Just recently," Stella sobbed into Mrs. Gyraud's microphone, "I began to question some odd things about our personal finances and then, coincidentally, I found a check from one of those shyster lawyers I think Buck Grand talked about—not a kick-back of a million dollars but a big enough check that something told me it was irregular, so I hid it! It has driven Maury crazy trying to find it, though he never spoke of it, so I knew it was important! — and shady!"

"Oh, God, Stella," Maury cried out, "you k-killed my son and now you're ruining me! And, God, I've got to get out of here! I'm suffocating!" He looked a bit green. He was beginning to feel nauseated, apparently.

The screens were now flashing feverishly with a quartet of George's pictures that linked the digging of the butter clams, the transport of the "clam juice," and the dead lab rats with a new shot of Maury taking a cracker loaded with a seafood spread from a tray held by Ramona. "You put something in that seafood spread?" Maury hissed. Then it struck him:

"Omigod!" he cried out. "Those dead rats weren't enough of a test for you! (Gasp) You had to put clam juice (Gasp) into the seafood spread! That's why I feel sick and breathless like Evelyn!" Maury seemed to physically shrink as he realized he could have been poisoned the same way he poisoned Evelyn. The assembled guests seemed to realize what might be happening too and some stepped back from the stage and the TV monitors, convinced they were going to see Maury collapse and die, and not keen on seeing it quite so close.

"(Gasp!) I'm having trouble breathing!" Maury said. "I should have known better than to eat the seafood hors d'oeuvres! Y-you're killing me the way I poisoned that tramp Evelyn – Oh, God. – I can't get my breath – the paralysis is starting. Please, please, call 911."

ADRIANNA:

A howl like that of a pained animal pierced the mansion's vast space—shocking the guests as they realized it was from Maury, whom some were almost ready to pity. Then the microphone picked up the sound of retching as he stuck a finger down his throat to make himself vomit and cleanse himself of as much of the toxin as possible. Mildred snatched a trashcan and gently held Maury's head over it.

"I'm not a bad person," Maury begged us, Buck in particular, to believe. Maury seemed unconscious that his voice continued to boom throughout the house (and was being recorded by George's equipment as well). "I just rid us of a terribly common woman whom we all despised! She was (gasp!) preparing to blackmail me!

"Don't let me die that terrible way. I was so scared at your dinner, you know (gasp!) when I realized I had licked that spoon -- and probably p-poisoned myself! That's why I called 911 so fast!"

It was the confession we had worked so hard and long for! Buck had gotten it!

Maury now fell back in his chair. "Maybe (Gasp!) it would be best to die. Reputation gone; I've lost Phyllis (Gasp!) and soon I'll die and lose all my beautiful things, won't I? Buck. My trees, my marine specimens, my German mugs, my family paintings!"

EVELYN:

Observing Maury's confession, I jumped up and down, unseen as I was!

But, in the wake of this confession, our Buck got soft in the head! He must have thought of Spencer's crazy maxim to be kind to the damn fool loser, which I think is about the dumbest thing you can do. I say, squeeze 'em for all they're worth!

But Buck—who didn't learn to do this in the Marines I'm betting you—put his hand on Maury's shoulder and said, "You won't die, Maury.

"We duplicated the way you produced the paralytic shellfish poisoning, just to be sure it could be done. But that was just with rats. We didn't put it in the seafood spread. What you're suffering from is a simple dose of fluid extract of Ipecac—the stuff you give kids to make them vomit when they've swallowed something poison— and it was in your two martinis, not the seafood."

"But the tingling, the difficulty breathing – "

"Suggestibility and your old problem, hyperventilating. You told me you were susceptible to it when Mary Ann nearly passed out, remember? Here's a brown paper bag."

"Oh, Buck," Maury said through the bag, "how could you set me up like this? You've been a friend—you've been a *guest*. Maury began to cry. "All I ever wanted was a quiet Virginia farm, a greenhouse full of flowers, a son, my collections, and peace. Oh, Buck, Buck, Buck, what shall I do?"

Buck stood up tall and straight. "I'll tell you first what you're *not* going to do. My Marine friends Mildred and Hal are here because some people envisioned you speeding off in your Mercedes or your antique MG and deliberately crashing it and killing yourself down near Charlottesville, or somewhere else you love. But we are not going to let that happen.

"You're going to live to cooperate with the authorities and get a bunch of bad lawyers disbarred at the least. Maybe, some of them, I hope, will be put behind bars. Your cooperation in that, plus any evidence you have of Evelyn's possible blackmailing, may help you reduce your jail time."

ADRIANNA takes over:

Oh Buck, what a lovable damn fool! I thought, just like Evelyn did, only with the added "lovable." But, believing that Buck and the two other Marines had Maury well in hand and the action in the little auditorium was over, I left the room and headed in the direction of the front door, near where Ernie Bell and Mrs. Gyraud were watching one of the screens. And where I expected one or two city police to soon enter and take over.

What happened next, I couldn't have expected. I heard it over the speakers and saw on the screens that were everywhere, and nearly lost whatever composure I still had.

A guttural noise erupted from Maury that was half laugh and half hate. He simultaneously reached into the jacket in his lap, as if the old-fashioned gentleman was getting a handkerchief to wipe his wet eyes and face.

But Maury pulled a gun from that jacket and in the same motion swiped Buck in the jaw with it, knocking him to the floor, bloodying his face, and holding him and Hal and Mildred at bay.

Maury snarled, "You underestimate me, Buck. I have options that don't involve either jail or killing myself.

"All of you, keep back. Remember: I've killed Evelyn and, indeed, I'll shoot to kill anyone who tries to stop me."

To prove it, he shot Buck where he lay on the floor.

Chapter Twenty-four: I, ADRIANNA, SAVE THE DAY

ADRIANNA:

I heard the shot and nearly collapsed on the spot. Maury would be aiming to kill, I was sure, but I could see in the monitor that Buck was alive and getting up. Maury had hit Buck's artificial leg, it turned out.

Not knowing that, Maury had backed quickly out of the little auditorium, slamming the door behind him.

He waved his pistol, scattering those of us in the living room and foyer as he fled toward the front door and his car. Buck was up and after him as fast as he could move. Hal and Mildred were not a moment behind.

"Stop that man!" Buck yelled, like a character in an old B movie.

But Maury was not stopped. He bolted toward the open front door and porch. Desperation fueled him as he brushed aside a much bigger man and darted between Ernie Bell and Mrs. Gyraud, toppling them in opposite directions.

I stood trembling just beyond them.

I had heard and now saw the gun and I barely stifled a scream but, like a robot, I put my little foot forward, catching Maury's larger foot, as he tried to speed by.

I got quite a bruise! But it was worth it. Maury flew head first into the hard edge of the partially open front door.

His weapon discharged again, the bullet firing harmlessly into the ceiling. Stunned, Maury slid quietly to the floor, briefly unconscious. The gun fell from his hand and skittered along the floor as grains of plaster showered down.

Hal, Mildred and Buck all pounced. They knocked the wind out of Maury. And, to a degree, out of each other. Two policemen, having heard the shots, rushed in and took Maury into their charge.

I picked up the gun and blew on its muzzle as I'd seen done in movies. I laughed at myself and handed the gun to Mildred, who gave it to Hal, who decided Buck should have it.

Buck turned it over to the police as a dazed and winded Maurice Woodrow glared. "You low-born bastard," Maury said, with all the vitriol he could muster.

So much, Buck might have thought, for being charitable! But Buck mopped the blood from his jaw with a pocket pack of Kleenex I handed him and tried again:

"Be the gentleman you are, Maury. Help the police. Give evidence. You'll be treated well and maybe you'll be out much sooner than you think."

Maury didn't answer. In his anger, he may not have heard. He lunged toward Buck and tried his best to spit in his face. The police, however, yanked him back.

"You called this perp a gentleman?" the taller cop asked.

Buck did not answer.

I answered for him, "Not any longer!"

After the D.C. police drove Maury away in handcuffs, future Vice President and Claims Department Director Edward Chase and just about everyone else shook Buck's hand and mine, George's, and Spencer's "for a job well done," as was repeated again and again. Some said it even better: "for an *impossible* job well done."

"I'll want this team on my side — loyal as they've always been to you!" Chase told Spencer.

Buck gave me a knowing look. For my part, I smiled as smugly as I could, as if I had never for a minute doubted Jeffrey Spencer's innocence.

The Founding Sisters pulled Buck down to their height and kissed him on the cheek that wasn't bleeding, and Buck in turn kissed and thanked them. "We could never have done this without your grand party, your cooperation, your secrecy, and your faith in us."

"All true," I said.

"We hid behind our chairs during the shooting," the Smith sisters admitted, "but Brother slept right through it."

Chapter Twenty-five: NO RELATIONSHIP

EVELYN:

I would have felt even better if I were alive but even as one of the dead I felt happy to have my murderer outed and carted off! Meanwhile, my reluctant hero Buck and his brainy Adrianna headed for the now-so-familiar Sibley emergency room.   Buck's cheek was sown up and Adrianna's ankle examined.   Then they headed happily to Buck's apartment, any remaining pain masked by the joy of victory.

Party noise greeted them. A core group of co-conspirators and well-wishers had entered Buck's famously open-door apartment, carrying left-overs from the Smiths' party to eat and drink.

George and Ramona and the other party folks high-fived and embraced Buck and Adrianna, as if aware that the team's "triumph over evil," as Adrianna put it, was perhaps a rare experience in the world of commerce.

Jeffrey Spencer said that the story of how Buck used the principles in their book to put a team together to unmask my killer should be written up as an addendum "to our business memoir as Mary Ann here likes to call it." The two had their arms around each other and, still clinging romantically, left together a short while later, no longer appearing to be worried about the Athena relationship rule, not among this group of friends at least.

Hal and Mildred remained to the last—*very* inebriated I'd say, yet obviously hungry for each other. The "new Buck," as I'll call him, only drank half of the drink he had been handed, but it had been a long and heady day and after a while his eyes could not stay open. His head drooped and he was out. Hal and Mildred stumbled about helping Adrianna put him to bed. They managed to remove his artificial leg and his clothes down to a pair of camouflage-print briefs. I watched, admiring the man's battered but still impressive body in those remaining briefs, which turned out not to camouflage much.

"Marine-issue?" Adrianna asked Mildred and Hal, just before covering the night's hero with a sheet and blanket. They didn't answer. They were debating whether they could make it safely to either one of their homes. They decided not.

"I have a sleeping bag in the gym big enough for two if they're tight," Hal said. Mildred hit him hard on the bicep and said, "Oh, we're tight all right." She agreed that the cozy sleeping bag would do quite well.

"But, Hal," she said, "you do know I have a history of, well, being with women."

"Hell, Mildred honey, so have I," Hal said with a grin, as, with muscled arms around each other's muscular shoulders, they departed.

ADRIANNA:

Wondering how "that" would work out, I looked about at the after-party mess. "Yi, yi, yi, I can't leave things like this," I said and managed to refrigerate the remaining food and put the glasses and plates in the dishwasher and start it (without remembering to put in the detergent pod). At length, I went into the bedroom carrying the remainder of my drink. I looked unsteadily upon the recumbent. Despite the leg that ended just below the knee and the newly repaired cheek, he looked big and strong and peaceful, though he was still, I knew, something of a tormented soul. Nevertheless, I smiled.

EVELYN:

Maybe she was thinking of Buck as I was:

I had seen an angry, explosive man—almost as helpless and dead as I am — come to life in the pursuit of my killer and under the influence of Jeff Spencer, that master of organization and management. Buck could now organize and manage, most especially himself.

Yes, he was sometimes too generous—foolishly so with Lou, perhaps, and certainly with Maury, and, Adrianna probably thought, with the beautiful Sylvia.

But I kind of liked that he was one of the rare men who looked on women as equal partners in the office and elsewhere, even, it seemed, in bed. Maybe Adrianna was thinking likewise.

I believe she had intended to wrap herself in a blanket and sleep on the sofa.   Adrianna, as a professional working woman, probably had less time or inclination to get into sexual relationships, thinking (as did Athena Insurance) that they were likely to be messy and unprofessional, and to end unhappily.

But now, her speech slightly slurred, she spoke into the last of her Scotch and soda.

"I am a law-yer, Adrianna Canter, Esquire," she said, "and I (cough) want to state a legal o-pinion:

"A m-moment of pleasure—a one-night stand, or an overnight—should *not* be, repeat *not*, be construed as a 'relationship.'"

She finished her drink and removed her jewelry, shoes, stockings and dress. She peeled back the sheet and blanket that covered Buck with and slipped in beside him, wearing bra and panties.

"What the hell," she said – and removed her remaining undergarments as well. She tossed them on a chair by the bed.

"That's more like it," she said as she cuddled herself around her man, enjoying the feel of heat from Buck's body. She whispered in his ear, "What we'll do tomorrow morning, Buck, we'll just cut the bull-pucky and–"

Before she finished the sentence, she slept.

Chapter Twenty-six:

ONE MORE DETAIL

EVELYN continues:

If "Heaven Can Wait" and "Topper" and a couple of other old movies are accurate, now that my death has been resolved. I should be going, maybe disappearing like the Cheshire Cat, one part of me at a time. But I'm still here, even though there's no more to my murder story, is there? That's funny. Yes, I'm still here.

Life is real but I'm not living. Death is real but I'm not with the dead. I wonder which part of me will be the most enduring. Not my brain, I guess. Maybe it'll be that part men have been so hot for, whatcha think? I'd like to keep it around as long as possible, though I don't suppose I have any more use for it.

However, far from fading away I'm still in this ghostly state where I can see and hear what's goin' on— and tell you all about it.

For example, I watched Buck and Adrianna waking up in the morning and, after all this time knowing each other, just merging into each other. I sure enjoyed watching that.

In the bed.

In the shower.

Back in the bed.

Yes, indeed. That little Adrianna, now that she has finally opened herself to having sex with the guy, well, she's gotten pretty aggressive about it. A couple times, she's run her hand right down Buck's chest and under his Jockeys! I think Buck might prefer to be the controller— say that word fast three times aloud—but it looks like he can also lie back and take it easy.

As for Adrianna's plan for "a moment of pleasure," but not a relationship? No way.

On Monday, with Buck nodding his agreement, Adrianna called Mary Ann and said, "Buck and I are taking the week off to be together, fully together if you know what I mean, *enjoying* each other, and we can't come back to Athena until the relationship rule is changed. Tell Pulsudski and the Smiths that the relationship rule as it is now wouldn't stand up in court anyway, I'll bet my lawyer's license on it." She lightly patted Buck's privates as she said all this, and Buck lightly patted hers, but she nevertheless managed to speak slowly so that Mary Ann could take down her lawyerly language to the effect that when a relationship does develop, "each party is required to report it, in confidence, to both their supervisors, and each party in the relationship must avoid any action that would influence the performance rating, pay or benefits accruing to the other party."

With a smile in her voice, Adrianna said to Mary Ann, "Please make this a priority. You know, hurry. I think Buck may want to do some things pretty soon that are not only disapproved by Athena's rule but are not even legal in some states." The two women giggled.

"Never1" Buck said, producing that big, wide grin of his.

As the happy amateur crime-solvers continued to *enjoy* each other, Adrianna once or twice slipped and called Buck "Daddy." But he didn't care. She could call him that—or Phileas Fogg, or Santa Clause in those moments as far as he was concerned. And, a far as she was concerned, he could call her "Mommy" or "Sister" or anything else but Sibyl, I'll bet. For they were both into it, I mean, deep. I could tell by how wildly Adrianna responded. I mean, she was really high on the Richter scale.

Would it last? The "Relationship Rule" would get modified for these heroes, I was sure, but would Adrianna and Buck marry—or even stay together? He still had his PTSD, his anger, his self-indulgence, and one day probably he might start drinking heavy again. I'm not wishin' it. I'm just sayin'.

To tell the truth, I think I'd have liked to have seen him end up with Sibyl. Sexy and sweet and generous and very, very smart, too, you know? Quoting Congreve! After I heard about that, I had to Google the guy!

Adrianna, I'll just bet, will prod Buck to go to law school, whatcha wanna bet? Will he or won't he?

Now it is Wednesday of their week of rule-breaking love-making and I'm watching with interest, but I'm still puzzled that I'm here.

Buck and Adrianna are lying in bed together kind of resting in that happy haziness after, you know.

Buck suddenly rises up in the bed, attaches his leg, and gets up and paces around the apartment naked, finally pouring himself a cup of coffee in the kitchen but so distracted he does not offer Adrianna one. Returning, he stands before Adrianna, who eye him and smiles, though she seems slightly puzzled.

"Maury," Buck says, "didn't poison Evelyn to death."

"What?" lawyer Adrianna, says. (And I'm certainly agape, too.) "You handed him over to the police with a recording George made of Maury's confession, a confession witnessed by more than a hundred people."

Climbing into the bed Buck whispered into Adrianna's ear, "Maury killed Evelyn all right. He tried to kill her with his natural poison, but his and Dr. Gorse's 'perfect murder' didn't work. The doctors thought Evelyn was on the mend. I thought she was too. So did Maury, I'm sure. You weren't there but in Alaska our expert Kupik said that quick medical care often can save a person by supporting their breathing until the toxin dissipates, the lung muscles lots of time recover, and the patient often can breathe again."

Demonstrating he wasn't one of those people who can't walk and chew gum, Buck tickled Adrianna's breasts, kissed her chest between them, and said, "I think Maury realized that in his rush to get medical care himself, he had helped save Evelyn, despire her much higher consumption of the toxin. And he was terrified. Remember, he thought Evelyn knew he had been leaking key information to opposition lawyers and getting kickbacks.

"Crafty as she is, he'd think, she might even have proof.

"And Maury would realize if she guessed he had tried to poison her she might want revenge."

Buck walked his hand down Adrianna's smooth belly. "So, he had to finish the job. He came into your room, I speculate, and got your extra pillow instead of using the extra one in his own room, and he used it to smother Evelyn. Then, discarding the pillow who knows where, he ran to the nurse's station to alert them to the racket from the alarms, giving himself a kind of alibi, much as he had done when he tasted the poison bouillabaisse."

"You really think that's what happened? You're serious!" Adrianna says. "Hmm. Odd but I had a funny dream that I saw Maury in my room with a pillow. But he saw you and left!"

Buck said, "I was sleeping on the lounge every night."

"That's right, you were. My hero! Come here."
She took Buck's hand and kissed it. "I'll give you a
reward."

I could happily continue watching and listening, but
that seems to be the true and final end of my story: I
survived the perfect crime! And then I was smothered to
death. I don't remember a pillow, but I do remember
struggling at the end.   So that was Maury, the old fraud!   I
didn't think he had it in him!

Of course, I'd like to know how that Buck-Adrianna
thing works out in the long run, but maybe now that *my*
story is over, I won't be able to stay any longer—

Let me just say before I go. Life is good; hold onto
it. They talk about Eternal Rest. Rest is the last thing I
want to do.

Hmmm.

Well! That kind of tickles —

Where are the pretty clouds, the gowns and the harps?

(Oh, Hell. Hell. Hell.)

But maybe this won't be so bad. Maybe I can find an
angle, find a way to help whoever runs this place.

Pouf.

###

While red tides do contaminate shellfish and Alaska's
Butter Clams do hold the poison for as long as two years, in
other respects this is a book of fiction not based on any
known murder. My appropriation of some real institutions'
and people's names should not lead the reader to think they
necessarily acted as written here, in real life. However, it
has been widely reported that the Trump Administration
was quick to let the Obama era CDC director go, and that
his replacement was short-lived after she made
controversial stock purchases. – WG.